# Around Which All Things Bend

*A Novel*

Nancy Perpall

Archway Publishing books may be ordered through booksellers or by contacting:

Archway Publishing
1663 Liberty Drive
Bloomington, IN 47403
www.archwaypublishing.com
844-669-3957



ISBN: 978-1-6657-2611-5 (sc)
ISBN: 978-1-6657-2610-8 (hc)
ISBN: 978-1-6657-2612-2 (e)

Library of Congress Control Number: 2022912287

Print information available on the last page.

Archway Publishing rev. date: 08/22/2022

# *Chapter 1*

Keep your eyes wide open before
marriage and half shut afterwards.
—*Benjamin Franklin*

It's been said that lovers cannot see each other's weaknesses and shortcomings, and if they do, the glare causes them to turn quickly away from each other. What Alex Whitgate struggled with was why it had taken him so long to see something that was so clear to him now.

His iPhone on the bedside table lit up with an incoming call. Set to "Do Not Disturb," it neither rang nor vibrated. When the call disconnected, a message banner appeared on the screen. It was Gwynn. Almost immediately, the landline in the downstairs study rang. Although the rooms, stairs, and his closed bedroom door slightly muffled the ringing, it reverberated in his ears.

As he pulled on his blue jeans, he heard a knock on the door and his mother's strained voice. "Alex, Gwynn just called. She asked me to tell you she *has* to speak to you. She sounded hysterical. What's going on?"

Pressing his lips tightly together, he continued to dress. Then, taking a deep breath, he said, "Dang it. Mom, tell her that I've already gone out to the upper pasture, and there's no cell reception."

He heard his mother mumble something, and then, sounding exasperated, she said, "Really, Alex, Gwynn knows you use a satellite phone when you go up there."

"Tell her I left the satellite phone home."

"You want me to lie to the girl you're marrying in four days? What in heaven's name is going on?"

He heard another knock on the door but didn't respond.

"Alex, what's happened?" his mother called with an anxious voice.

After tugging on his boots, he stood up and rubbed the back of his neck. Alex felt a vestigial flicker of anger loop through his mind as he thought about what *had* happened. "Mom," he said in a harsher tone than he'd intended, "I'll be right down and explain everything."

A few minutes later, he opened the door, walked down the long hall, and descended the sweeping staircase. When he entered the kitchen, his mother was leaning against the sink, staring out the window above it. He felt his chest clench as he noticed how frail and tired she looked. Definitely not the beautiful, strong, stalwart matriarch Mary Whitgate was known to be. Alex watched as she turned slowly, crossed her arms, and narrowed her green eyes. "Well?"

Alex walked to the coffee pot, gripping the handle so tightly his knuckles blanched. After pouring himself a mug and one for his mother, he motioned toward the table. After taking a deep breath, he said, "Why don't you sit down."

"Humph. Telling someone to sit down before they'll tell you what they have to say isn't a good sign," she said sourly, taking a seat.

After placing the coffee mug in front of her, Alex kissed the crown of her head and took a chair across from her. Pressing his back against the chair, he said, "I know this is going to be a blow to you. But the wedding is off."

"What?" she exclaimed, placing her hand to her throat.

"Gwynn and I broke up."

"You what?" Mary cried.

"We had a fight, and we broke up."

"Why? What happened?" she stuttered. "A fight? Over what?"

Alex straightened, hooking his thumb inside his belt. "It's complicated."

"It's complicated?" Mary said, her voice an octave higher. Opening her palms to the ceiling, she raised her arms above her head. "That's all I get? 'It's complicated'?" Then, taking a breath, her eyes laser focused on Alex, she exhaled and, grabbing onto the table's edge, leaned in. "Let me tell *you* what's complicated. Expecting two-hundred and fifty guests in four days, working for months to get this ranch ready for the reception, preparing the house for your guests, who you may remember are arriving in a few hours, and working with Gwynn and the wedding planner for the last six months—"

Alex raised his palm to her. "Mom, I know how hard you've worked, and I appreciate everything you've done. But I'm not going through with it."

"But why? Why suddenly out of the clear blue do you decide, 'I'm not going through with it'?"

Alex pushed his chair back, stood, and, walking to the kitchen window, poked at the air in the direction of the capacious reception tent erected next to the carriage house and the huge fountain standing sentry to the tent's entrance. "Mom, it's not out of the clear blue."

"Well, it seems that way to me," she huffed, placing her elbow on the table and her hand to her forehead.

"Don't tell me you haven't seen what a circus this wedding has become. I mean, that tent is big enough for one. And this wedding has turned into one." Alex's eyes narrowed. "This is fucking Montana, and that stupid fountain she insisted on looks like it belongs in front of a casino in Monte Carlo."

Shaking her head, she said, "Alex, watch your language."

Shrugging, he continued. "And she's been spending money as if she's planning a Super Bowl halftime performance starring herself." Then after a pause, he added, "And last night when I went to pick her up for dinner, she excitedly presented me with monogrammed toilet paper."

Mary's eyes grew wide.

"Fucking monogrammed toilet paper. Oh, and a bill for a hundred and fifty dollars."

Mary cleared her throat but let the obscenity go. After a long beat, she swallowed and said, "Um, well, she may have gone a little overboard with the wedding. But we did tell her we were paying for everything and gave her wide berth throughout its planning." Appearing befuddled, she shook her head again. "Monogrammed toilet paper? There really is such a thing?"

"Yeah," he said, slowly nodding. "And leave it to Gwynn to find it."

"Alex, please, don't tell me you broke up over monogrammed toilet paper. Gwynn sounded so desperate to speak to you, maybe she realizes it was ... um, what's the word?"

"Idiotic?"

"Well, yes. Silly. Maybe she intended it as a joke."

"Yeah, the joke's on me. I've been a fool."

They sat in silence for a long moment, looking at each other.

"Well, I feel like one too," Mary said, looking up at the ceiling as if the answer she was looking for was on it. "You're telling me to cancel this wedding without knowing the real reason why."

Ignoring the comment, Alex said, "Did I ever tell you how we actually got engaged?"

"No, I guess not. I was surprised. I just remember the two of you came in, and Gwynn showed me the door knocker of a ring on her left hand."

Alex gave a grunt of a laugh and said, "Yeah, well, we went to the mall to get a wedding present for a friend of hers, and she said, 'Let's go into the jewelry store for laughs and look at rings for the fun of it.'" With his chin nearly to his chest, he shook his head. "Anyway, we walked into the jewelry store, and Gwynn latched onto a saleswoman as if she were a life raft. The woman sat us down and brought out trays of engagement rings. Gwynn looked so excited; you'd think she'd struck gold like Grandpappy Whitgate did up on the mountain."

Alex watched as Mary's brows furrowed; she opened her mouth as if to speak, then closed it.

"What?" Alex asked.

"It's blindingly obvious to me that you're trying to avoid telling me what really happened. I'd like to know the truth." After a long silence, she added, "I think I deserve to know."

He cleared his throat. "OK, you want to know the truth?" He looked down at the coffee mug and up into Mary's eyes. "Gwynn told me at dinner last night that she wants you to move out and into the carriage house."

Mary's eyes grew wide. "What?" At first, her face reddened and then turned a shade of white. After a few moments, she let out a sigh so forceful Alex noticed the lapel of her silk robe move. "Really? Gwynn actually said she wanted me out of my own house. Does she know I'm the one who owns it?"

"I don't know what she knows, but that was the last straw."

"I don't know what to say. I wouldn't have thought she'd feel that way about me."

"I've come to realize that she doesn't feel much about anybody but herself. I mean, at first I thought I'd misheard her and asked her to repeat it. She did. When she saw the look on my face, she said, 'Alex, it's not like I'm asking her to live in a kennel outside.'" Then, using air quotes, he said, "'The carriage house is five thousand square feet of meticulously renovated and exquisitely decorated living.'"

"So, you're breaking up with her because of me," Mary said mournfully.

"No, Mom, I'm breaking up with her because of her. I'm not sure now what I'm looking for in a life partner, but I know what I'm *not* looking for, and that is satisfying someone else's needs as if they're the center of the universe," he said with aggressive finality.

As Mary's phone buzzed with an incoming text, she repeated, "She actually said she wanted me out of my own house?" Shaking her head, she turned the screen toward Alex. The text was from Gwynn.

*PLEASE MAKE ALEX CALL ME.*
*WE HAD A HORRIBLE FIGHT LAST NIGHT*
*WE SAID THINGS WE DIDN'T MEAN*
*HE SAID THE WEDDING IS OFF BUT I KNOW*
*HE DIDN'T MEAN IT*
*HE CAN'T*
*I HAVE TO TALK TO HIM*
*PLEASE HE'LL LISTEN TO YOU*

Alex shook his head. "No. I'm done," he said, putting his mug in the sink. "Besides, I have to meet Cody and go over some plans for the roundup and culling the cattle herd."

"Wait. Wait. Sit back down for a second, Alex. Don't you think you should at least try to talk to her? I mean, you've come this far with her. There must be something between the two of you that made you want to get married." Mary sniffed and dabbed her eyes with a tissue she'd pulled from her pocket.

Alex rubbed the stubble on his chin and thought, *Yeah, the sex was great.*

Returning to his seat, he said, "Mom, what made me go along with getting married was that's what every other Whitgate male has done. Serve your country, come back, get married, and start a family. Pop out some heirs to inherit our family's fortune."

Mary sat looking at the tissue in her lap.

"Mom, what's going through your head? You have a funny look on your face."

"I was just wondering. If Gwynn hadn't asked you to have me move out, would you have gone through with it?"

Alex pulled at his chin. "I don't know. It was as if what you always say about everything happening for a reason happened. And suddenly things seemed crystal clear to me." Then after rubbing his index finger across his lips several times, he said, "It even crossed my mind that maybe Dad was looking down from above and sent down a reason so I'd open my eyes."

Mary's eyes glistened. "Maybe he did. It wouldn't surprise me." She wiped her eyes and said, "Sometimes I think I can feel his presence. And then I realize that it's because he still lives in my heart."

Alex reached over and took his mother's hand. Squeezing it, he swallowed and said, "He lives in mine too, Mom. He lives in mine, too."

It was Mary's turn to swallow. She cleared her throat and blew her nose. "You are all I have left of him, Alex. And when you came back from Afghanistan with ten fingers, ten toes, and no physical injuries, I was so grateful. But you seemed different … I don't know … disengaged."

"Disengaged. Yup. Good word for it."

"Well, I thought getting married and starting a family would help you. Make you happy. That's why I was so excited when you got engaged. But if getting married is going to make you miserable, then you're doing the right thing. Because it will make you both miserable after a while."

"About that I have no doubt, Mom. Getting married with doubt in my heart and divorce in my head is the recipe for disaster."

"I understand. But I'm a little concerned about whether Gwynn understands the wedding is really off. Do me a favor and consider going to talk to her. I think she needs to know that your mind is made up." She hesitated and took a deep breath. "It is, isn't it?"

"Yes. I have no doubt that this is the right thing to do. For me and for Gwynn."

Raising an eyebrow, she sighed. "I doubt she'll see it that way, Alex. If I were her, I'd probably chalk it up to prewedding jitters and expect it to blow over since it is so close to the wedding."

Alex's chest expanded with an overdue sigh. He walked to the back door, took his Stetson off the hook, turned to look at Mary, and touched the brim of his hat, tipping his head slightly. Then he was out the door.

# *Chapter 2*

Heaven has no rage like love to hatred turned,
Nor hell a fury like a woman scorned.
—*William Congreve*

Alex found Cody Stone, the ranch manager, waiting in Alex's office. Cody's tone was light as Alex approached him. "What's up with you, Alex?" Cody asked, pushing the brim of his Stetson up.

"Why do you think something's up?"

"The sour look on your face. And you're late."

"I had to talk to my mother about something," Alex said.

Cody rose from the chair he'd been sitting in and walked toward the coffeepot on the counter behind Alex's desk.

"Um, you might as well know. I broke up with Gwynn last night. The wedding is off."

Cody stopped, turned to face Alex, puckered his lips, and let out a shrill whistle. "Damn. Jesus H. Christ. Holy shit." After vigorously shaking his head, he blurted, "Whew. That was close."

"What do you mean?"

Cody grimaced. "Look, I wasn't going to come between you and your fiancée with my opinion of her. But next time you think about getting married, ask yourself what you're most looking forward to and compare her answers to yours."

"What are you talking about?"

Cody shifted from foot to foot.

"Didn't you hear me? What are you talking about?" Alex exclaimed.

Cody looked at the floor, then up at Alex. "Um, I overheard Gwynn talking to her friends one night at The Cedar Tavern. One of them asked her what she was looking forward to the most about getting married—"

"And?" Alex snapped impatiently.

"And she didn't mention you."

"What did she say?"

"She said she couldn't wait to move into Cloudlands and redecorate, have money, get a new car, have a couple of kids, be Mrs. Alex Whitgate. Nothing about love, partnership, sharing your lives together."

Alex pressed his lips together so hard he felt his teeth bite into them. Then he took a deep breath, walked around his desk, and sat down. After a long silence, he looked up at Cody. "And why didn't you tell me this?"

Cody took a deep breath and leveled his eyes at Alex. "Look, you're one of the smartest men I've ever known. You're a decorated combat veteran. You're a savvy businessman and a first-rate rancher. If you didn't see in her what she was after, then who was I to say anything?"

"Still, don't you think you should have told me?"

"Look, I overheard it just last week," Cody said defensively. "And look at this place. I thought things had gone too far."

Alex leaned back in the chair and closed his eyes. After a long moment, he opened them. "Tell me, given what you heard, what's your bet on whether Gwynn thinks I'll still go through with it?"

Cody stretched his neck back and forth. "My bet would be she probably thinks whatever you guys fought over will blow over and that you'll go through with it to save face."

Alex put his elbow on the desk and a fist to his mouth. After a long moment, he looked up. "Yeah. My mom thinks maybe that's what Gwynn thinks, and I should go over there and make sure she knows it's off."

Looking down, Cody nodded. "Good advice." Then, looking up, he said, "Mind if I give you some other advice?"

"Now you offer some advice?"

"Do you want it or not?" Cody shot back.

"Shoot."

"An angry woman can be a lot like a bucking bronco set on fire. And Gwynn's going to be one angry filly. If her nose starts to flare, get the hell out of there."

Alex exhaled a half chuckle as he rose from his chair. "Will do."

"Good luck," Cody called as Alex walked to the door.

Alex turned and, touching his index and middle finger in salute, swallowed hard and closed the door.

★★★★

As Alex pulled into the driveway leading to Gwynn O'Brien's house, the stone in his stomach sank. He'd had no intention of seeing her again, certainly not this morning. Foolish in a small town after what he'd done to have thought that, he chided himself. He glanced at his watch. It was a minute before nine a.m. He had two hours before he had to pick up his army buddies at the airport. He wasn't looking forward to telling them they'd made the trip for nothing. Just another consequence of what he'd done.

Clenching his jaw tighter than a sprung bear trap, he wondered how he was going to convince Gwynn he'd meant what he said. As he placed his Stetson on the passenger seat, he thought about all the times he'd fearlessly knocked doors down in Afghanistan. It was disorienting to approach knocking on this door with nothing but timidity and regret. Introspection was something he usually liked to avoid, but he couldn't help but wonder what weakness and shortcomings in him had led to ignoring the red flags he'd seen over the last few months.

As he climbed the stairs to the porch, the door swung open. Gwynn stepped out, wearing a tight white T-shirt and skinny jeans. Her corn-colored hair was pulled back into a ponytail. She stared at him, her cobalt-blue eyes bright. "Oh, Alex, I'm so happy you came. I've been sick about last night. I am so sorry. So very sorry," she said in an excited utterance.

Alex stepped back as Gwynn reached for his hand. "We have to talk," he said.

Looking around, she said, "Not out here. Nosey neighbors."

Without another word, she turned and entered the house. He hesitated for a long moment, then followed her into the foyer. After closing the door behind him, Gwynn pressed her body against his. For an instant, he felt the tension ease in his body. He felt her curves, smelled her familiar scent, and took a deep breath as her lips moved across his skin. While his body told him to linger in this space, his gut warned that this was the place where he'd ignored all those red flags, signaling that she used sex as her manipulative tool. As he stepped away, Gwynn grabbed his hands, pulling him back to her. She slipped them under her shirt, cupping them to her breasts. Dropping one hand, she stroked his groin and with a throaty whisper said, "Let me make it up to you, Alex."

In one swift motion, he grabbed her wrists and held them chest high in front of her. Jarred, she pulled her hands away from him and stood back, her mouth twisted, wild emotion in her face. "What is wrong with you?" she cried.

His heart thumped. He knew exactly what he shouldn't say and said it anyway. "You. You're wrong for me. And we are wrong for each other. That's what I came here to tell you. And that's the only reason I'm here. I told you last night, and I'm telling you again. Gwynn, I can't marry you."

Gwynn froze. "All this because I asked you to have your mother move out. Forget it. I'm sorry I said it."

"It's not that, Gwynn. I'm not going to marry you because I'm not right for you," he said, taking another step back.

She seemed frozen in place. Staring at him with wild eyes, she said, "What do you mean? Of course, you are. You're everything I've ever dreamed of."

He took a step back. "I'm not the man you dreamed of. The man you dreamed of will make you happy. I'm not that man."

Suddenly she flew at him, crying, grabbing him as hard as she could. "You are, you are. Please, please, stop saying that. We're getting married in four days. That will make me the happiest I've ever been. Nothing could make me happier!"

Alex placed his hands on her upper arms, pressing them close to her body. "I'm sorry," he said, holding her still. "I am so sorry. I never wanted to hurt you, but I know I'll hurt you much worse in the future if we don't end it now."

When her breathing became regular, she whispered, "I'm sorry for whatever I've done to make you feel this way, but I know we can work it out."

"Gwynn, there is nothing to work out."

Tearing herself away, she stepped back, looking like a pure, white ghost with fire in her eyes.

Alex felt her gaze burning into him. Then he saw her face crumple and turn red as she lurched toward him. "This can't be happening!" she screamed. Then, reaching out to strike him, she hollered, "You can't do this to me! Please, Alex. Please."

Dodging her fist, he quickly walked the few steps into the kitchen. He could hear Gwynn breathing heavily behind him. He took a ready-for-action stance at the end of the kitchen table next to the backdoor. He'd seen her flare up at her mother, Diedre O'Brien, and the wedding planner when they tried to talk her out of something she wanted but never saw her so out of control. A cold sheen of sweat collected on his neck and forehead, but he didn't wipe it away.

She stood at the other end of the table, which was covered with wedding gifts. Leaning both hands on it, tears welling in her eyes and a vein in her forehead bulging, she sputtered, "Please. Don't do this to me. Please, I'm begging you! Let's just go through with the wedding, and we can work everything out afterward."

With his hand on the doorknob, his voice low and steady, he said, "I'm sorry, Gwynn. I am so sorry. I can't do that."

He was halfway out the door when a crystal candlestick whizzed past him and smashed against the wall. He dashed to his truck and was backing out of the driveway by the time she made it to the front porch. In his rearview mirror, he could see her rage-filled face. Alex thought she must be screaming louder than a tent revival preacher as the crows clinging to the treetops next to the driveway took flight.

# *Chapter 3*

O beautiful for spacious skies,
For amber waves of grain,
For purple mountains majesty,
Above the fruited plain!
*—Katherine Lee Bates, "America the Beautiful"*

The dashboard clock read 9:27 a.m. It seemed like he'd been with Gwynn much longer than twenty-eight minutes. It was peculiar. It was like the time warp in battle when some ancient part of the brain slowed things down so he could respond to what was happening around him faster. Now he wished he could fast-forward time; then the fallout would have fallen out, and it would all be over with. Later, Alex would always remember how he had tempted fate by thinking on the way over to Gwynn's to confirm the wedding was off that she would agree it wasn't right for either of them and get on with her life. Someone up there must have read his mind and didn't like his attitude. *Oh, really? You don't think there will be any consequences to you? Well, we'll see about that.*

Feeling gut punched by Gwynn's reaction, Alex decided he needed a beer, turned the truck around, and headed for The Cedar Tavern. He turned off the radio and studied the distant glaciated mountain peaks piercing the sky, the buffalo grazing on the plains to the left and the right, and the cattle and sheep feeding on growing grass around scattered remains of human habitation. He slowed to look at the rusted tractor, which seemed swallowed up whole by tall grass on the side of a small, abandoned house, its paint stripping off and roof caving in.

He wondered why the farmer and his family had left their home and wondered what would have happened if his namesake, Alexander Whitgate, had done the same in the spring of 1862. His ancestor had camped at the base of Blue Ridge Mountain, mining the stream below for gold. But he had been out of luck and out of food.

As the story went, he decided to pray and, looking up, saw a family of elk standing on the terraced granite steps above him. He grabbed his rifle and climbed toward them. As he leveled his gun, the soil beneath him shifted, and the rifle discharged. The elk loped away as Alexander climbed in pursuit. When he reached the ledge where the elk had stood, he noticed the glint of something shiny in the shattered rock. The bullet had struck a gold vein and, as rarely happens, a sister vein of silver. It was a lucky break that changed his fortune and the lives of his progeny yet to be born—Alex was the last of them.

His cell phone chimed with a text message. It was his mother.

*CALL ME WHEN YOU CAN.*

She picked up on the first ring.

"What's up, Mom?" Alex said.

"I was just so anxious to find out how it went with Gwynn," she whispered as if asking for classified information.

"Can you call Diedre and ask her to go over to be with Gwynn?"

"Is Gwynn OK?"

"No … no, actually she's not," he said, feeling his chest tighten. "You were right. She thought our fight would blow over."

After a brief silence, Mary said, "She knows now it won't, right?"

"She knows," Alex said flatly.

"Well, I was waiting to make sure before I called the wedding planner."

"Call her and make sure she tells Deidre." He heard Mary heave a sigh. "Mom, I'm sorry for putting you through this. I really am."

"I know, Alex. But in a strange way, I'm relieved."

"Relieved?"

"Yes, relieved. You seem like you're coming out of a fog."

"Maybe I am. A fog I didn't know I was in."

"Well, it will work out, you know—"

"Yes, I know, Mom, everything happens for a reason. I'll call you when I'm on the way with the guys."

"I look forward to meeting them. Drive safe."

A few minutes later, Alex entered The Cedar Tavern. Knobby pine-paneled walls were covered with scenic paintings of Montana's landscapes and deer, moose, and longhorn antlers. His aunt was behind the bar, getting ready for the lunch crowd. Looking up, she saw Alex, and her face lit up. She began singing, "Here comes the groom, here comes the groom ..."

Alex frowned and put his hand horizontally across his throat, palm down. He yanked it sharply in the direction of his elbow.

Peg's face fell as she pointed to the barstool in front of her. She was his mother's sister and could have been her twin. She had his mother's green eyes, fine features, petite size, and huge heart. Alex noticed that the corners of her down-turned mouth twitched slightly as she raised her eyebrows and reached across the bar, tapping her finger in front of him. "Out with it before you choke," she said.

Alex removed his hat and sat down. "You mean to tell me Mom didn't call you yet? That's a first."

Peg stepped back, pulled a glass from the shelf behind her, and filled it with draft beer. Placing it in front of him, she said, "No, she hasn't told me anything. My phone died, and it's in the kitchen charging."

Alex took a long pull and placed the glass on the bar. "I have to drive to the airport so I can't have much, but that hit the spot. Thanks."

Peg shifted from one foot to the other and tapped her index finger on the bar. "OK, now. Give it up. What's going on?"

"Gwynn and I broke up."

Alex watched as Peg wrapped her arms around herself. Then he heard her let out a series of sounds. "Huh, huh. Oh-oh. Oh-oh. Oh, dang it."

Alex almost smiled. "That's probably the nicest thing I'm going to hear about it."

Peg walked around the bar and sat down on the stool next to him. "How did your mother take it? She's worked so hard getting the ranch ready for the reception. And she's so excited about the prospect of grandchildren."

"She's disappointed."

"You know I love you, Alex, like my own son, but I have to ask. Why did you let it get this far?"

Although Alex had just gulped down a mouthful of beer, his throat felt dry. "Why? That's a good question," he said, looking into the bottle. "Once I resigned myself to the idea of marriage, I sort of accepted this was how it was going to be. Then suddenly, as if a lightning bolt struck me, I asked myself, 'What the hell am I doing?' When I didn't have an answer, I called it off."

A warm smile spread over Peg's face as she placed her hand on his shoulder and squeezed. "I understand," she said, giving him a concerned look. Then she leaned in and kissed him on the cheek. "There's one thing you can't be when you're about to get married, and that's unsure. I made that mistake … twice."

Alex remembered Tex Patterson, her first husband. After he had run off with the cashier from the feedstore, his sons, Jake, and Jesse, rarely saw their father. And then there was her second husband, Wyatt

Greninger, who do-si-doed out of town with the long-legged, thirty-something member of the Greningers' square-dance group.

"Well, I'm not happy it took me this long, but my eyes are wide open now."

Peg put her hand to her throat the way his mother always did before she was going to give him advice. "You know, you don't marry the person you think you can live with. You marry the person you don't think you can live without. And if you're not sure you can't live without them, that's your answer."

"One thing I'm sure of is that I can live without Gwynn." He waited a long beat before asking, "How much of a stir do you think this is going to cause?"

Peg put her hand on this shoulder. "Look, Alex, buried under this bar are this town's skeletons. Wait and see. This will just be another one added to the pile." She hesitated a moment before she said, "I never said anything, but I didn't care much for Gwynn."

Alex stared blankly at her. "For crying out loud," he barked. "Why didn't you say anything?"

"Because it wasn't my place."

"Aunt Peg, you just said you loved me like a son. So why couldn't you have said something if you had a concern about me marrying Gwynn?"

"Because no mother *ever* thinks *anyone* is good enough for her son. And that's the truth. I think your mother had some concerns about her, but her eyes were glassed over with visions of—"

"Grandchildren," Alex said, finishing her thought. Shaking his head, he glanced at his watch. "I'd better get going. Will you tell Jake and Jesse they won't be needing the tuxes? I'll give them a call later."

Clearing her throat, she said, "Sure."

Then, taking a final sip, he said, "I'm sure the gossipers are going to be piling in here and piling it on me. Better stock up on the beer."

"Yup. People love a scandal. An invitation to your wedding was like finding the golden ticket to Willy Wonka's chocolate factory. Folks around here are goin' to enjoy devouring every morsel of gossip like it was a sumptuous dessert. Yes, sir, this place is goin' to be buzzin' tonight," she said, chuckling. "But don't let them turkeys get you down 'cause I got your back, hear?"

Bending to kiss her on the cheek, he said, "Of that I have no doubt. Everyone should have an Aunt Peg."

# Chapter 4

The light of friendship is like the light of phosphorous,
seen plainest when all around is dark.
—*Robert Crowell*

The roar of a plane touching down on the tarmac announced its arrival at the Billings Logan International Airport. Alex made his way to baggage claim, their rally point, and eagerly scanned the crowd. It had been only ten months since he'd last seen them, but it seemed like ten years. First came a group of briefcase-toting and backpack-carrying young- to middle-aged adults. They were followed by a few mothers and fathers with their squirming, young children being pushed in strollers, which were more heavily padded than some Humvees he'd traveled in. As an old couple, holding tightly onto each other, slowly passed by, Alex spotted his friends, and his face relaxed with a grin.

Donovan Bryant was carrying a large backpack. He was tall, broad shouldered, square jawed, and slender. Alex smiled as he saw Donovan's deep-set, light-hazel eyes light up as he waved at Alex. Donovan's Mediterranean coloring gave him the look of many nationalities, but Alex never bothered to ask what Donovan's was. Behind Donovan was Nick Wilson, who was carrying his backpack. Alex noticed a roundness to Nick's features and a look of softness to his arms as if he's dropped the workout obsession he'd been known for. He also noticed Nick had the look of someone who knew his way around a buffet.

The two gathered around Alex, saluted, and said in unison, "Reporting for duty, Captain."

Returning the salute, Alex barked out a laugh. "I'm here to inform you that there's been a tactical retrograde."

They looked at each other before Nick snorted and said, "One good thing about the army. They teach you how to dodge a bullet."

Donovan shot Nick a look. "So, the wedding's off?"

Nodding, Alex said, "Yeah." At the sound of another plane landing, he added, "Do you need to get any bags?"

"No, we packed light since you said you were taking care of the tuxes and all," Nick said.

"Let's go then," Alex said.

When they reached Alex's four-door Ford 150, Donovan slipped Nick's backpack off, put it in the back of the truck, and without a word climbed into the back seat, leaving the front for Nick.

Alex started the truck and stopped. He blinked. Then he took a deep breath and elbowed Nick in the ribs. He turned to face them. "You know, guys, while driving here, I worried about telling you that you came all this way for nothing."

"For nothing?" Nick exclaimed. "We're together again. I don't know about you, but that's not nothing to me."

"Me either," Donovan said.

After swallowing hard, Alex said, "Thanks guys."

When Alex pulled onto the highway, Nick exclaimed, "Holy shit. The blue sky goes on for fucking ever."

"Yeah, genius, that's why they call Montana 'Big Sky Country,'" Donovan said.

An easy silence fell in the truck until Donovan cleared his throat. Alex looked in the rearview mirror and saw a pensive look on his face as he stared out the window.

"Donovan, what are you thinking?" Alex asked.

"I can't help but think it would be easier to split an atom than split from a bride a few days before the wedding. Mind telling us what the hell happened?" Donovan said.

Alex laughed. "Well, she almost split my head open with a candlestick."

"Come on, out with it. What happened?" Nick asked impatiently.

Alex threw Nick a look and cleared his throat before continuing. "Let's just say I realized we had two very separate agendas in getting married."

"Can you be any vaguer?" Nick said sarcastically.

"I wanted a family, and she wanted my family's money," Alex said without hesitation.

"Shit, it doesn't sound like either of you wanted each other," Donovan said.

Alex turned his head quickly to glance at Donovan, then went back to the road. "Christ, you're right."

"You know," Nick said, "it would be a hell of a lot better for us if someone blew up the unspoken 'guy code.' You know, real men don't talk about their feelings."

"The more you care, the less you share," Donovan said.

"What did you really care about, Alex?" Nick asked.

"Not making a mistake. But from the very beginning, I knew in my gut I was making a mistake and went along with it," Alex said.

"You were settling," Donovan said.

Alex shrugged. "I can see that now. It just seemed like the next thing I should do." Then he waved his hand toward the windshield. "And as you can see from how underpopulated this place is, there aren't that many eligible women to choose from," he said.

For a few miles, the only sound in the truck was the hum of tires on the road. As they reached the crest of a small hill, they left the flat prairie behind them and approached a driveway entrance.

"What's that?" Nick asked, pointing to the thousands of fruit and shade trees that graced the sides of the long driveway.

"The entrance to the ranch," Alex said.

"Are you shittin' me?" Nick asked.

Donovan leaned forward, pulling himself up to get a better look. A few minutes later they pulled into the driveway shouldered by stone pillars supporting statues of elk preparing to leap. Carved into a cement square in the middle of the left pillar was the word *Cloudlands*.

Alex pressed an opener clipped to the sun visor, and the massive iron gate slowly opened. "Is this where we're staying?" Nick asked.

Alex nodded. "Your home away from home."

"Oh, I think I'm going to like it here," Nick said.

As they approached, the structure hidden by the trees came into view. The house had five windows across each wing separated by a three-story-high, massive front entryway. On either side of the house were high arches that had served as carriage entrances. Alex drove through the one on the left and entered an expansive courtyard. What had once been stables were now converted garages. Beyond the courtyard were a carriage house, the reception tent, and gardens.

As Alex pulled the truck to the back entrance to the house, Mary stepped out the door, followed by Maria Lopez, the Whitgates' housekeeper.

Alex noticed his mother's face seemed pinched, and she wasn't smiling as she raised her hand and waved him over to her.

# Chapter 5

If you ever find yourself in the wrong story, leave.

—*Mo Williams*

"What is it, Mom?" Alex asked.

Fiddling with her earring, she said, "Gwynn called."

"And?"

"I felt I had to answer it."

"And?" Alex said with an impatient frown.

"And I'm very concerned about her."

"I am too," he said, rubbing his knuckle between his eyes.

Touching Alex's arm, she said, "I'll have Maria show the boys around and to their rooms. We need to talk about this."

Alex nodded and called Donovan and Nick over. After introducing them to his mother and Maria, he explained that there was some ranch business that needed immediate attention.

After Donovan and Nick left with Maria, his mother steered Alex to the pool off the study on the east wing of the house. The pool was expansive, as was the enclosed cabana for changing and an open lanai for lounging. The lanai was furnished with a long, white upholstered couch, two side chairs, a concrete coffee table, striped floor-to-ceiling curtains tied back at its four white columns, and a mirrored wall behind the sofa.

Mary took a seat on the couch and motioned Alex to the side chair closest to her. "Gwynn called right after I spoke to you. Since you said she was so upset, I felt I had to pick up."

"I understand."

"Well, I wish I hadn't."

"Why," Alex asked shifting in his seat.

"She was hysterical. I could barely understand what she was saying."

"What did she say?"

"What I could make out was that she wanted to apologize to me for asking you to have me move out of the house. She begged me to forgive her."

Looking down, Alex removed his Stetson and held it between his hands, turning it over and over. When he heard his mother take a deep breath and looked up, Mary was biting her lip.

"Um," she continued, "she begged me to talk you into going through with the wedding."

Alex shoved his jaw to one side. "What did you say?"

Mary pursed her lips. "I was afraid to say anything, afraid she'd misinterpret whatever I said. I asked if she was alone. She said yes, and I told her I was going to hang up and call her mother. I told her she shouldn't be alone."

"I thought I asked you to call Diedre when we spoke earlier."

"I did. It went to voice mail. And so did this one. I had to leave a message."

"What did you say?"

"That something happened between you and Gwynn. I hated telling her on voice mail, but I told her the wedding was off and that her daughter needed her."

Alex threw his hat onto the coffee table and pressed his hands together, placing them between his knees.

After a long moment, Mary handed Alex her phone and said, "I called Blair Mathews. This is the email Blair already sent to the guests to be followed up with a phone call."

The email said,

CANCELLED

Due to unforeseen circumstances, the wedding of
Gwynn Elizabeth O'Brien
and
Alex Thurston Whitgate
will not take place. We apologize for
any inconvenience and thank you
for your understanding.

You will be contacted in the near future to arrange
the return of all wedding gifts previously sent
and to arrange compensation for any expenses
incurred as a result of this late cancellation.

"I feel terrible about hurting Gwynn, but I feel total relief reading this."

Mary put her hand to her mouth and sighed. "That's good, but I doubt that's how Gwynn will feel when she sees it."

Alex swallowed the lump he felt in his throat. "I don't know. Maybe if she sees in print the wedding is canceled, it will help her come to terms with it."

Suddenly Alex heard laughter coming from the house and stood. He extended his hand to his mother, and she rose to her feet. Forcing a smile, she pointed to the door to the study. "Let's go and feed your friends. They must be starving. Maria prepared a feast with your favorite dishes: chilaquiles, tacos gobernadora, mole sauce."

"Unfortunately, I've lost my appetite."

"Well, it doesn't sound like they have."

Taking his mother's arm, they went into the house. Entering the dining room, Alex noticed that Maria had taken several leaves out of the table, contracting it to an intimate size. He smiled to himself when he saw the table was set with Puebla Talavera Mexican pottery dishware. "You didn't have to go to all this trouble, Mom," Alex said, putting his arm around her and giving her a quick squeeze.

"Of course, I did," she said. "They're your friends, and I want them to feel as special as they are to you."

Donovan sat on one side of the table and Nick on the other. Each had a beer in front of him and was engaged in animated conversation. As Alex took a seat next to Nick, Maria brought him a beer.

"So, what's all the chatter about?" Alex asked.

Donovan and Nick looked directly at Alex. "We can't believe we're actually here. Together again. In the lap of luxury," Nick said.

Mary took her place at the head of the table, where a glass of white wine had been placed. "Well, it's wonderful to have you here," Mary said.

"So, how long have you lived here?" Nick asked, emptying his glass.

"Thirty years. I moved in when I married Alex's father. But the Whitgates have lived here since it was built in 1842 by Alex's great-great-great-grandfather," Mary said. "Oh, wait. I think I missed a *great* in there."

"Is that why it's so big?" Nick asked.

"Yes, the idea was that each family would have privacy in their own wing," Mary explained, exchanging looks with Alex.

"So, who lived here when you were growing up, Alex?" Donovan asked.

"Just my family. My father's older brother was killed in Vietnam. He was engaged but not married. Since my father died, it's been just me and Mom," Alex said.

Nick sat back in his chair, giving Maria room to place a plate in front of him. "Thank you," he said, looking up at her. "Can I have another beer?"

"Si," Maria said, placing a plate in front of Donovan.

"I'm curious," Nick said. "How did your ex feel about moving in?"

"Why do you ask?" Alex said.

"Just wondering," Nick replied.

"Just wondering about what?" Alex said.

"He's wondering about the red flags he saw in his own marriage," Donovan said.

"I mean, I came back to find my wife had had an affair with my best friend and announced she was pregnant. Then she fought for me to keep her on my health insurance to pay for her and the baby's medical care," Nick said. "I was an idiot. She was always making demands before we got married, and I ignored them." As if to himself, Nick added, "But, oh my, that woman could suck chrome off a tailpipe."

Mary sat up stiffly and blushed as Alex and Donovan exchanged wide-eyed looks.

Alex cleared his throat and said flatly, "Gwynn wanted my mother out of the house."

Mary's face flushed.

"There ya go," Nick pronounced. "Demands are the death knell to a marriage."

# Chapter 6

In each loss there is gain,
As in each gain there is loss,
And with each ending comes a new beginning.
—*Buddhist Proverb*

Diedre O'Brien reached her daughter's house within minutes after listening to Mary's voice mail. Although she had yet to find out why the wedding had been called off, she had her suspicions.

She'd raised a monster. From the moment Gwynn was born, Diedre had indulged her baby's every demand. Constant arguments between her and Gwynn's father had led to him leaving. Although arguments were mostly about Diedre's lack of interest in him since Gwynn's birth, they had bitter fights over how Diedre parented Gwynn. Or didn't, according to him.

While Barry O'Brien adored his little girl, he was afraid that without setting limits on Gwynn, she'd grow up having an inflated sense of her importance and be entitled, be demanding, and lack empathy for other people.

The words he'd said during the argument right before he left looped in Diedre's head. "You're ruining her, Diedre. Someday she's going to destroy her own future because of her selfishness, and you'll have no one to blame but yourself."

A cold chill came over her as Diedre recalled the morning Barry had left as if it were yesterday. She'd gone into Gwynn's bedroom to tell the five-year-old that Daddy was moving out. Diedre remembered Gwynn rubbing her eyes with her little fists and how Gwynn's eyes grew big when she saw her mother crying.

"Mommy, why are you crying?" Gwynn asked.

Diedre said through sobs, "Daddy is leaving *us*."

"Is that why you're crying, Mommy?"

"Yes, precious."

"Don't worry, Mommy. I'll make him stay."

"No, little one. He's leaving us for good," Diedre explained, wiping her eyes.

"I can stop him," Gwynn said, springing out of bed and running down the hall.

Her father was opening the front door when Gwynn pulled at his pantleg. "Stop. Stop. You can't go. You can't," she cried.

He knelt to look at her. "It will be OK, princess. I'll be back for you, and we'll have fun," he reassured her. "I'm not leaving *you*. This is not about you, but Mommy and I need a time-out. Never, ever forget how much I love you, Gwynn."

He opened the front door with Gwynn in tow, tripping over her pink, ruffled nightgown as she followed him down the stairs.

"Gwynn, come back inside right now," Diedre shouted. But Gwynn ignored her.

Gwynn kept following her father and calling over and over, "Daddy, come back inside right now!"

Diedre remembered seeing the tears streaming down Barry's cheeks. Without turning to look at his little girl, Diedre watched as he quickly put his suitcase in the car and backed out of the driveway. That was the last time without a court order Diedre allowed her daughter to see her father.

Now twenty years later, as Diedre climbed the stairs to Gwynn's front door, she knew Barry's prophecy had come true.

The door was ajar. Calling Gwynn's name, Diedre pushed the door open to find the foyer's floor littered with broken china, crystal, and glass. She looked into the kitchen and saw the table turned on its side.

She shuddered, remembering a similar scene in Gwynn's New York City apartment last year after the man Gwynn had been living with left her. That was when Diedre talked Gwynn into returning to Montana and joining Diedre's real estate company. Diedre was so happy when shortly after Gwynn returned, she met Alex at The Cedar Tavern. And shortly after that, they were engaged. But now this. Again.

Diedre walked down the short hall past the bathroom and knocked on Gwynn's bedroom door, calling softly, "Gwynn, it's Mom. Come out. We need to talk."

"Go away," Gwynn screamed in return. "I hate you."

Diedre felt her daughter's words carve a hole through her. She turned the doorknob. It was locked. Inhaling deeply, she shook her head and walked back through the kitchen, gingerly stepping over the remnants of Gwynn's rage and heading out the back door. Walking around the house, she peered into Gwynn's bedroom window. The shade was pulled halfway down, but she could see the top of Gwynn's head sticking out of the covers.

She returned to the kitchen and began to cleanup. Then she tackled the foyer. She glanced into the sitting area to the left of the foyer, the only intact room. She walked to the upholstered chair next to the fireplace and collapsed on it. Placing her head in her hands, she wept.

A flood of memories filled her mind. She thought about how she had spent the small inheritance she'd received from a maiden aunt to fund a custody battle with Barry. Diedre's mother had warned her not to prevent Barry from seeing Gwynn because "a woman can't have a good relationship with a man unless she has one with her father." A myriad of emotions swelled inside her. She thought about all the questions Gwynn had when filling out forms requiring information about her father after Diedre had successfully cut him out of Gwynn's life. She thought about all the Father's Days when she'd distract Gwynn by taking her to a double feature movie or an amusement park. She thought about how over the years she'd begun to realize preventing Gwynn from seeing her father may have been the best thing for *her* and the worst thing for Gwynn, the person she loved most in the world. The person she would kill for.

# Chapter 7

We don't heal in isolation, but in community.

— *S. Kelley Harrell*

They'd been at the table for an hour before Mary excused herself. "I hope you boys don't mind, but I have a number of things to do this afternoon."

Alex stood, followed by the others. "Is there anything I can do?" he asked.

"Yes. Enjoy yourselves." She smiled broadly and said, "Alex, why don't you take them up to the billiard room? The fridge and bar are stocked. It'll be more fun to visit there."

Donovan and Nick looked at each other when they entered the massive billiard room. In the center was an antique pool table made of burl walnut lit by two large, conical brass lights. On one side of the room were floor-to-ceiling bookshelves; at its end, a stone fireplace was framed by floor-to-ceiling Palladium windows. Photographs of Montana's historic back bars and ski scenes by local artists hung above a round game table surrounded by four swivel tub chairs.

Donovan whistled. "This what I call a pool table," he said, approaching it.

"And that's what I call a bar," Nick said, licking his lips.

Alex opened the paneled refrigerator door. "I'm only going to serve the first one. After that, you're on your own. What will it be?"

After he handed out beers, taking one for himself, they walked to the cue stick rack on the wall. "Pick your weapon," Alex said.

"Straight pool?" Nick asked.

They agreed. "Good by us," Alex said. "Nick, how about you and Donovan play first, and I'll play the winner?"

Nick adjusted his pants while Donovan pulled out a coin from his pocket and handed it to Alex. "How about you do the honors?"

"Call it," Alex said, tossing the coin over the table.

Winning the toss, Donovan chalked his cue and slowly leveled it.

"You know," Nick said, "you level that cue stick as if it's a fucking M4 carbine. And you're aiming at that cue ball as if it's a fucking al-Qaeda operative."

Donovan didn't look up, nor did he speak. He kept his shoulder totally locked during the shot and hit the ball square in the center, sending the number one ball into the right pocket and the number five into the left.

After gulping down a mouth full of beer, Nick said, "I surrender." Then he sat down in the tub chair next to Alex.

"You chicken shit," Donovan said, laying down his cue stick on the long side rail of the pool table. Carrying his beer, he joined Alex and Nick at a table.

Nick sat staring at the beer bottle he kept turning in his hand.

"What's up with you?" Alex asked.

Nick looked up. "I feel like there are ghosts in the room," Nick said.

"Ghosts?" Alex asked.

"Henry and Miguel," Nick said, his voice slightly cracking.

"I may not be able to see them, but I'm never without them," Nick said.

Nick's words evoked a memory so strong in Alex that he felt physically pulled back into the night Henry and Miguel had been killed.

It had been the last mission before they were to leave Afghanistan. They were sent to capture or kill a senior al-Qaeda agent, who'd recently popped up on the radar in the Hindu Kush mountains. As the team leader, Alex was in charge of the mission. The moonless night was cold. Through the greenish night-vision goggles, the outline of a cluster of houses came into view as they made their way down a ravine. There was one house that was fairly well isolated from the four others in the village. A dog barked as they approached it.

Suddenly a man appeared in the doorway of the isolated hut and immediately sprayed bullets with his M4 carbine. Return fire dropped him instantly. Then the doors on two other houses flew open, and women and children ran out, screaming and shouting, followed by another man with a gun crouched behind the women and children. He bolted into a hut next to an alley. As they approached the hut, a burst of gunfire erupted. The man wasn't alone.

Although Alex had reviewed intelligence reports from a range of classified sources and studied the terrain, he made a split-second decision to change the plan, directing Henry to make his way to a rock wall directly across from the hut and pour cover fire into the hut's door and window. Alex moved forward and threw a grenade through the shattered window, praying there were no kids inside. He signaled Miguel and Henry to climb onto the flat roofs of the huts next to the one sheltering the barricaded fighters and watch for a back exit. Then he directed Nick to guard the women who'd removed sniper chest racks from the bodies of the dead fighters.

After a brief firefight, the enemy gunfire ceased. Before they entered the buildings and identified the dead, Alex motioned Donovan to return to where the women and children huddled. He signaled Henry and Miguel to jump down the back alley and check behind the huts.

Alex saw a young boy suddenly appear from behind a tree, standing about ten feet from Nick. The boy suddenly pulled a grenade from his pocket and was about to pull the pin. Alex leveled his gun at the boy. His finger was on the trigger when a burst of fire from Henry, who'd appeared with Miguel, shot the boy, bringing him down. As the two moved in to check the boy, a group of al-Qaeda fighters appeared at the perimeter, opened fire, and took down both Henry and Miguel.

As another firefight ensued, Alex had signaled his men to pull back and called in artillery from a nearby firebase, which took out the enemy group holding the perimeter of the village.

It was a few minutes before anyone spoke. Nick cleared his throat. "Too many nights I've relived that night. Sometimes I think I can see them. And imagine them there while I drink to their memory."

"Well, you're here with us now," Alex said. "And we'll drink to their memory with you." The three stood and, raising their bottles, said in unison, "To Henry and Miguel. We'll never forget you, guys."

# Chapter 8

Anger is an acid that can do more harm
to the vessel in which it is stored
than to anything on which it is poured.
—*Mark Twain*

Deidre shuddered when she heard the door to Gwynn's room open. With her ear cocked, she slowly rose from her chair and walked into the kitchen. It was there that she noticed a knife missing from the block that had been pulled to the edge of the counter. With her heart in her throat while fearing Gwynn may harm herself, she ran to Gwynn's bedroom, screaming Gwynn's name. The room was empty.

She covered her mouth with her fist. The last several hours weakened everything inside her except her motherly instinct to protect her daughter. Turning on her heel, she yelled for Gwynn to answer her.

She called Gwynn's name as she ran out the back door and rushed around the house to the driveway. Gwynn's car was gone. Frantically, she called Gwynn's phone. It went to voice mail.

★★★★

Gwynn glanced at her phone as it rang and at the knife handle sticking out of her handbag. She looked at the road ahead. In between experiencing a tortured sleep, waking up with her head spinning, and trying to process what had happened, she knew there was no going back. It was over—at least for now. But Alex was going to pay for her humiliation. She wasn't entirely sure what she was going to do or how she was going to do it once she got to Cloudlands. All she felt was a volcanic anger propelling her forward. She didn't doubt one thing: Alex always considered his words carefully, and he was slow to anger. If he said it was over, it *was* over. But not for her.

"Maybe it's over for you, you fucking asshole, but it's just beginning for me," Gwynn said to the windshield. She thought about the embarrassment that would surround her now. She thought of all the people who would keep their distance and lower their voices when they saw her. But she didn't need to imagine what they'd be saying. *Well, heh, heh, heh, that bitch got knocked off her high horse, didn't she?* Gwynn knew she'd played it all wrong. She'd become as controlling as her mother. Laughing, she said in a singsong voice, "Like mother, like daughter. Losers. We're nothing but fucking losers."

Turning into the driveway at Cloudlands, she saw Cody Stone's truck parked horizontally across it.

Cody radiated self-assurance and a certain kind of sexy male energy she found attractive, even though he was old enough to be her father. She couldn't look at him without thinking of him roping a steer or breaking a young horse. He was tall and trim, and he wore a short-sleeved denim work shirt and blue jeans. His forearms were tanned and corded with muscle. He smiled and approached her vehicle, motioning her to roll down her driver's window.

Gwynn's eyes were puffy behind her reflective sunglasses. Her nose was running, and she didn't want him to see her like this. She shook her head. "No," she said through the glass.

He stood next to the driver's door window and knocked on it. "Hey, little lady, I heard you had a bad day."

She didn't have to ask how he knew. She was sure that within five minutes of Alex's canceling the wedding, everyone with a pulse in the county knew what had happened. But the understatement made her smile despite herself. Absently she wet her lips with her tongue and pulled down the visor to check how bad she looked.

Cody shook his head and pointed to his ear. "I can't hear you. Roll down the window," he shouted.

She cracked the window, her voice hoarse. "Just let me through."

She glared at him. But he'd always been nice to her. Most recently when she'd stopped by to see Alex, and he wasn't home. She'd thought she'd drive down to the stables some distance from the house to see a part of the property she'd yet to explore and would soon own. Cody was in the stable, brushing down a large chestnut horse. She remembered that she'd tentatively reached out to stroke the horse's nose but pulled back when the horse snorted and tossed its head.

Grinning, Cody said, "Try offering the back of your hand first. Like this."

Gwynn mimicked his movement, and the horse responded by cautiously sniffing her hand and blowing warm air on it. Cody placed an apple in her flat palm and told her to offer it to the horse. The horse devoured the apple in one bite, spraying Gwynn's face with juice and apple fragments. Laughing, Cody had offered her a neckerchief to wipe her face and told her he'd teach her about horses and how to ride. Lessons that would never happen now, like so many of her plans.

Now, slowly, Gwynn rolled the window down.

Cody leaned in and eyed the knife in her handbag. "Well, little lady, what you fixin' to do? Slash some tires?"

She laughed. "No, a throat."

Cody winced. "I'd stick to tires."

"OK, I will, if you get out of my way," she said with a grin.

"Oh, come on. You don't want to go and do anything that will make him the victim, do you?" Cody said, rubbing the back of his thick neck.

They measured each other in silence. Cody said sadly, "Gwynn, I've come to realize that many things that happen to us in life just don't make any sense to us at the time. They happen, and then we're left in the aftermath to deal with the new reality we find ourselves in." He bent down so he was eye level with her. "Way I see it, you have so much goin' for you. You're goin' to be fine."

Gwynn looked away as a tear escaped from under her sunglasses. Cody handed her a folded neckerchief from his back pocket. She took it and slid it under her sunglasses. She motioned for him to take it back.

"Keep it. I have a drawer full of 'em."

A shadow of a smile crossed her lips as her cell rang.

"Do you have to get that?" he asked.

"No," Gwynn snapped. "It's just my mother. Again."

He reached in, gently squeezed Gwynn's shoulder, and said softly, "Answer it. She's probably worried."

Gwynn looked at the phone and hesitated before answering.

Cody smiled and stepped back from the car to give her privacy.

"What's your problem, Mom? I'm fine," Gwynn said, disconnecting the call.

Cody looked up at the setting sun casting a crimson light in the west.

Gwynn threw the phone on the passenger seat as she watched Cody watching her. She saw how earnestly he was looking at her face and asked sharply, "What?"

"Something else I've learned in life is that breakups aren't always meant for makeups. Sometimes their meant for wake ups. I think one day someone will walk into your life and make you see why it never worked out with anyone else."

Gwynn let his words seep in. They felt like a balm to her broken dreams. She nodded, sat for a second, and backed out of the driveway. As their eyes locked, Cody tipped his Stetson at her.

When Gwynn pulled into her driveway and saw her mother waiting on the porch, she angrily slapped the steering wheel with her palms.

★★★★

Diedre meanwhile willed herself not to run down the steps and throw her arms around her baby girl.

Head down, eyes swollen, Gwynn slowly climbed each step of the stairs. Diedre stood and opened the front door. They walked into the kitchen, but neither spoke as they took seats at the table.

Finally, Diedre asked, "Can I get you anything?"

Gwynn looked up from her intertwined hands, her lips parted as if she were about to sip from the brew of the three witches at the opening of *Macbeth*. She said in a high voice, "Go. I want to be alone." She paused. Then, Gwynn barked, "If you really want to help me, leave."

Her mother's head snapped up. Tears ran down Diedre's cheeks as she slowly rose from the table. Taking the missing knife from Gwynn's handbag, she returned it to the knife block, turned, and leaned against the counter. "I've been thinking. It may be good for us to get away. You've always wanted to go to Hawaii."

"What are you talking about?"

"It may be good to get away and not have to answer a lot of questions about what happened. It will give you time to heal."

Gwynn stared at her mother for a long moment. She rubbed her face with her hand and let out a long sigh. "Hmm. It might be good to get away. I'm not up to answering all the questions inquiring minds are going to have."

"So, you'll go with me?"

At first Gwynn just stared into space. Then she began nodding. Finally, she said, "Yes." Pausing, she added, "Yes. It will give Alex time to cool off. And time to miss me. I know he's going to miss me. And that will give me some time to think about a plan to make him forgive me." Gwynn put her head on the table and with a muffled cry added, "He has to."

# Chapter 9

In good times, your friends get to know you.
In bad times you get to know who your friends are.
—*Unknown*

Alex awoke to find offensively bright sunbeams filtering through a crack between the curtains. His temples pulsated like drumbeats. He walked over to the window to close the curtains and looked down at the swimming pool below. Like on most mornings, his mother was doing laps.

He watched her white bathing cap bobbing toward the far end of the pool and thought of everything she'd been through these last few years: his father's death, Alex's deployment, and now this disappointment. It was no secret she'd always wanted a house full of children, but for her, it hadn't been meant to be. Alex knew his mother's hope for his marriage was grandchildren. But after what Cody had told them about Gwynn showing up with a knife, she said she knew Alex had made the right decision.

The sound of echoing footsteps in the hallway shifted his thoughts to the day. He wanted to take the guys on a trail ride to his grandfather's cabin on the Blue Ridge Mountain and hoped they weren't as hungover as he felt. A few minutes later, he joined Nick in the dining room. He chuckled as he watched Nick surveying the breakfast buffet Maria had set out on the long sideboard at the far end of the room.

"How are you doing this morning?" Alex said from the doorway.

Nick used his middle finger to reply as he piled food on his plate. A breakfast burrito, eggs with chorizo, bacon, ham, and refried beans. Picking up a silver spoon, Nick held it up. "Tell me, asshole, which one of these was in your mouth when you were born."

"Only if you tell me which one of those legs is hollow," Alex said with a chuckle.

"No. I'm serious. I always thought it was bullshit about you being rich. You never acted like it. But here I am, a grunt in the lap of luxury because I was lucky enough to have you as my captain."

"And I was lucky enough to have you in my unit," Alex said, strolling in and placing his hand on Nick's shoulder. Taking a breath, he said, "If you must know, *that* silver spoon is hermetically sealed in Plexiglas on a shelf in my mother's library." He waited a beat before asking, "Now, tell me, where's the shovel that was in your mouth when you were born?"

Nick gave him a lopsided grin and placed his plate on the table. "You really are an asshole. And the shovel is hermetically sealed on a shelf in my mother's garage. By the way, do you eat like this every morning?"

"No, Nick," Mary said as she entered the room. "We usually eat in the kitchen and fix breakfast ourselves. But for you and Donovan, I wanted everything to be special because you are special to us."

Smiling, Nick nodded and took his seat as Donovan walked into the room.

"Good morning, Donovan," she said.

"Morning, ma'am," Donovan replied.

"OK, then, let's get our food and join Nick at the table. I want to see if you guys are up for a trail ride today," Alex said.

"A trail ride?" Donovan said.

"To Blue Ridge Mountain, to my grandfather's hideout," Alex said.

"Who was he hiding from?" Donovan probed.

"The law?" Nick asked.

Mary and Alex laughed. Donovan shot a sideways glance at Nick, who shrugged.

Mary shook her head. "Not the law. Alex's grandmother, Martha." Smiling, she added, "Although Martha *was* notorious for laying down the law. While his grandfather never complained to anyone about her, he simply disappeared from time to time. We suspect it was to get away from her."

As Mary walked toward the sideboard, she added, "Alex was the only one he took up there. And he left it to Alex in his will."

"I'd like to see it," Donovan said.

Alex asked, "What about you, Nick?"

Nick's words were obscured by his chewing. "Flmmp, flath …"

"Just nod. Yes or no," Alex said.

Nick nodded.

After breakfast Alex arranged for Cody to bring the four-seater golf cart to the courtyard. Alex introduced Cody to the group and climbed into the driver's seat. With everyone aboard Alex drove the half mile to the stables, with Cody following in another golf cart Maria and Mary had loaded with saddlebag provisions for the ride.

Alex and Cody matched each rider with a horse of suitable temperament and size. Donovan, who'd ridden in the past, was given a more forward-walking horse, Tucker. Nick's mount was Lady, who'd been there, done that on trial rides hundreds of times. Alex's horse, Sundance, a large chestnut thoroughbred gelding with a pure-white blaze down his face, stomped his front right hoof and nodded repeatedly as Alex approached his stall.

As soon as everyone in the group was mounted, Alex arranged Nick to ride behind him and Donovan in the rear. They rode slowly on flat land, following a small, gurgling stream. Alex remembered the first time he had ridden this trail fourteen years earlier, half of his life ago.

Before ascending the steeper mountain trail, Alex halted the group. Turning Sundance around, he walked by each of them, asking whether they were OK to go on. Satisfied, he returned to the lead, and said, "If at any time you want to stop or rest, just yell out. We're not in any hurry. It will take about half an hour to get there. It may be a little uneven, but these horses are as sure footed as mountain goats."

They rode up twisting, rocky paths, around spreading groves of towering pines separated by a clear mountain stream, and into a clearing. A stacked stone wall with a hitching rail and water trough in front of it abutted a wooden bridge leading to a rambling adobe house built against the mountain rising sheer behind it.

"OK, dismount," Alex called, slipping off of Sundance and hitching him to the post. Alex untied two saddlebags and slipped them over his shoulder.

Nick climbed out of the saddle, falling to the ground.

"You OK, brother?" Alex asked.

"My fucking legs feel like jelly," Nick said as Alex helped him up.

"Mine do, too," Donovan said, stumbling.

"Well, I have something that will take care of that," Alex said, heading toward the bridge.

An intricately carved cedar door opened into a large, lofty room, which was raftered in ancient, peeled tree trunks. The walls were plastered white, and the dark floors were covered with bright Navajo rugs. The furniture was massive, carved, and painted in the Spanish style. There was a fireplace in the corner with a curved, raised hearth, and the deep window ledges were filled with flowering plants. A well-appointed kitchen at the far end of the room was separated from the living room by a long pine table. Adjacent to the kitchen was a wood-burning stove and a large Spanish cabinet, carved and painted with bright-red flowers. A brightly painted screen separated a bedroom alcove from the other areas. At the far end of the room, a circular staircase led to a loft.

"Holy shit," Nick said. "This is really cool. I could live here the rest of my life."

"But how would you get up here, jelly legs?" Donovan asked.

"Easy," Nick said, "'cause I'm not leaving."

Alex carried the saddlebags to the kitchen and unpacked the lunch Maria and Mary had prepared, setting it out on the table. He went to the cupboard and pulled out the tequila, Cointreau, lime juice, and salt. He poured the mixture into the blender, added ice from the ice maker below the counter, and filled the pitcher, then four margarita glasses. Before long the pitcher was empty. As Alex stood to replenish it, he said, "You know, the times in my life when I've felt most connected to someone was when we were in combat."

Nick nodded and Donovan said, "I know what you mean."

"Without saying a word, we knew what each of us had to do, and we watched each other's back," Alex said. "Being with you makes me realize how detached I've felt since I got back. Like I'm just going through the motions of doing what's expected of me. Going along to get along." Alex paused gripped by a thought. *Maybe Grandad felt the same way after he came back from the South Pacific. Maybe he built this place as his retreat from the world and not just my grandma. Maybe she was frustrated with him because she wanted more from him. More than he could give her.*

"You're not alone, Alex. I've felt the same way," Donovan said.

The room grew silent. The only sound was the distant call of a sage grouse's low coos and pops.

Nick dropped his head. "And I feel adrift. Empty. Like my body may have come back but my mind is still over there. I've found the fastest way not to feel this way is to get drunk. So, I'll have another one of these," he said, lifting the margarita glass toward Alex.

Twirling the stem of the empty margarita glass, Donovan stood. "I could use another one too."

Alex filled their glasses.

"You know, I've given what we went through over there a lot of thought," Donovan said. "I don't think it was the guns and gear that got us through it. I think it was the love we have for each other."

Nick bit his knuckle.

"You OK, buddy?" Alex asked.

Looking into his glass, Nick said, "I've pickled my liver trying to find an answer to why I didn't die instead of Henry and Miguel." Looking up, his eyes luminous with tears, he said, "I wish I had." And then their loss welled up and out of him in agonized, bitter tears.

Alex and Donovan pulled their chairs to form a tight circle around him, each reaching to touch Nick's shoulders. They sat like that until Nick looked up and wiped his eyes with his shirt.

Alex waited a long moment before speaking. After wiping his eyes, Alex said, "Look, Nick, none of us ever know why things happen to us. But I have no doubt you're here because you're meant to be. And you never doubt that we're here for you."

Nick stood, followed by Alex and Donovan. After clicking their glasses, Nick said, "To the best fucking friends anyone could ask for."

Just then, Alex heard the horses whinny and went to the window to see Cody with Lucia Hernandez and Casey Hunt, the best riders on the ranch, tending the horses. Alex opened the door, waving them in. Cody gave him a thumbs-up, but a few minutes later, only he stepped inside.

"Don't tell me Mom sent you up here to make sure we didn't get too drunk to ride back down the mountain," Alex said.

Cody shrugged. "She told me not to make it obvious."

Alex's chest heaved as if he were suppressing a laugh. "What, you're supposed to say you were just riding by and decided to drop in?" He shook his head. "Oh, and Lucia and Casey just happened to meander by you on the trail?"

Cody looked at Alex with resignation. "Well, you know your mother." He went on, "Your aunt has something planned for you at her restaurant at seven thirty. Your mother was worried that you'd stay up here too long and be late."

Alex's face registered a tinge of dread. "Oh, yeah, I forgot about that."

Glancing at Alex, Cody said, "It's so your cousins and your aunt can meet your friends. Shaking his head, he added, "And being your mother's sister, Peg doesn't take no for an answer."

Turning to Nick and Donovan, Alex explained, "I think I've told you guys about my aunt's restaurant, The Cedar Tavern. The food is really great, and the place is where most people go to swap lies."

Heading for the door, Cody said, "In this town, the truth isn't exciting enough for most folks. They depend on what happens in the lives of their neighbors. From what I gather, your mom and your aunt decided the best way to shut down the gossip about canceling the wedding is to show up tonight and show 'em you don't give a rat's ass about the gossip."

"Good strategy," Donovan said. "It's the old 'The person who cares the least controls the most' approach. My mother taught me that when kids at school made comments about my mother being White and my dad being Black."

Alex and Nick exchanged glances. Alex had never heard Donovan mention race before.

# Chapter 10

For every bad there might be a worse:
and when one breaks his leg let him be
thankful it was not his neck.
*—Joseph Hall*

At seven thirty sharp, Mary, Alex, Donovan, Nick, and Cody entered The Cedar Tavern. Peg, looking vexed, met them at the hostess stand. The place was packed. Each table was filled. Laughter and chatter layered one on top of the other. As the group walked by the bar, Alex noticed heads turning to stare at him. Alex knew a few couples from high school, who'd married shortly after graduation; the rest were townsfolk. Alex grinned, waved, and said, "Hi, guys. Great to see you all. Enjoy your evening."

After his greeting, most ducked their heads, turned back, and studied their drink or resumed conversations.

Peg guided the group to a private room, with expansive windows and two large French doors that opened onto a large fieldstone patio enclosed by a four-foot-high stacked stone wall edged with boxwoods. At the far end of the room was a walk-in stone fireplace, flanked by bookshelves. Donovan walked to the first set of bookshelves. It was lined with rare first-edition books about the history of Montana, from the Lewis and Clark expedition to Montana becoming a territory and then a state. The other bookshelf contained framed photographs of young men in military uniforms. There were several small shadow boxes displaying medals. Inscribed on a brass plate fasted below the medal was the name of the recipient and the year it had been earned. There were several Purple Hearts, Distinguished Service Crosses, and a Bronze Star. From the dates, he could tell Whitgates had served in the First and Second World Wars, the Korean War, and Vietnam. He looked over at Alex, who was in deep discussion with Cody, Peg, and his mother about something. Donovan saw Nick looking out the window toward Blue Ridge Mountain as it jutted out of the prairie, its peaks appearing to pierce the sun as it slowly descended behind it.

Donovan caught Nick's eye and waved him over to study the bookshelf.

When Nick whistled as he studied the medals, Alex looked up and joined him.

"The Distinguished Service Medal is my Uncle Bob's," Alex said.

"How'd he earn it?" Nick asked.

"He was in command of a platoon establishing night ambush sites. They were attacked by a large force of North Vietnamese supported by heavy mortar fire. Outnumbered and out armed, my uncle established a hasty defense, firing his weapon into the main point of the enemy attack." Alex paused, studying his uncle's photograph. "They recovered a rocket launcher from among enemy casualties. He directed the new launcher team to a better position, where they could fire on the enemies' machine-gun positions. He stayed behind, covering his men with machine-gun fire from the oncoming Vietcong. This enabled his men to gain a protective position, where they turned them back, thwarting their plan to kill not only the entire platoon but also our guys, who were encamped a mile away."

"Did your father serve?" Nick asked.

Alex nodded. "Non-scholarship ROTC with Individual Ready Reserve. He always regretted, to my mother's dismay, that he was never called up for active duty."

"So that's why you were ROTC in college?" Donovan asked. "Family tradition?"

Alex shook his head and let out a long breath. "Family tradition. Yeah, well, that's why I've done a lot of things. I knew you guys were trying to figure out why I'd joined the army ever since I heard through the grapevine that the asshole, Caden Watkins, googled me and found out about my family's wealth."

"He googled everyone. He was always looking for ways to find where someone was vulnerable and exploit it publicly for laughs," Nick said, scratching his neck.

"Is there something wrong?" Donovan asked, glancing at Peg. "She seems distressed."

"The chef is out sick, and the extra servers she hired for tonight didn't show," Alex said. "My cousins, Jake and Jesse, were supposed to join us, but they're helping in the kitchen. I was looking forward to you meeting them." Alex paused. "Yeah, and Butch Nichols, the bartender's wife, is about to have their baby. So, he may have to leave."

Donovan snorted a laugh. "I know all about staff not showing up. I told you guys about my mom's restaurant in Charleston. We have that problem all the time. Tell me what I can do to help. I grew up in a restaurant. And I have a food handler permit."

"I can, too," Nick said. "That's a long bar we passed. I can handle that."

Alex raised an eyebrow at Nick.

"You can trust me. After this afternoon I feel better than I have in months," Nick insisted.

Alex looked into Nick's eyes. "I do trust you. You don't happen to have a food handler's permit."

Nick shook his head.

Alex looked over at his mother and Peg. "This isn't going to be an easy sell to my aunt though." He caught the questioning look on Nick's face. "Not because of you, Nick. Because you're her guest, and you don't have a food handler's permit."

Alex managed to convince Peg that Maria and his mother had fed them so well during the day that nobody was hungry. Although she protested, Alex suggested she cook them a real western-style breakfast after the dinner crowd was gone, and Peg grudgingly agreed.

Alex and Peg walked over to Nick and Donovan. Alex thought he saw a flicker of fear registered behind Peg's eyes. Pointing to Nick, Donovan, said, "Don't worry, Miss Peg. Nick was best mixologist on the base, and I've been waiting tables since I was knee high to a grasshopper."

"OK then. Alex, take them through the patio to the locker room. There are extra Cedar Tavern T-shirts to change into, and I'll meet you in the kitchen. I'm embarrassed to have you do this, but I appreciate it."

Peg turned to Cody and Mary. Cody asked, "What I can do to help you, Peg?"

"Me, too. Give me a job," Mary said.

Peg gave her sister a chin chuck and kissed her on the cheek. With a wink, she said, "OK. Mary, you can man the hostess station, and Cody, you can bus tables."

Cody smiled slightly and tipped the brim of his Stetson. "Pleasure, ma'am. Do I have to change?"

"No, you look authentic," Peg said, smiling.

When Peg entered the kitchen, she saw Alex at the corner table explaining the computer software he'd programmed for the restaurant to Nick and Donovan. Jake was at the chef's station, and Jesse was on the line; both were a blur of movement. Stainless steel was everywhere: appliances, countertops, backsplash, sinks, pots, and knives. Peg organized the kitchen following the Auguste Escoffier "brigade system." A trough for dirty dishes was located next to the back door. Stationed at its side was a deeply tanned young man, who wore earphones and hummed to himself while he scraped food into the trash and loaded the dishwasher.

Alex had programmed the software according to Peg's specifications. Each code represented the ingredients to the food ordered, and on a seating diagram, a flashing dot indicated the location of the guest who'd ordered it. Hanging down from the ceiling were computer screens at every station and at the pickup location for the order. Based on the code that flashed on the screen representing what was ordered, Jesse and Jake flew into action.

"If everyone is OK in here, I'm going out front," Peg said. "Call me if you need anything," she added, walking through the swinging door.

A few minutes later, Nick was at the bar, filling orders. Donovan was waiting tables in the front of the house. Alex remained in the kitchen, acting like a sous-chef for Jake and Jesse.

The only spoken words were those focused on the orders they had to fill. The dishes, once prepared, were placed under heat lamps. Within minutes the door would swing open, chatter from the dining room filtering the air, and without a word, Donovan or another server would pick up and disappear with the plated order.

It wasn't until the orders began to trickle in that Alex thought this night was supposed to have been a pre-wedding celebration. "I have to admit I got in over my head with Gwynn," he said.

Jake and Jesse looked at each other and rolled their eyes. "You think?" Jake said, smirking.

"All I can say is that it's going to be boring after all the shit dies down," Jesse added.

"Don't worry. There's a support group for gossipers who meet regularly at the bar out there. They'll find something or someone else to talk about soon enough," Jake said.

Alex laughed as he looked up while an order code on the screen flashed, and he went back to work.

The kitchen closed at ten and the bar at eleven. Things began to slow down at quarter of ten. By ten thirty the stations were being cleaned and the trash bagged.

Peg came in as Alex, Jake, and Jesse were taking off their aprons. Smiling broadly, she gave each a hug. "I can't believe how well tonight went. But if it hadn't been for you guys and Alex's friends, the shit really would have hit the fan," she said. "And you, Alex. Your program avoided total chaos tonight. I can't thank you enough." Waving toward the door, she said, "Now come on out. There are only the usual suspects in the bar, and there's a table set for you all in there."

Behind the bar, Nick polished glasses lined up on the counter as a few stragglers nursed their drinks.

"Where's Butch?" Jake asked.

"His wife called around eight, and he ran out of here like a bat out of hell," Nick said, laughing.

Jake smiled. "Butch has been so excited about becoming a father. I'm really happy for him."

"Hey, Alex," Nick called, walking to the end of the bar and waving Alex over.

"What's up?" Alex asked.

"I overheard some news about your ex, if you want to hear it," Nick whispered.

Alex shrugged. "It's only a matter of time until I do. I might as well hear it from you."

"Apparently, she's leaving for Hawaii with her mother tomorrow, so she didn't have to be here for what was supposed to be her wedding day," Nick said.

"Who'd you hear that from?" Alex asked.

"Two ladies were talking about it," Nick said. "They're pissed that they're not going to the wedding or getting to see Cloudlands."

"Oh," Alex said, letting out a breath he didn't know he was holding. He waited a beat and added, "Good. That'll be good for Gwynn."

"Do you want to hear what else they said?"

Alex shrugged. "I don't know. Do I?"

Nick nodded. "They said they thought she was after your money."

*If they said that, there has to be more,* Alex thought. "That's not all they said, is it?"

Nick's Adam's apple moved up and down as he wiped another glass. "Well, they did say they thought you were a shit for dumping her at the last minute." He laughed, then added, "One of them smiled and seemed to be licking her lips as she said, 'Well, the upside is, it means Alex is back on the market.'"

Alex rubbed the back of his neck. "Yeah, well, that's not likely. Come on, let's sit down. I need a beer."

They walked to a large circular table in the corner set with glasses and two pitchers of beer. Alex noticed two women at a nearby booth looking at him. As Nick poured the beer, Donovan collapsed in a chair and blurted out, "Alex, you programmed that computer system?" Leaning on his elbows, hands clasped, Donovan said, "Boy my mother sure could use something like this at her restaurant." After clearing his throat, he added, "Any chance you might be able to come to Charleston and do the same thing for my mother?"

Alex studied Donovan as if trying to decipher his words. For as long as he'd known him, Donovan had never asked anyone for a favor. He noticed Donovan's jaw tighten as he waited for Alex's reply.

A slow smile spread across Alex's face. "Are you kidding? For you ... anything." His smile grew broader as he realized he'd just been handed a way to escape the small-town drama for a while.

# Chapter 11

Only those who risk going too far can
possibly find out how far they can go.
—*T. S. Eliot*

A week later, Alex stood next to the conveyor in baggage claim at the Charleston International Airport. He spotted his suitcase as it rounded the corner toward him. He was bending forward to pick it up when a hand came around him and lifted it off the conveyor. He looked over his shoulder to find himself face-to-face with a grinning Donovan.

"What's up with valeting my suitcase?" Alex said, pointing to the end of Donovan's arm.

"Now, you're my guest, brother. You have anything else to collect?"

"Only this," Alex said, bending over to pick up his backpack.

"Great. Let's go. I'm parked in short-term right across the street."

As the automatic sliding doors opened, a wave of heat and humidity Alex thought was hot enough to burn his bones washed over him, and the bright sun's rays cast a burst of light, causing him to squint. "Holy shit, it's fucking hot!" Alex said.

"You'll get used to it."

"When? When I'm finished baking like a loaf of bread?"

Donovan sputtered a laugh. "December. Then you'll only feel like you're baking like a fruit cake."

"Great. I'm only here for a week."

"Well, the place you're staying in is air-conditioned, and so is the restaurant."

Alex shrugged. "Good to know."

They were quiet as they walked to Donovan's truck. The unspoken code of camaraderie between them—silence—was more bonding than words.

Leaving the airport, they merged onto I-26 and a concrete bridge came into view. It was just high enough for small boats to navigate under. On either side of the bridge, marshes stretched out as far as the eye could see.

"This is really beautiful. It's not Montana, but it's open and expensive, and you don't feel hemmed in," Alex said, looking out the window.

Once over the bridge, they drove a short way, took an exit, and turned onto a road bordered by creeks, marshes, and palmetto trees. Alex looked out the window as lush, tropical growth seemed to morph from light green to deep green to an iridescent shade of green.

They drove a few miles and turned onto a pebbled driveway, where huge oak trees stood sentinel on either side, their intertwining branches reaching for each other like yearning arms. The canopy overhead created a tree tunnel. At the end of the tunnel, a huge white house with two wings and a grand front staircase came into view. A piazza ran across the full length of its front, and it had a Palladian entrance, Doric columns, and a fan window in the attic.

The sun's yellow-gold light cast long shadows under the great limbs of several more majestic oaks guarding the house's entrance. The gray Spanish moss hanging from their limbs floated like gossamer drapery.

"This is spectacular. I don't know why you were impressed with the ranch. This looks just as grand," Alex said.

"I think it depends on what you're used to. I'm used to this type of architecture. It's Lowcountry. Your house is in a class by itself. Between the scope of the land surrounding it and its outline against a sky that goes on forever, it's something I'd never seen before."

"Well, I've never seen anything like this before. Um, I take it back, it looks like Tara in *Gone with the Wind*."

Donovan smiled, steering the car to a parking area beside a large side porch. "Tell my mother. She'll love hearing it. She bought it after the financial crash in 2008 with an eye toward making it either a bed-and-breakfast or a wedding venue she'll run after she retires."

"Perfect setting for either one. Where in Charleston is your mother's restaurant?"

"Downtown across from White Park and the harbor. It's about half an hour without traffic."

"Where am I staying?"

"Downtown, in the converted carriage house behind the restaurant."

Alex's jaw slid to the left as he took in an audible breath.

Donovan's brows furrowed. "You all right?"

Alex paused a moment before answering. "Yeah. Just thinking about Gwynn telling me she thought my mother should move into the carriage house on our ranch. Even now I can feel my temperature soaring when I think about it. Like I'm ready to break into a sweat."

Donovan put his hand on Alex's shoulder and opened the car door. "Bygones. Come on. Mom's waiting for us."

Alex followed Donovan through a side door that funneled them into a paneled butler's pantry. When Alex saw the huge gourmet kitchen it opened onto, with two copper pots on the stove, an ambrosial fragrance emanating from them, he thought about how much his aunt and his mother would love it. On the far wall was a door-less pantry stocked with earthenware jars of rice, grits, wheat flour he figured were essentials for a southern cook. The screen door to the loggia on the back porch opened, and a tall, thin woman stepped in. Her dark, ginger shoulder-length hair was striking against her translucent, white skin. She smiled broadly as she walked to Alex, her Bermuda-blue eyes dancing. "Alex, thank you for coming. We're excited to have you."

"Pleased to be here, Mrs. Bryant," Alex said, extending his hand.

Opening her arms for a hug, she said. "My name's Charlotte, but everyone calls me 'Lotte.'"

She stepped back after a brief embrace. "I hope you're hungry. I made lunch. Donovan, why don't you get something for y'all to drink and sit out on the loggia. I've set the table there."

Donovan opened the double-door refrigerator and lifted a beer toward Alex, who gave a thumbs-up. Donovan pointed to the screen door, and Alex followed him onto a terrace with a floor made of ancient handmade bricks laid out in a basket-weave pattern overlooking a bronze, fluted three-tiered fountain, with water flowing into a large basin from two of its tiers.

The fountain was surrounded by a lush, circular garden rich with the scent of lavender and confederate jasmine. A minute later the screen door opened. Lotte carried a deep-dish lined with a red-checkered cloth napkin cradling buttermilk fried chicken and another dish brimming with cheese slaw salad. Donovan jumped to his feet, taking the dishes from her and placing them on the table.

Alex and Donovan stood until Lotte was seated. "This food looks amazing," Alexsaid. Pointing to the fountain, he continued, "And this house and garden—I feel like I'm on a movie set."

Lotte beamed. "Thanks. It's taken a lot out of me and my bank account, but it's my passion, other than my restaurant."

"Donovan said you may turn this into a bed-and-breakfast or wedding venue. I have to tell you that after last week, the last thing I could ever imagine becoming excited about is a wedding venue. But even I'd be tempted to get married to have a wedding here. Or stay here if it's a bed-and-breakfast."

Lotte studied Alex for a moment. "I understand from Donovan that you live in a pretty spectacular place yourself."

Alex shook his head. "Yes, but I didn't have anything to do with building it. You created this."

Donovan sat back and smiled.

Lotte blushed. "Thanks, Alex. I appreciate your kind words." She cleared her throat. "So, tell me how you came to write a program for a restaurant, with you being a rancher."

"Well, during one parents' weekend in college, my father and I attended a lecture on AI, artificial intelligence, and farming. The use of drones and computer programs to keep track of the herd and crops. In Montana we're plagued with blister beetles that feed on potato, sugar beet, and alfalfa hay. After that my father wanted to start using drones to look for stunted crops, signs of pest and weed damage, downed fences. He also wanted to test soil and count the herd with it—things like that. So, I began to study cloud computing, predictive analytics, and various new ways to conduct, operate, and manage a high-tech ranch. I learned how to write programs for it."

"Your father must have been very proud of you," Lotte said.

"He was and proud to be the first in our parts to start using AI to run a ranch. When I came home for breaks, we'd work on it together." Alex looked down for a second. "Those are some of the happiest memories I have. It was the first time I was teaching him something."

Lotte smiled, looked at Donovan, and said, "When we parents see our child succeed at something we couldn't have done, we feel a sense of redemption for all the mistakes we've made while raising them."

"Thanks. You can be equally as proud of Donovan's construction company," Alex said.

"I am. Very proud of him," she said, smiling at Donovan. "I'm proud of both of my children. I'm eager for you to meet Brooke. She lives here with me. She can show you around Charleston. She used to give tours at the visitors' center downtown. She's the family historian."

"I look forward to meeting her," Alex said.

"Donovan told me that it's your mother's sister who owns the restaurant," Lotte said.

"Yes, my Aunt Peg. She bought the restaurant after her last divorce. She heard what I'd done at the ranch and asked if I could write a program for her restaurant."

"Alex has been asked to write programs for other restaurants, and he's declined. I didn't know that when I asked him to help us," Donovan said.

"How did you find out?" Alex asked.

"Nick."

Laughing, Alex said, "Yeah. Nick. He wanted to stay and help my aunt until her bartender returned from family leave. I told him he could stay up at the hideout or in the carriage house. He chose the carriage house." Alex pulled at his jaw. "Did Nick tell you he's seeing Lucia?"

"No," Donovan said, his eyes growing wide.

"Yeah, she's teaching him to ride, and I think maybe some other things. And he started exercising again."

"He sounded good when I talked to him." Arching his eyebrow, Donovan added, "But he made no mention of Lucia."

"You know Nick," Alex said.

"Yeah, aren't we glad we do?" replied Donovan.

Alex replied with a thumbs-up.

# Chapter 12

GLENDOWER. I can call spirits from the vastly deep.
HOTSPUR. Why, so can I; or so can any man.
But will they come when you call for them?
—*William Shakespeare, Henry IV, act 3, scene 1*

After lunch Lotte walked Donovan and Alex to the porch next to the parking area. "Once you're settled in the carriage house, we can meet at the restaurant, and I'll show you around," she said.

"G-r-eat," Alex stuttered, looking past Lotte to the bank of oak trees next to the driveway.

"What's wrong?" Lotte asked, following Alex's eyes.

Pointing to an oak tree on the edge of the driveway, he said, "There, under the oak. For a second, I *thought* I saw the profile of a girl leaning against its base. But then she … disappeared."

Lotte broke into a broad smile and exchanged a look with Donovan. "Welcome to Charleston, South Carolina, one of the most haunted destinations in America."

"Yeah? Well, my ranch is close to one of the top ghost town destinations in Montana, but I've never actually seen a ghost. I mean, if that's what I saw—" Alex said, stretching his neck to look toward the tree.

"Yes. That was Clarissa. She's from the plantation next door. She's harmless. In a hundred and fifty years, she's never hurt anyone. We only see her when a new young man comes by. Which is rarely. She's looking for the Irishman who jilted her," Donovan said.

Alex nodded as he studied the tree and the large, knotted base that extended like a giant antediluvian foot. He noticed the Crayola-green leaves, deep-ridged bark, and silvery moss hanging from its limbs, which seemed a deeper shade than the trees it stood next to. "Good to know she's harmless, but who is she?" Alex said, the vertical lines between his eyes deepening.

"She was an enslaved young, gullible girl, who fell in love with the plantation's Irish gardener," Lotte said.

Alex rubbed his chin as he shot Donovan a look.

"The Irishman talked Clarissa into stealing her mistress's jewels, promising to take her away with him. But after she did and gave the jewels to him, he left, telling her to wait under the oak until he had returned. He promised her he'd be back after he sold the jewelry and buy her freedom."

"Nice guy," Alex said, grimacing.

"Wasn't he though?" Lotte remarked.

"Well, anyway," Donovan continued, "to cover her crime, Clarissa attempted to set the house on fire, but she wasn't much of an arsonist or a liar. When interrogated, she confessed to both the theft and arson, and was hanged. Legend has it, she waits for the Irishman's return underneath the oak."

"Do you believe in ghosts?" Lotte asked.

Alex shifted his gaze from the tree to Lotte. Scratching the side of his head, he said, "In answer to your question, I consider myself open to the possibility."

"That's good because the house the restaurant is located in was once considered one of the most haunted in Charleston," Lotte said.

"My father got into studying ghosts after he bought the house because it was haunted, like a lot of old houses around here," Donovan said.

"Well, Clarissa is harmless, and so were the ghosts in the house downtown, so let's get on with our day," Lotte urged.

"You remind me of my mother," Alex said.

Lotte regarded him with an affectionate look. "She's an 'either conquer something or be consumed by it' kind of girl, is she?"

"That she is," Alex said.

"I think I'd like her," Lotte said.

"Yes, you would," Donovan agreed, smiling.

# Chapter 13

When your mouth stumbles, it's worse than feet.

—*Oji Proverb*

Alex looked out over the marina on the right side of the Ashley River as they crossed the bridge connecting the Charleston peninsula. "Welcome to the 'Holy City,'" Donovan said as he turned onto Calhoun Street. "Know much about Charleston's history?"

"What everyone else knows. The Civil War started here."

Donovan winced.

"What's the face for?" Alex asked.

"Charleston is more than the place where the Civil War started." There was a long beat before Donovan added, "Ya know, Charleston is a lot like our mothers. She gets the wind knocked out of her, but she comes back strong."

Alex smiled. "Educate me about 'her'—Charleston, that is."

"Well, of all the early American cities, and before Pierre L'Enfant ever thought about laying out DC, Charleston and Philadelphia were the only planned cities. Charleston was a commercial experiment cooked up by a group of English lords."

"That I do remember."

"Were you aware their plan included the *entire* Carolina territory, which was originally the land in both North and South Carolina?"

"No."

"As I said, Charleston was a commercial experiment. The English lords broke the territory up to make more money from the trade that was established."

"Interesting."

"I think what's really interesting is how they found potential settlers to come here. I mean, the sea journey was perilous, and the hardships the settlers faced in an uncivilized land were pretty miserable. This was before advertising executives like *Mad Men*. Anyway, to make it attractive and worth the risk, they hatched schemes to entice people into making the trip."

"Such as?"

"Like allowing the settlers of any religion complete freedom to worship as they chose. A decision based solely on the hope that it would increase profitability by attracting more varied settlers like carpenters, blacksmiths, farmers, tailors, and the like. And it did. It brought French Huguenots. Protestants of all denominations, Jews, and Catholics came here to be free to practice their religion."

Donovan turned toward Alex, lifted his hand above his head, and said, "And that's why they call Charleston, 'the Holy City.'" Pausing, he continued, "But there was *nothing* holy about their idea of the headright system."

"Indentured servitude?"

"A bastardized concept of it," Donovan said, shaking his head. "You see, while White indentured servants, like those who came over in the *Mayflower,* could work for a designated number of years, repay their sponsor, and then get the land grant they had been promised, there was no opportunity for a kidnapped African whose fee for their passage was included in the price they were sold for." Donovan looked over at Alex for a second. "And since Africans weren't paid or given any record of what they owed, there was no way out of enslavement unless their owner agreed to allow them to self-purchase. There was also manumission when a slave owner voluntarily freed a slave."

"Why would an owner do that, to make them feel good about themselves?"

Donovan pursed his lips. "The motivations were pretty complex, but for whatever reason, some slaves were freed, and that gave hope to other slaves."

"The whole subject of human trafficking turns my stomach. And I don't know much about slavery in the South, but my grandfather was a student of the slavery in the American West. He taught me a lot about what Native Americans went through and how thousands of them were enslaved in Colonial New England. He said there was a period in the late sixteenth century when more Native Americans were exported as slaves to Europe through Charleston than African slaves were imported."

"Well, you can't understand Southern culture without understanding its relation to slavery," Donovan said, glancing over at Alex.

Meeting Donovan's eyes, Alex said, "And you can't understand human nature without understanding humans can be the kindest, gentlest, most generous species on earth and at the same time the cruelest and most murderous."

Donovan pulled onto a cobblestone street in an upscale neighborhood and said, "Well, moving from Charleston's cultural history to its geographical history, we are crossing Broad Street into an area called 'South of Broad.' This is where most of the architecture that brings millions of tourists from all over the world is located, along with my mother's restaurant."

Alex noticed a street sign on the left read "East Bay," and another sign on a fenced driveway said the "Carolina Yacht Club." There were boats of various sizes moored to docks in the club's private enclave that were cut from a slice of the harbor.

"Nice boats," Alex said.

"That's a private sailing club. It's been here since the late 1800s. Like most of the private clubs in Charleston, it's by invitation only.

I've been invited to join, but the only boat I want to own is a badass fishing boat. What'd you think? Can you see that docked alongside those?" Donovan chuckled to himself. "Anyway, that's the Cooper River that flows into the Atlantic."

As they rounded the corner, Donovan said, "Just ahead on the right is my mother's restaurant, Serenity."

Alex looked at the huge Greek Revival mansion with a three-story piazza surrounded by ancient oak trees and said, "It looks serene."

"From the outside. It can be chaos in the kitchen, which is why I really appreciate you being willing to bring calm to it."

Alex looked over at him. "Thank *you*."

"For what?" Donovan said as he pulled into the driveway next to Serenity.

"For giving me an excuse to get out of town." Alex paused. "The way things have happened, it's convinced me breaking up with Gwynn was meant to be."

They pulled up in front of a stone carriage house at the end of the driveway. After Donovan put the truck in park, he turned to Alex and said, "Here it is. Your home away from home. We'd better get goin'. Mom and my sister will be here before we know it."

"How come you've never talked about your sister?"

Donovan took his cell phone from the dashboard holder, swiped it, and turned it toward Alex. Alex's assessing eyes widened as he shook his right hand vigorously as if to cool it. "Ooooh. Holy shit. She's a stunner." He waited a beat and added, "I bet she beats 'em off with a stick."

Donovan pursed his lips and nodded. "You'll see. She uses her wits." He held his hand out for his phone, but Alex had it in a tight grip, staring at the screen. As Donovan opened the truck's door, he said, "Yeah, that's why I never showed her to you guys. Can you imagine the ribbing I'd have taken from that asshole Watkins? Anyway, she just broke up with someone she'd been seeing. He wanted to get more serious, and she didn't."

Handing the phone back, Alex got out of the truck. He lifted his suitcase from the back, slung his backpack over his shoulder, and followed Donovan to the front door. As it creaked open, Donovan stepped aside. When Alex entered, he looked around the room, took his Stetson off, and hung it on the hook next to the door. To the right of the door was an enormous mahogany secretary elegantly ornamented with decorative drawer pulls and reeded panels.

"That's some fine piece of furniture," Alex said.

"That it is. It was made by an enslaved craftsman."

"Why isn't it in your mom's house? It looks like that's where it belongs," Alex said.

"That's right. You were only in the kitchen and loggia. Well, next time I'll show you around. I think my mother's family collected every piece of furniture Sherman overlooked on his march to burn the South to hell. She doesn't have any more room in the house, and since we only let our guests stay here, she thinks it's safer than in storage. It's mine whenever I get the time to build my house."

Alex noticed Donovan smile as he opened the sloped, hinged panel that became the desk resting on extendable beams. He pointed to the middle, where there were a series of small drawers. "It used to be in my grandfather Donovan's study. He'd hide candy for us in the secret compartments behind these drawers."

Alex chuckled. "Looks like our grandfathers had something in common. But mine hid himself. So, your grandfather was named Donovan, too?"

"Donovan was his surname. My mother is Irish and German and a bit of this and that. Like me."

"If I told you the genetic concoction I'm made of you'd laugh your 'genes' off."

A quizzical look passed over Donovan's face.

"Dang, Donovan. *G-e-n-e-s*, get it?"

"You're an asshole," Donovan said, breaking into a laugh.

"What's so funny?" a voice from the doorway asked.

Alex looked up, and there she was. He felt a quick spark of attraction stir in his groin as their eyes met. A moment later, he heard his heart beating in his ears.

Donovan glanced over at him and smiled. "Alex, this is my sister, Brooke."

Before he could string words together, she said, "Nice to meet you, Alex. I've heard so much about you."

"Nice to meet you, too. I've heard a lot about *you.*" *Damn,* he thought, *you sound like you're trying to sell her something.*

She cocked her head, raised an eyebrow, and stared at him. "Oh, really? My brother rarely tells his friends about me. He's *so* protective."

"Oh," Alex said, thinking he sounded like she had caught him in a lie, which she had. "Yes. He said you're a true southern belle." Another lie. This one he was about to pay for.

She tucked her long, deliciously rich auburn hair behind her ear. Her sun-kissed cheeks glowed with a slight reddish tint as she placed her right hand on her hip, bringing Alex's eyes to her well-proportioned curves.

Alex noticed she was squinting at him and looked to Donovan for help, but Donovan winced. Then Alex offered, "Sorry, Brooke, did I say something wrong?"

Silence.

Alex noticed the vaguest hint of a smile cross her full lips. His military training told him her smile wasn't one of amusement, delight, or acceptance. It was defiance.

Alex began to speak, but she raised her hands to silence him. "Let me educate you, cowboy. A southern belle is a myth of the postbellum South. Its purpose was to boost the morale of White women who'd lost their slaves so they could cling to their lost antebellum racial and class hierarchy. A southern belle is someone who isn't supposed to lift a finger. She's educated enough to make clever conversation but not smart enough to challenge a man."

At that moment Alex felt like Andy Dufresne in *Shawshank Redemption*. Like he was stuck in the middle of the five hundred yards of shit.

Suddenly, Donovan was at his side, his hand on Alex's shoulder. "Come on, Brooke. He meant it as a compliment."

"A compliment?" Brooke snarled.

"Yes, a compliment, so give it a break. He's good people."

Her expression didn't change as she fished around in her handbag, pulling out a key fob. "Here." She tossed the fob to Alex. "This is the key to my mother's jeep. You can use it while you're here."

"Hey, look," Alex said. "I'm sorry I—"

Brooke cut him off. "Forget it. Just come over to the restaurant when you're ready." She turned on her heel and walked quickly to the door.

As it closed, Alex exhaled. "Whew."

Laughing, Donovan said, "Well, that's the other reason why I never told you guys about her. As my grandfather used to say, 'That girl is like a mule sometimes. And that mule kicks.'"

# Chapter 14

If you start off on the wrong foot, the
farther it goes, the wronger it gets.
—*Anonymous*

Alex followed Donovan to the back door of the restaurant. Lotte was sitting in her office off the kitchen. Brooke was nowhere in sight. Alex's heart dropped. Pushing his disappointment out of his mind, he stood in the doorway to Lotte's office and said, "Ma'am?"

A mischievous smile tugged at the corner of Lotte's lips. "Southern belle?"

"Uh, yeah, I didn't mean anything by it."

"I know. And I'm sorry. I'm the one who stoked that fire. I hate the term and have schooled my daughter too, as well," Lotte said, standing. "Don't worry. It'll pass. She said you already apologized."

"OK, then. How can I help you?"

Lotte's face brightened. "Oh, God, if only you could. I struggle with keeping up with the inventory, the alcohol for the bar, the wine from the cellar, especially the accounting. And the dining room is always packed, and the kitchen crew works feverishly, trying to keep up with the orders. It gets chaotic, and I can see it's taking its toll on the staff."

Alex nodded. "Same problem my aunt had. Have you looked at any online demos to see how a computer program works to facilitate guest orders, inventory, and such?"

"No. I have a technological phobia. But I know I need to get over it."

"Well, the first thing is for us to go to a few websites that sell restaurant computer programs and look at the demos so you can give me an idea about your specific needs," Alex said.

She made a clucking sound and said, "OK. That sounds like a great idea. Unfortunately, something's come up that I have to deal with before we open soon. Can we start tomorrow?"

"Sure. You tell me what time, and I'll be here. And that will also give me a chance to preview some demos before we meet," Alex said.

Donovan appeared. "I'll show Alex around, and then I thought I'd take him to the Boll Weevil."

"Sounds like a plan," Lotte said. "So, Alex, can you meet me here tomorrow around noon?"

"Yes, ma'am," Alex said, smiling.

"Let's go," Donovan said. "You need to study the layout in the kitchen before we go?"

"No. I noticed it's set up pretty much like my aunt's."

"Well then, I'll give you a quick tour of the house and the wine cellar," Donovan said.

Alex followed Donovan to the main dining area located in the former ballroom of the converted mansion. "This is *really* nice," Alex said, noticing that the twenty tables in it were spread far enough apart to give the guests ample space for private conversations.

"Mom was going for 'southern elegant,'" Donovan said.

Alex took in the long mahogany bar running the length of one wall and the six booths on a step-up platform running the length of the wall opposite it. "This room drips with class and tradition." Alex paused, eyeing the crystal chandeliers hanging from the ceiling, the oriental carpets laid over well-worn wooden floors, and the stunning oil paintings hanging at focal points against pale-yellow walls.

"I'm glad you see the beauty in it," Donovan said.

"These rooms are more than beautiful. It's like a place where you could bear your soul," Alex said.

Donovan smiled. "That's what my mother said she wanted when I renovated it."

"You did this?"

Donovan nodded. The corners of his mouth and cheeks lifted slightly, and the skin around his eyes crinkled as he scanned the room. "Yup. After I got back. Took a couple of months at night so my mom didn't have to close the restaurant."

"Let's go. I'd like to try to get a place to sit before the Boll Weevil gets too crowded."

After walking a few blocks over cobblestone streets, Donovan noticed Alex's footing was unsteady. "Cobblestones and cowboy boots are a hard match."

"No shit," Alex said.

They turned into an alley and emerged on a street next to the harbor. Alex looked out at the harbor's surface, dotted with ripples from the breeze on the incoming tide, and took in a deep breath of sea air laden with a distinctive fishy odor.

"Hey, cowboy, giddyap. We're almost there," Donovan called from a few yards ahead.

Alex looked from the harbor to Donovan, who stood next to a large door with the carved relief of a bug on it. Donovan stepped aside and opened it, saying, "Welcome to one of the oldest bars in the city and the invisible point of demarcation between tourists and those who serve them. Waiters, barmaids, housemaids, valets—you name it. This is where they come to gripe, gossip, and get away for a few hours before they have to go back to whatever it is they have to do all over again."

Alex stepped into the bar. The air was thick with the smell of beer. The room's walls were made of ancient red brick. The room itself was long and wide. The mahogany bar started a few feet from the door, curved slightly, and ran the room's length. It featured square paneling below the drink rail, a brass footrest, and tall wooden barstools. Behind the bar on either side of a long mirror were shelves holding liquor bottles and various sizes of glasses. In the center was a statue of a woman holding a pedestal with a large bug perched on top. The bug was showcased by a spotlight. Leather upholstered booths lined the walls. Behind a wall of glass, Alex saw a kitchen crew working over flaring grills.

Donovan and Alex snaked through the crowd, three deep in some places, to get to the bar. Donovan waved at the bartender, a burly man with heavy-lidded eyes, who raised a hand the size of a baseball mitt in acknowledgment. A few minutes later, he placed two bottles of Charles Towne beer in front of them and asked, "Want me to put it on your tab?"

Donovan nodded, handed Alex one of the bottles, and pointed to the back of the room. As Alex followed Donovan as he bobbed and weaved through the packed room, Alex noticed most people wore rumpled T-shirts, shorts, and flip-flops or sneakers. He looked down at his jeans and boots and made a mental note to go shopping. When he looked up, *she* was standing in front of him, grinning like a Cheshire cat.

"You lookin' for a southern belle, cowboy?" Brooke asked.

"No, ma'am. I'm looking for an independent woman who knows her own worth," he said.

He couldn't help but smile at the way she titled her head, accentuating her chiseled features. She looked at him from under long, black eyelashes he thought resembled spider's legs. He couldn't help but smile at how she seemed to enjoy giving him a hard time. "OK, cowboy, let's start over."

Brooke extended her hand. Their fingers met, and her expression changed as if she were seeing him for the first time. "Hi, I'm Brooke Bryant."

"Hi, Brooke, nice to meet you. My name is Alex Whitgate, but most people just call me an asshole," Alex said with a lopsided grin.

"A man who knows who he is. How novel," she said, walking toward the group Donovan had joined.

Alex followed her. They approached the group, some of whom were sitting, and some were standing along the back wall. Alex noticed an attractive woman standing next to Donovan; she looked as if she were holding onto every word one of the guys in the group was saying as if it should be put in a time capsule.

Brooke walked ahead and whispered in the girl's ear.

"Holy fuck, he's hot," the girl blurted out as Alex approached.

He noticed the girl's coloring was strikingly opposite Brooke's. She had blonde hair, light-blue eyes, and pale-white skin.

"Hi, I'm Hollis Hillburn. I'm Brooke's best friend," she said as Alex smiled, assessing Hollis's skinny mid-calf jeans and off-the-shoulder white top.

"Nice to meet you, Hollis," Alex said, extending his hand to her.

As he and Hollis chatted, Alex noticed Brooke watching them.

Eventually Donovan, Brooke, Alex, and Hollis took a booth. After a few hours of eating and drinking, Brooke tapped Donovan on the shoulder. "I think we'd better get going. You have to drop me off at home, and I have an early class tomorrow," she said.

Donovan shot Brooke a look, but she didn't look back, her gaze remaining on Alex and Hollis, who sat next to each other.

Donovan cleared his throat. "OK, sis. I have to walk Alex back to the carriage house and get my truck. Want me to pick you up here in a few? I'll text when—"

"Oh," Hollis said, interrupting Donovan. "Going already?"

"Yup," Alex said.

"I hope I see you again," Hollis said, handing him her card.

Alex glanced at it. "You're a nurse?"

"Yes," Hollis replied. "If you need any attention while you're here," she said, pausing and smiling broadly, "just give me a call."

Brooke scowled. "If you two are finished playing doctor, it's time to go, Donovan."

The first thing Alex noticed when he stepped outside was that the sea breeze from the harbor had cut the humidity. "Neat place," Alex said as they crossed the street. "But what's with the bug on the pedestal behind the bar?"

"Why don't you tell him, Brooke? You're the family historian," Donovan said.

She raised her eyebrow at him. "Sure. That's a boll weevil. The statue is a replica of a monument in Enterprise, Alabama. That's where the bar's owner is from. In the 1900s, the farmers' cotton crops were decimated by the boll weevil. The entire town's livelihood depended on cotton, and things looked pretty dire until someone from the state inspecting the damage suggested they try growing peanuts instead. Peanut farming turned out to be a great deal more lucrative than cotton, and the town became more prosperous than ever before. The town's founding fathers decided to build a monument to the boll weevil to show that something disastrous can actually be a catalyst for something better to happen."

They fell silent as they walked.

"Do you believe that?" Alex asked after half of a block.

"What?" Brooke asked.

"That something good can come from a disaster?" Alex said.

"I do," Donovan said.

"What about you, Brooke?" Alex asked.

Brooke had been walking slightly ahead of them and turned to look at him under a gas-lit streetlamp. The mist blowing in from the harbor and flickering light from the lamp gave her face an ethereal quality. Alex was savoring her beauty when she said, "I think in natural disasters, probably yes. Things that went unnoticed or were outright ignored are often addressed. But in the wake of an emotional disaster, I think the odds are fifty-fifty. I think a person has to be ready to make positive changes. To get over what happened to them."

Quiet filled the night air. When they reached the driveway to the carriage house, they walked to Donovan's truck. As Alex opened the door for Brooke, he said, "Thank you for taking me with you tonight. I enjoyed meeting your friends."

"Obviously," Brooke said as she pulled the door closed.

As the truck backed out of the driveway, Alex laughed and said, "That mule kicks all right." Still chuckling, he entered the carriage house.

He sat down at his computer and googled "How do you stop a mule from kicking?" To his surprise, he had found an article. He read that a mule kicks out of fear of being hurt. He thought about Brooke and wondered what she was afraid of.

# Chapter 15

Overcome space, and all we have left is Here.
Overcome time, and all we have left is Now.
—*Richard Bach, Jonathan Livingston Seagull*

The next morning Alex wakened to the sound of seagulls. Sitting up, he scanned the room he'd barely examined before falling into bed. There was a bookcase on the wall next to the bed, and a high-def TV hung on the far wall. He pulled on boxers and a T-shirt and walked to the kitchen to make coffee. From the window above the sink, he noticed a bird feeder hanging from the limb of an oak tree. A squirrel crouched on a nearby branch, ready to pounce. Suddenly the squirrel jumped onto the top of the feeder and shook it until the seed fell. Jumping to the ground, it scraped the seed into its paws, sat back on its haunches, and munched away.

Laughing, Alex said, "You bandit. You know what we do with bandits where I'm from? You'd be somebody's lunch." While the coffee brewed, he sat the kitchen table, staring at his computer and thinking of Brooke. After filling a cup with coffee, he took a sip and gagged. Pouring it into the sink, he went into the bedroom and brushed his teeth. After dressing, he walked across the street to the park. Leaning on the railing, he looked at the bright-orange ball of sun rising over the harbor. Suddenly, several large dolphins burst from the water, shooting plumes of spray in the air before disappearing. He narrowed his eyes to focus on the sleek, gray skin of several dorsal fins rising and falling close to each other and noticed that gulls were trailing them.

"Hey, Alex," Donovan called.

Alex turned to see Donovan walking toward him with two steaming cups of coffee. "Well, my prayers have been answered. I made the worst coffee ever," Alex said.

"It's not you. The stuff on the counter is espresso, not regular blend. I realized I forgot to tell you," Donovan said, handing Alex a cup.

"No worries. Remember the mud the Afghan interpreter made us when we were up in Kandahar," Alex said, taking a sip.

"How could I forget?" Donovan said, putting his hand over his mouth and feigning vomiting.

"I mean, we appreciated the gesture, but man." Alex closed his eyes, hunched his shoulders, and shook his head frantically as if he had a neurological condition.

"I don't think my GI tract has been the same since then," Donovan said, leaning on the railing and looking out over the glistening water. "This is what I used to think about when all we saw was sand, dirt and dust."

Alex leaned on the railing next to him. "I used to think of the snow-covered peaks of Blue Ridge Mountain."

There they stood, shoulder to shoulder, watching ripples upon ripples of water form steps on its surface leading to the horizon.

After a long moment, Alex glanced sideways at Donovan. "Was it my imagination, or was Brooke annoyed that I was talking to Hollis?"

Donovan grunted. "Probably. Hollis seemed too keen to meet you. Brooke was probably concerned."

"About what?" Alex asked.

Donovan shifted from foot to foot. Looking directly at Alex, he said, "Hollis is a piece of work."

"What do you mean?" Alex asked.

"She acts a little wifty sometimes. She's my sister's best friend. Those two have been together since kindergarten. They'll fight like cats and dogs one day, and the next they're BFFs again." Donovan added, "They drive me crazy."

"I can only imagine." Alex chuckled.

"You're lucky you don't have a sister."

*I don't know about that,* Alex thought. Being an only child was lonely. He remembered frequently asking for a baby brother or sister until his grandmother told him his mother had lost the place where babies grow when she had him. In a momentary epiphany, Alex realized maybe his mother was recasting her longing for her own babies into a longing for grandbabies.

"You, OK?" Donovan asked.

"Yeah," Alex said. "I just figured out something that's been bothering me."

"This place has a way of doing that. So, what are you going to do until you meet Mom?"

Alex pointed to his jeans and boots. "Clothes shopping."

Donovan chuckled. "Good idea. Walk down King Street. You'll find shops where you can buy whatever you need."

"What I need to buy is into your philosophy. 'The person who cares the least controls the most,'" Alex said, rubbing the back of his neck.

"You still feeling guilty about your ex?"

Alex nodded and looked toward the harbor. "When there's nothing to distract me, it's like regret about what I did to Gwynn creeps in and stakes out a place in my mind."

"Not caring isn't the answer. You need to come to terms with the fact that there were two of you in that relationship. Ask yourself, are you feeling guilty over breaking up with Gwynn because she still cares about you, or are you embarrassed you made a mistake because you realize she didn't?"

Alex looked over at Donovan, whose face was open, as if acknowledging they'd just shared a moment unlike any they'd shared before. "When did you get so philosophical?" Alex asked.

Without skipping a beat, Donovan looked over at Alex and said, "When I saw the pain in your eyes at the airport in Montana."

Alex pressed the back of his hand to his lips and waited a long beat before he said, "When I first met you, Donovan, I knew there was something special about you. I just didn't know how special you were or how special you'd be to me."

They stood there for a moment in silence, looking out over the ocean.

Donovan's cell chimed. Glancing at it, he said, "Um, I've got to get going. I have a meeting at the job site."

Alex raised his right hand and touched his index and middle fingers to his forehead, motioning a salute. "Thanks for the advice and the coffee."

After showering and taking inventory of the clothes he'd need, Alex set off for King Street. He walked through an alley and onto a sidewalk too narrow for two people. He made his way around a group, who were carrying cruise-line shoulder bags and appeared to be studying a posted breakfast menu. As he passed a woman's dress store, he heard someone call his name. "Alex, wait up." He turned to see Hollis's smiling face.

She looked way too happy and was walking way too quickly toward him. *She looks almost predatory*, Alex thought.

"Hey, there, cowboy," she said breathlessly.

"Hi, yourself, Hollis."

"What are you doing here? I thought you'd be at Serenity, doing the computer thing for Miss Lotte."

Alex placed his fingers into his jean belt loops. "I have to get some clothes. These aren't working for me here. And some shoes for these streets."

"Oh, I can help you with that. My mother owns that women's store on the corner, and I know everyone on the street." Slipping her arm under his, she moved so close to his body that he thought she must have suction cups on it. And suddenly, the narrow sidewalk accommodated two.

"Really, Hollis, I appreciate it, but Donovan told me what store to go to," he lied. "I wouldn't want to inconvenience you," he added.

"Oh, no trouble at all. I was just dropping something off for my mother. I'm on middle shift today. I'm sure you've heard of southern hospitality. Please, it would be my pleasure to help you. Trust me, you won't be sorry."

*I already am*, he thought.

Two hours later, he had to admit, she knew clothes and every proprietor on King Street, with whom she had negotiated an employee discount for him since he'd be working at Serenity. She'd also arranged to have the packages filled with his old clothes and boots delivered to the carriage house.

Alex glanced down at his watch. It was 11:45. "I have to be at Serenity at noon, but I'd like to thank you somehow."

"When do you leave?" she asked.

"I'm not sure. A week or so. As soon as I finish the program for the restaurant."

Looking crestfallen, she said, "Oh."

"Yeah, I have to go back to work," he said.

"I didn't get a chance to ask you last night. What is it you do?"

"I work on a ranch."

"Oh, so you really are a cowboy. That's cool," she said. "Tell you what."

The lines between Alex's eyes deepened. "What?"

"You can thank me by taking me to dinner one night before you go."

Alex made a sound that could have been confused with indigestion. When he didn't say anything, Hollis said, "I'll text you a couple of dates. Let me know what works for you."

Scratching his head, he said, "Look, I have to go. Thanks again for helping me." Although Hollis insisted he ditch the Stetson, he felt as if it was still there, like a phantom limb. He brought his hand to his hairline and nodded to her, quickly stepping away.

# Chapter 16

If the highest aim of a captain was to preserve his ship,
he would keep it in port forever.
*—St. Thomas Aquinas*

Trying to shake the feeling he'd just been ambushed, Alex picked up his computer from the carriage house and entered the back door of Serenity.

"Hey, you," Lotte said as she walked toward him. "Where'd you get the khakis and white shirt? That's the uniform our servers wear, except for the tie I designed."

"I ran into Hollis on King Street. She picked it out."

Lotte smiled and nodded. "I see."

"Ready to look at some demos?" Alex asked.

"Yes. And is there anything else you'll need to do the job?"

"I'd like to work as a waiter and observe for a night or two. That way I'll get more of an idea of your specific needs. And I'll need an inventory of everything you'll want the program to track."

"Well, then, let's start. We open at five thirty and gather at four for a family-style staff meal. That's when I give the assignments and instructions for the night, and I'll introduce you to the team then," she said.

After showing Lotte several programs and working through a couple so she could see how helpful they'd be, Alex said, "I'm going to go through your inventory and catalog things."

Several hours later, Alex was looking over his notes at a table next to the sidewalk when he looked up to see a woman he could have sworn was Gwynn walk by. Jumping up, he ran to the front door; finding it locked, he ran out the back door and onto the sidewalk. The woman was nowhere in sight. *Couldn't be*, he thought. *She's in Hawaii.*

When he turned to go back to the restaurant, Lotte was standing behind him. "Are you all right?" she asked.

Alex shook his head, and then hit his palm to his forehead. "I think seeing Clarissa has me seeing ghosts."

In the kitchen, they sat at a small table next to the back door. "You think you saw a ghost?" Lotte asked.

"No. Not a ghost, my ex-fiancée. At least someone who looked like her."

"I should tell you about this house. People thought it was haunted when my husband bought it in the seventies. That's how he could afford something in this neighborhood."

"Was it?"

"It was. But my husband wasn't afraid. He knew all about ghosts. That man knew things the way the moon knows the ocean tides. He believed there's a thin veil between life and the afterlife, and sometimes a soul gets caught in it. He learned this from his grandmother, Sadie Bryant, who learned it from hers, Maya, an African slave from Ghana. He bought the property, convinced he could get rid of the ghosts." She sat back in her seat, a broad smile growing on her face. Closing her eyes, she shook her head and sighed. "God, I loved that man."

Alex studied the floor as he waited for her to continue. It was a few moments before she did. "It took him a couple of months to get rid of them."

"How'd he do it?"

"First, he painted the front door, shutters, and porch ceiling powdery blue to keep the haints out."

"What's a 'haint'?"

"It's a restless spirit of the dead, who hasn't moved onto the next world. They're thought to be more malevolent than regular ghosts. A regular ghost, it's believed, is preoccupied with resolving their unfinished business on earth. But haints steal energy from the living." She chuckled again. "My husband said haints were like bad memories that sap a person's energy."

"Good analogy."

"It is, isn't it?"

"How'd he get rid of the ghosts?"

She laughed. "He called his grandmother, of course. She said to get rid of ghosts you have to ignore them. No matter what bizarre things happened. When James saw ceiling lights going on and off, and tools go missing or fly at him, he ignored it. At the same time, he burned sage in every room to clear the air. He sprinkled salt on the entrance to the house to keep them out and burned white candles for positive energy. He also filled the house with white roses to absorb negative energy, and like I said, he painted the front door, shutters, and porch ceiling blue."

"What did the blue do?"

"It's a special hue of blue called 'haint blue.' It represents water to confuse the haints. They can't cross over it." She chuckled. "But people did. They flocked in to see if they could catch a glimpse of a ghost at the 'Haint House.' That's what my husband named the restaurant."

"Interesting name. Why'd you change it if it attracted people?"

Through a wry smile she said, "While most people in the South know about haints, Charleston was suddenly becoming an international travel destination for people who had no clue." She put her hand to her mouth and laughed into it. "Of course, I hadn't taken into consideration that people would think 'Serenity' was a spa. But with a little advertising, it became the place to be seen."

"Well, what I think I saw couldn't be my ex. She's in Hawaii."

"Are you sure she's in Hawaii?"

"That's what I was told."

Lotte took a breath. "Maybe you'd better check." After a long moment, she said, "Mind if I tell you something?"

Nodding he said, "Go ahead."

"If that *was* your ex-fiancée, I think you should be careful."

"Why do you say that?"

"Because I'm a woman who's seen a thing or two in my life and in the hospitality business." Pointing out the window, she said, "You see the courtyard out there?"

Alex looked out the window. "Yes."

"That's a wedding venue. So, I'm well-schooled in helping brides plan their 'special day.' And let me tell you, a fiancée isn't something you have one day and discard the next without some severe repercussions. It's *the law of the land,* so to speak."

Alex grimaced as Gwynn's rage-filled face flashed through his mind. He spent a moment in pensive silence before asking, "What is the usual punishment for such an offense? Sackcloth and ashes? A hair shirt? The firing squad?"

Lotte laughed. "Look, Alex, all I'm trying to say is that it wouldn't surprise me if your ex-girlfriend … what's her name?"

"Gwynn."

"Followed you here." She paused. "It would be normal for her to want to know what you're up to and to get some sort of revenge."

"So, what's with the coffee break?" boomed a voice from the doorway.

Lotte smiled and turned to face the large, muscular man who had the whitest teeth Alex had ever seen. Turning back to Alex, she said, "Sorry, I've been babbling like the Whitewater River. Calvin, come over and meet Alex Whitgate. He's the one who's going to computerize us."

Alex stood and extended his hand. Calvin sauntered over, stopping in front of him. "So, you're the one who called off the wedding at the last minute, huh?" Shaking his head, he said, "Man, wish I'd called off a wedding or two. I wouldn't have had to buy back my house twice." Extending his hand to meet Alex's, he added, "Nice to meet you. You think you can bring order to chaos?"

"With your help. You're the key component to the program's success."

Throwing his head back, he looked in Lotte's direction. "You hear that, Miss Lotte?" Calvin said.

"I heard it, Calvin," Lotte said, the laugh lines around her eyes deepening.

"Well, if I had a stake in this business …," Calvin said through a wide-mouthed grin.

Lotte shot Calvin a mischievous look. "Calvin, we've been through this. I'd give you a kidney before giving you a share in the business. You know how I feel. And you know the saying 'Business partnerships are sinking ships'?"

Lotte and Calvin laughed as if they were in on a private joke.

# Chapter 17

Unquiet meals make ill digestion.

—*William Shakespeare, The Comedy of Errors, act 5, scene 1*

When the staff sat down for the team meal, Lotte introduced Alex, explaining his presence. After going over the specials and reviewing which guests had reservations for a special occasion, she gave the team members their table assignments. Then she stood, quieting the team with a clink of her water glass. After lining each one of them in her sights, Lotte said, "As a reminder, the people we're serving tonight aren't here just for the food. They're here because we make them feel like they matter. That's our job. Whatever first world problem they're having, it's up to us to fix it. And do not forget that even when this place is packed, our guests want to feel like they're the only ones here."

Alex watched Lotte smile warmly as she waved her hand in the air to dismiss the staff. Abruptly the room grew loud with the sound of chairs pushing back from the table and the clatter of plates being cleared. Half an hour later, the doors opened, and those with early reservations appeared. Lotte also mentioned that this was also the crowd that had tickets to sold-out art openings at the Gibbs Museum, readings at the Charleston Library Society, and shows at the Dock Theatre. She cautioned that those guests would be most mindful of time. The later guests, she'd explained, were ones who came to unwind and expand their routine. "They just want to take their time," she said. "Let them. Do not rush them to turn the table."

Alex was assigned to the front of the house. After picking up the orders for a table next to the window that overlooked the garden, he asked, "Is there anything else I can get you?" When the customers declined, he headed back to the kitchen to pick up another order for one of his tables.

As he walked past a table by the kitchen door, he overheard a large-breasted woman wearing a pink dress too small for her complain to her rotund female companion about a quintessential first world problem. "I thought this should have more fish in it. It tastes too eggy," the woman said.

Alex glanced down at the small china bowl in front of her and recognized it as one of the specials. He thought about the food he'd had to eat in Afghanistan and fought the urge to blurt out, "Madam, what you're eating is fresh-caught mackerel sautéed in a warm ponzu, a tangy soy sauce made with fresh citrus juices of lemon and orange, with a plumcot, and a sous vide egg yolk jam, which requires the yolk to be cooked in a controlled temperature over a very long time. You're an idiot. It's just as it's supposed to taste. By the way, if you don't like eggs, why did you order it?" But he smiled broadly as he realized she was obviously enjoying calibrating the level of her dissatisfaction more than she would have if her "problem" would have been addressed. So, he kept silent and walked into the kitchen just as Calvin's amplified voice sliced through the cacophony, calling, "Pick up."

By the end of the evening, Alex had mentally mapped out the program he felt would meet Serenity's needs. There were six wait staff, two bartenders, and six in the kitchen, excluding Calvin, and two young women who worked the reception desk. As Alex waited for Lotte at the bar, where he'd been told to help himself to a drink, he thought most of the staff would have no problem buying into using an iPad for orders and payment. He'd noticed most of them peeking at their phones during their shift. Calvin and Lotte were going to be his challenge.

As he sipped his beer, he thought about the couple seated at a table overlooking the harbor. While serving them, he couldn't help but notice the glorious sunset ablaze against the blue sky in shades of purple, orange, and pink. Yet neither looked up or spoke to each other. They kept their heads buried first in the menus, then their cell phones, and then their meals.

Alex looked into the bottle and wondered what had happened to the couple that they'd stopped talking to each other.

"Well, you seem deep in thought," Lotte said, breezing into the room.

"I was just thinking about a couple I served tonight. They spent a lot of money on a dinner neither seemed to enjoy."

"Really? What did they order?"

"I didn't mean the meal as the problem. I meant each other."

"I'm sure you saw that at your aunt's restaurant."

"Well, her restaurant is a lot different than yours. Everybody knows everyone else, so you don't get stuck just talking to the person you're with."

"Well, my theory is that they stop talking to each other because the very thing they loved about each other is the same thing they want to get away from now."

"Hmm. That's depressing."

"That's reality. Marriage takes a lot of work. Not everyone is willing to do it." She shook her head. "Enough of that. I want to thank you for helping out tonight."

"No need. I'd do anything for Donovan. And the bonus is that I finally got to meet you and your *beautiful* daughter," Alex said.

"Ah, yes, Brooke. She is beautiful. She definitely won the genetic lottery," Lotte said as she walked around the bar and poured herself a glass of wine.

Alex sat silently for a moment, waiting for her to say something further. Then she did.

"Ever since she was little wherever we were, strangers would come up and fawn over how beautiful she was." Lotte took a sip of wine. "I know they had the best intentions, but Brooke hated it. She said it made her feel as if she had an embarrassing medical condition."

"I understand."

Lotte studied Alex's face for a long moment. "You do, don't you?"

"Not for how I looked. What made me feel like I had an embarrassing medical condition was how wealthy my family is." Alex took a sip of beer. Wiping his mouth, he added, "When I was little and out with my mother, what I remember were people's furtive looks as if we had extra limbs or something."

Lotte laughed.

"Can I ask you something?"

"Sure," she said, tilting her head toward him.

"I called my mother and asked whether she knew where Gwynn was, and she said as far as she knew, Hawaii. Do you think I should call Gwynn and make sure?"

"Well, um, no. I don't," Lotte said, looking pensive.

"Why do you say that?"

"Because if she's here and doesn't want you to know, she'll lie. And if she's in Hawaii and you call her, she may get the wrong impression. Like there's still a chance for the two of you."

Alex found himself smiling. "I can see where Donovan gets his wisdom."

Lotte closed her eyes briefly and put her hand to her mouth. After a long exhale, she said, "Not from me as much as from his father. James was a very special man with deep insights and a very clear way of expressing them."

They were quiet for a moment, the only sound in the room from the traffic in the street.

Lotte reached across the bar and patted Alex's hand. "Alex, you seem burdened by your breakup with Gwynn. Have you thought about talking to someone about it?"

"I talked to Donovan this morning."

"I mean a professional. Brooke is a clinical psychologist. She's working on her PhD. She could recommend someone."

"Oh. Brooke's a psychologist?"

"Yes. You seem surprised."

"I guess I am."

"Because she seems defensive?"

Alex raised an eyebrow and tipped his head slightly, shrugging.

"I think Brooke went into psychology to understand herself as much as to help other people. She might just be the one to help you." Glancing at her watch, she stood. Placing her wine glass in the sink, she added, "Well, it's something to think about."

# *Chapter 18*

The sun has only one day. Live this
day in a good way so that
the sun won't have wasted precious time.

*—Navajo proverb*

Streams of light falling across the bed woke Alex the next morning. Pulling himself up, he sat against the headboard and thought about his conversation with Lotte. After a few minutes, he walked to the kitchen and opened the pantry door. Sitting right in front of him was the regular coffee. While he filled the coffee carafe with water, he looked out the window for the squirrel. "You know we have a lot in common. We're both rats," he said aloud as he turned back to the bedroom to get dressed.

After filling a mug with coffee, Alex walked across the street to White Point Park. He had learned from the short history printed on the back of Serenity's menu that the park was named for the bleached oyster shells found at the tip of the peninsula. He also learned Serenity was housed in an architectural landmark built in 1833 by a wealthy planter, and the Confederates had used it to defend Charleston harbor during the Civil War.

Standing at the railing, Alex listened to the gentle lapping of water against the seawall. He thought somewhere out there, the Ashley and

Cooper Rivers joined the Atlantic Ocean and formed the currents that sent the waves he was looking at back into the harbor and out again. *Sort of like my thoughts about Gwynn*, he thought. *I shove them out of my mind, and they flow right back in.*

"Hey, cowboy," he heard a woman's voice call.

He turned around to see Brooke coming toward him, carrying steaming cups of coffee.

"Good morning," she said, extending a cup to him. "Donovan said you may not have found the regular coffee and asked me to bring you some."

"Um, I found it," he said, raising his mug. "But thanks. I could use another cup." He glanced into her eyes as he reached for the cup and thought they looked softer. After a long moment when nothing clever to say came to mind, his stomach rumbled.

Brooke tilted her head slightly. "Well, I brought you something for that," she said. "Some warm croissants and homemade jelly are back at the carriage house. Want some?"

"Are you kidding? I'll race you."

Pointing down, she said, "Not today. I have flip-flops on."

Alex followed her across the road and onto a gravel driveway that crunched under their feet. Walking slightly behind her, he noticed how shiny her hair was. When she reached the door to the carriage house she stopped and looked back.

When Alex reached the door, he maneuvered around her to open it and let her step inside. As she passed by him, he took in a deep breath and savored the subtle, faint scent of roses.

Walking toward the stove, Brooke said, "I put the croissants in the oven to keep them warm. A bakery on King Street makes them." She didn't look up as she took out plates from a cabinet and the croissants from the oven. She placed them, along with a mason jar of jelly, on the kitchen table.

"Well, you're in for a treat," she said, waving for him to take a seat.

Alex took his place at the table and waited for Brooke to sit down before devouring the food and licking the jelly from his fingers.

Brooke sat back in her chair and looked at him. "I have to confess something."

"What's that?"

"Donovan didn't ask me to come. My mother did. And the croissants weren't my idea. They were hers."

Alex's face fell as he sat back in the chair. "I see. Well, maybe it wasn't your idea, but you did it."

"I did it to please my mother. I didn't want you to give you the wrong idea."

A minute ago, he'd thought they'd turned a corner. *And now?* He shook his head to clear it. After a long moment, he said, "Trust me. I don't have the wrong idea."

"I didn't want to come here under false pretenses. My mother thought you may need someone to talk to."

"Did she tell you why she thought that?"

"She told me that when she was talking to you last night, you seemed burdened. She thought I could refer you to a therapist I know."

"I appreciate the thought, but I won't be here long enough to start with a therapist."

"That's what I told her, and then she asked if I would ask you how you'd feel about talking to me."

Looking into her face, he saw she was searching his. Her eyes seemed to have taken on a clinically compassionate look. He blew out a long exhale and shrugged. "Well, if you're as insightful as your mother and Donovan, I don't know. I guess it wouldn't hurt."

"The point is to have what you're feeling hurt less," she said with a slight smile on her lips.

"Let me ask you something."

Raising an eyebrow she said, "What is it?"

"Your mother said you were studying for your PhD and working on your thesis. I was curious. What's your hypothesis?"

"About you or my thesis?"

He chuckled. "Your thesis."

"It focuses on gender differences when experiencing a traumatic event, specifically in children."

"Interesting. What have you learned so far?"

"In a nutshell, I'm sure you know PTSD isn't limited to war. And without getting too technical about the difference in the psychobiological reactions of men versus women, my research shows it seems to be associated with the sex chromosomes XX in women and XY in men. What has been reported is about sixty percent of men and fifty percent of women will experience a significant trauma at least once in their lives. While the number of people who develop PTSD is relatively small, only seven to eight percent, women are twice as likely to develop it. As it pertains to children, a trauma in early life has the most impact and may interfere with neurobiological development and significantly influence the personality development of the child. My goal is to develop a therapy strategy that matches the patients' age and gender identity."

His jaw slackened, and he shook his head.

"What are you thinking?"

"About the trauma I caused my ex-fiancée. I'm usually good at compartmentalizing," he said, shrugging. "But I don't seem to be able to be about this."

Brooke looked down as she clasped her hands. "Breaking up with someone right before a wedding would be a traumatic event for sure." Then looking up, she added, "But the impact on her according to the research depends on her past response to traumas and her resilience."

Alex's eyes shifted to the right as if he were trying to recall something. After pulling at his chin, he said, "All I know about Gwynn's past traumas is that her father abandoned her when she was little."

The room grew quiet for a long moment.

"Alex, sometimes the hardest thing and the right thing are the same. Let me ask you this. Do you think you did the right thing breaking up with your fiancée?"

Before answering Alex took in a deep breath and sat staring into space and shaking his head. "Yes, I did. For me. But I'm haunted by her reaction, how hurt and angry she was."

"That means you're normal. It's normal not to want to intentionally hurt another person. But you're not responsible for another person's happiness. You're only responsible for your own."

It was out of his mouth before he could censor it. "Is that according to research or from a quote embroidered on a pillow?"

Brooke laughed. "From both."

Smiling Alex said, "Well, thank you for the coffee, croissants, and the therapy session. But I have to get started on your mother's program."

Carrying the plates to the sink, Brooke said, "Do you have to work all day?"

He shrugged. "I don't know until I get started. But since your mom's setup is so similar to my aunt's restaurant, it shouldn't be too difficult. I'm working off that prototype."

"Well, my mother also asked me to take you on a sightseeing tour and then to dinner at a competitor's restaurant this evening. She wants you to see the city and for me to have a chance to check out the competition."

"Calvin told me there isn't any competition."

"He's right. But we have to keep up with them, or they could be. I think that's why Donovan asked for your help. He's afraid Mom is falling behind." After loading the dishwasher, she leaned against the counter and said, "Well, does that sound like something that appeals to you?"

"It does, depending on how far I get."

"Okay then. I have to drop something off at the restaurant this afternoon, so I'll stop by and see if you're still up for it."

As Brooke walked toward the door, he called to her. She turned and looked at him with a wry smile. "Brooke," he said, "thank you. You were right. Talking about how I feel makes it hurt less."

When she turned, she was grinning at him with smiling eyes. "Good. Um, I'm sorry I gave you a hard time when we first met. You had a swagger and self-assuredness I tend to push back on."

"And now? What do you see?"

"I see someone who mostly has it together, who means well and is doing his best to figure out how to come to terms with having made a bad decision."

"I like what you see."

With her hand on the doorknob, she looked over her shoulder. "So do I."

Staring at the closed door, he thought, *Who beamed in that girl?*

He glanced at his phone. Despite the time difference, he knew Nick would be up.

Nick answered on the first ring. "So, how's it goin' in Ch-arle-ston?" Nick asked, feigning a southern accent."

"It's goin'," Alex said.

"Well, you don't sound too excited about it."

"I'm here to help Donovan's mother. It's not a vacation." Alex paused. "Look, I don't mean to sound like a dick. A lot's been happening." *Like my head is spinning over a girl I just met and one I just dumped.* "How's it goin' with you?"

"Good. Really good. I started exercising again. And wait for the drum roll—I stopped drinking."

Alex smiled so hard he felt his cheeks hurt. "Good for you, Nick. Good for you."

"When are you coming home?"

"I'm not sure. I'm just working on the program now." Alex took in a breath. "Nick, have you heard anything about where Gwynn is while you're bartending? Or in general for that matter."

"Not really. Last I heard, she was going to Hawaii. Why?"

"I thought I saw her here. In Charleston."

There was a short silence before Nick said, "I doubt it. From what I know, she's in Hawaii. Maybe it was a doppelgänger."

Alex rubbed his chin. "Maybe. But do me a favor and discreetly ask around, would you?"

"Sure. A neighbor of hers, Susan—I don't know her last name—is a regular. After a few large pours of vodka, she'll gush like a geyser."

"Thanks, Nick. Call me if you hear anything. And take care of yourself."

*A doppelgänger,* Alex thought. *Maybe, but what were the chances? Something doesn't feel right.*

# Chapter 19

No man can swim ashore and carry baggage with him.

—*Latin proverb*

When Brooke opened the door at three o'clock, Alex was sitting at the table just as she'd left him. His eyes laser-focused on the screen, his fingers flying over the keyboard. The only sound in the room: *click click click*.

She cleared her throat. "Hey, you."

Alex looked up. "Hey, yourself," he said. "Want to see what I've created for your mom?"

"Love to. But I'm not sure I'll understand it."

"Ah, that's the point. I designed it for anyone to understand. If you've ever played a video game, you'll get it. If you've been serving Slurpies at a 7-Eleven and get hired at your mom's restaurant, you'd get it." He took a deep breath, paused, and said, "I just hope Calvin and your mom do."

She sat down and began to scroll through the program. It was in 3-D with little icons specific to the item listed. It addressed food costs and purchasing order management for wine and spirits, and it tracked waste and theft. As she continued to scroll, her eyes widened. "This looks great, but how do you know where each guest's order goes?"

He reached over her shoulder and moved the cursor.

She sat back in amazement. The entire first floor of the restaurant came alive in 3-D. Each place setting at a table had a number, as did the booths in the bar area and each of the barstools.

"You did this … this morning?" she asked.

"Yeah. It wasn't that hard."

"Really?"

There was a short pause. "Yeah. It was fun."

"You have a weird idea of fun," she said solemnly.

Alex glanced at her. "Um, did you come back here to insult me? I thought we had turned a corner."

Brooke blushed. "I'm sorry. All I meant was trying to write a program for me would be like me trying to write pig Latin in Greek." Pausing, she added, "And, we did … turn a corner."

Looking back at the screen, Alex smiled. "Good to hear."

"Well, are you up for sightseeing and dinner?"

"I am, but I have to get cleaned up."

"That's fine. I'll just wait here," Brooke said, pulling out her cell phone and settling in the overstuffed chair in the corner.

Fifteen minutes later, Alex stood in front of her.

"You clean up pretty good," she said.

She rose, and they walked to the door. Holding it open, he nudged her and said, "Southern belles first."

Raising her eyebrow, she said nothing, and he followed her out the door, his eyes homing in on her sculpted shoulders, arms, and perfectly shaped backside.

"Let's go to the White Point first."

"Wherever is good by me," he said.

As they entered the park, they saw a group of tourists in a circle around a gray-haired woman holding a folded red umbrella high above her head. Alex and Brooke stood at the edge of the crowd with their shoulders touching.

The guide explained in a voice that could wake the dead that the area had been named "The Battery." Sweeping her umbrella from left to right, she said, "It stretches along the lower shores of the peninsular bordered by the Ashley and Cooper Rivers. Cannons were first placed here to protect against marauding pirates, then large-caliber cannons were installed during the War of 1812 when the British blockaded the harbor. Later it was fortified with larger longer-distance cannons by the Confederacy to protect against possible Union invasion." She turned toward the Cooper River and, lifting the umbrella, pointed it toward the harbor. "From here you can see Fort Sumter, named for General Thomas Sumter, a Revolutionary War hero. It was built after the British invaded Washington, DC, by sea. The attack on Fort Sumter by Confederate batteries on April 12, 1861, is generally agreed to have begun the Civil War."

Then, like a teacher using a pointer at the blackboard, she directed the end of her umbrella and boomed, "Out there in the Cooper River is Castle Pinckney; on the eastern side of the river is the World War II aircraft carrier USS *Yorktown*, Fort Moultrie, and Sullivan's Island, where Edgar Allen Poe was stationed in 1830." She looked out at the group and asked whether anyone had ever heard of his poem "Annabel Lee."

Several people raised their hands, and she pointed to a young woman at the front of the group. "It's about two lovers, one named Annabel Lee, who fall in love 'in a kingdom by the sea,' which is Charleston."

"Excellent!" the woman exclaimed. "Now let's walk on to the monument of William Moultrie."

Seeming utterly spontaneous, Brooke took Alex's hand, holding him back as he moved toward the statue. "Do you mind if we walk the other way?"

The split second of contact sent a spark running up Alex's arm and exited his mouth with the words "Wherever you're headed, I'm headed that way."

# Chapter 20

The axe forgets, but the tree remembers.
—*African proverb*

Gwynn's pulse spiked as she watched Alex with another woman. They seemed to be talking intimately to each other. About what, Gwynn had no idea, but she'd find out. It was why she was here. She had to figure out how to get him back. Her neighbor, Susan Wright, had been at The Cedar Tavern the night Alex and his friends were there. Susan had overheard the conversation about Alex going to Charleston to help with something at some restaurant called Serenity. Susan had been so angry that she wasn't going to get to wear the dress she'd bought to attend the wedding or get to see Cloudlands that she'd texted Gwynn about what she'd heard.

Gwynn approached the bench to try to overhear what they were saying, just as Alex and Brooke rose and crossed the street. They stopped in front of a house three doors from the place Gwynn knew, thanks to Google Earth, was Serenity. The woman with Alex pointed at the iron gate in front of it. Gwynn kept her distance though confident that, even if she were seen, Alex wouldn't recognize her in the short black wig and Jackie O sunglasses she'd just bought.

Meanwhile, the woman was pointing at different areas on the gate as Alex bent to study it. Curious, Gwynn flipped open the tour book she'd picked up and saw the gate featured in it. Holding the book up to shield her face, she read the gate had been made by a famous blacksmith, Philip Simmons. A map showed that the location of over his two hundred gates and balconies were scattered throughout the city. *Christ,* Gwynn thought, *who cares? You've seen one iron gate or balcony, you've seen them all.*

"Fuck," she said as a paneled truck parked in front of the house with the iron gate. Anxious not to lose them, she stepped off the curb into the street and heard screeching brakes. She looked up. Through the windshield, she saw the face of the man frozen with fear behind the wheel. Jumping back from the car's path, she tripped and fell on the sidewalk. Several tourists rushed to help her to her feet as the driver pulled over.

"Are you hurt, miss?" the driver asked. "Do you need to go to the hospital? Can I do anything for you? I'm so sorry. I glanced at my phone and looked up, and you were there."

"I'm fine. I'm fine, really. Thanks, everyone. I'm all right, really. I'm fine," Gwynn insisted, brushing off her clothes and their concerns.

"Shouldn't you sit down for a minute and make sure before I go, just in case?" he asked.

Gwynn strained to look around him and saw the paneled truck was gone, and so were Alex and the woman. Tears streamed down her face.

"Come on," the man said, putting his arm around Gwynn's waist. "Let me help you to a bench."

Gwynn nodded and leaned on his shoulder, pointing to the bench she'd seen Alex and the woman sitting on.

"Are you sure you're all right?" he asked again.

Gwynn heard the anxiety in his voice and said, "Yes. I'm fine." She took a breath and blurted out, "I'm not crying because I broke a bone. I'm crying because someone broke my heart," she said, removing her sunglasses and pulling tissues from her pocket to wipe away her tears.

Swallowing hard, he said, "Please, what can I do? I hate to see a woman cry." Turning to look directly into Gwynn's eyes, he said, "My name is Terry Mathews. And I'm a good listener if you want to talk about it."

Gwynn shook her head and looked at the thick blanket of cumulus clouds on the horizon.

"Well, do you mind if I sit a minute with you to catch my breath?"

Shaking her head again, she said, "No."

Terry studied her face. "You remind me of my little sister. Whoever hurt you must be a real idiot. I teach the sharpshooting class to the cadets at The Citadel. I could take him or her out if you want."

Laughing, Gwynn said, "It's him, and I already tried that."

"OK, good to know. So, what's your next plan?"

She shrugged and exhaled loudly. "That's why I'm crying. I don't have one."

"Well, I also teach tactics. Why not let me take you for a drink and get you something to eat? We can plan your attack." When she didn't answer, he added, "It's the least I could do. I shouldn't have been looking at my phone. If I hadn't been, I would have slowed down and let you cross."

"It's not your fault. I wasn't looking."

With a questioning gaze, he said, "You were in the crosswalk. You had the right of way."

Gwynn's eyes grew wide. "Oh," she muttered.

Terry stood. Extending his hands to her, he said, "Come on. I'll take you home."

"Um. I live in Montana."

"OK then, where are you staying?" he asked.

"Thank you. I mean it. But honestly, I'm fine. You can go," Gwynn said in a quiet voice.

"Look, little lady, I'm an officer and a gentleman, and I would never leave a damsel in distress. And a blind man could see you're in distress," he said, smiling with sincerity.

Gwynn perked up at hearing him call her "little lady." He reminded her of Cody. She cut her eye at him and smiled. "In a hotel nearby. I walked here, and I can walk back."

He shook his head and took her hands, pulling her to her feet and motioning for her to follow him to his car. She paused as she heard her inner voice tell her to go, that Terry was safe, and she told her inner voice that if he wasn't and she was abducted and murdered, Alex would see it on the Live at Five news and feel horrible about it. Smiling at Terry, she said, "My name is Gwynn O'Brien."

# Chapter 21

It is one of the beautiful compensations
of life that no man can
sincerely try to help another, without helping himself.
—*Gamaliel Bailey*

Minutes later the car rolled through narrow cobblestone streets and reached a pier overlooking the Cooper River. Terry opened the door of Fleet Landing and turned to Gwynn. "Do you prefer to sit inside or out?"

"I don't care."

"Outside, please," Terry told the hostess as she grabbed two menus and showed them to a table next to the water.

Pulling out a chair for Gwynn, he said, "Sit here. You'll get a great view of the sunset. I read an article recently that explained how watching a sunset can make you feel better emotionally. It's worked for me."

Gwynn sat back in her chair and looked intently at Terry. "Really? For me, I think it will take a wine glass the size of a baptismal font filled with nicely chilled sauvignon blanc."

A fresh-faced young woman appeared and placed glasses of iced water on the table. "Hi, there. I'm Savannah, and I'll be your server tonight." Smiling she added, "I overheard what the lady would like. What can I get you, sir?"

Terry ordered a beer for himself, and after confirming Gwynn didn't care what they ate, he asked for the lump crab bruschetta and calamari to start.

A few minutes later, Savannah hustled back with the drinks. With a practiced gesture, she placed Gwynn's in front of her and said softly, "Hope it helps, ma'am." The girl smiled at Terry and walked to another table.

Terry lifted his glass to Gwynn and took a sip. Gwynn put the wine glass to her lips and siphoned a third of it before putting it down. Several moments later and after many sips of wine, Gwynn found herself sighing a lot as she felt relief spread through her body.

"Feeling better?" Terry asked.

After inhaling and exhaling a sigh so powerful it could launch a paper plane, Gwynn said, "Yes. Thanks. Yes, I do." Then she placed her elbows on the table and leaned in. "Why are you being so nice to me? I'm not going to sleep with you." At first, he looked as if he'd swallowed a piece of gum, then pressed his hand over his mouth as it turned up.

"I mean, men don't usually pick up women and take them to dinner without expecting to have sex with them," Gwynn said tersely.

Smile lines around Terry's eyes and mouth deepened. He cleared his throat. "I wouldn't worry about that, Gwynn." Motioning Savannah to bring another round, he said slowly, "I'm gay."

She bit the insides of her cheeks, her eyes widened as she placed her hands in prayer position on the table and sank into the chair. Then suddenly she sat up and began looking around her chair.

"Did you drop something?" Terry asked.

"No. I'm looking for a hole to crawl into."

"OK then," Terry said. "Now that that's out of the way. Want to tell me what's going on with you?"

"Oh, nothing. Except I got dumped a few days before my wedding."

Terry gulped a mouthful of beer. "Are you sure you don't want me to take him out?"

"No. I want him back."

Terry reached over and patted the back of her hand, which was gripping the stem of the wine glass so tightly, he feared it might shatter. "The question is, does he want you back?" he said as Savannah appeared with the starters.

Savannah shot a look at Gwynn and asked, "Ma'am, another?"

Nodding Gwynn said, "You know it. Thanks, Savannah." She waited until the girl left and whispered, "In answer to your question, I don't know what he wants. All I know is, at the moment it's not me."

Terry looked quizzical. "Does he live here? You said you live in Montana."

She hung her head for a second, then looked into Terry's clear brown eyes. She hadn't studied his features before, worried he might misinterpret her interest in him. Now, feeling safe with him, she noticed he had a long, lean slightly sun-weathered face and thick, curly reddish-brown hair.

"No. I followed him here. We both live in a small town in Montana. He's here to help a friend with something. I just felt I *had* to see what he was up to." She leaned over the table. "I thought maybe away from everything, I could bring him to his senses." She looked up at him, trying to decide whether she should continue. "But then I saw him with another woman."

"When did he break up with you?" he asked.

"A week and a half ago. It still hurts so much," Gwynn said. "There are times when I feel this red-hot anger inside me that erupts like hot lava. Sometimes I get scared. I feel as if I can't control it."

Terry placed the bruschetta that had been an inch from his lips back on his plate. Pursing his lips, he measured his words. "Gwynn," he began, "don't be scared. You have what I call 'broken thermometer syndrome.' I've suffered from it, too."

Her eyes squinted. "What? What's that?"

Terry took her hand. "And just like a HVAC tech can adjust the house thermostat, a good psychologist can help adjust a person's anger meter by teaching them strategies to control it."

Tears rolled down her cheeks, and he handed her a pile of the extra napkins Savannah had left with the starters.

Terry cocked his head and fixed his eyes on her. "Gwynn, go back to Montana. The battle you're fighting is not with your ex. It's with yourself, and it can't be won by staying here and stalking him."

Gwynn shifted in her seat. Telling Gwynn what to do would normally have provoked a heavy frost from her, but getting angry with someone who had such unconditional sincerity would be like getting mad at a puppy.

When Gwynn didn't speak, Terry continued. "I've been where you are. As a gay man in a traditionally straight man's profession, you wouldn't believe the shit I've had to work through. Trust me, it's time for you to retreat, regroup, and plan your next move after you've had time to work through the smoldering anger inside you."

Gwynn recalled in slow motion the scene in her kitchen when she'd thrown the candlestick at Alex. Maybe that's why he refused to speak to her. She fisted her hands, bringing one to her mouth. *Maybe this guy is right*, she thought. She tapped her left heel on the deck several times as if to clear the mushroom cloud of uncertainty she felt. After a brief silence between them, Gwynn said, "So, I go home and then what? Just let this woman have what's mine?"

Terry thought about her words for a minute, then put both elbows on the table and leaned in. "No one owns another person. Each of us has to *earn* another person."

*That's what you think*, Gwynn thought. *I've earned him all right. Goddamn it, he belongs to me or nobody else.*

# Chapter 22

The first and foremost instinct of humans
is neither sex nor aggression.
It is to seek contact and comforting connection.
*—John Bowlby*

Brooke had chosen Halls Chophouse for a dinner after sightseeing. They settled in a booth in the back corner and recounted their day together of walking through narrow alleys and over the cobblestone streets past candy-colored houses Brooke called Rainbow Row as she explained the history of the city. She'd seemed particularly proud that despite being devastated by epidemics, earthquakes, hurricanes, floods, pirates, and wars, beginning with the Revolutionary War, Charleston always came back better than before.

"What did you like best?" Brooke asked after they'd placed their orders.

Without missing a beat, he said, "Being with you."

His words seemed to hang heavily in the air as he noticed her bring her hand to her neck.

"Did I say the wrong thing—again?" he said, breaking an awkward silence that'd slipped in between them.

Brooke said softly, "No. You didn't. I'm just thinking."

"Mind me asking about what?"

She looked at him with liquid eyes. Then she cleared her throat. "That the best part of mine was being with you—and what I should do about it."

"About what?"

"This is crazy. You're not even over a breakup, and you're only here for a few more days, and then you're gone."

Alex took a sip of the beer the waiter had just delivered. Then he studied her through narrowed eyes. "I thought you specialized in crazy. I mean isn't that what psychologists do? Deal with crazy?"

She laughed. "In others, not in yourself." She closed her eyes and shook her head. "Besides, we hardly know each other."

"That's not a problem. I don't know who I am anymore because I stopped being the person I was the minute I met you. So now you know all there is about me that no one else knows."

Brooke took a deep breath. "I'm sitting here, digging around my brain for an appropriate psychological strategy to deal with you. But I keep coming up empty handed."

"The way I look at it, meeting you was fate. When you came over this morning, it was your choice, just as it was mine to open up to you about how bad I feel about what I did to Gwynn. But the way I feel about you isn't a choice. It's beyond my control."

"But it takes time to get to know somebody to see if you laugh at the same things and delight in the weird things each other does. I feel as if our relationship has a time limit on it since you'll be gone before we know it … and each other."

"I hear what you're saying. But it's not like we're never going to see each other again and can't get to know each other after I leave. Christ, you don't get to Montana by covered wagon anymore. Jets land there now, and we even have cell towers, Wi-Fi, and indoor plumbing."

He took her laughter as a green light to go on. "Look, let's spend as much time together as we can while I'm here. And then if you have any interest in wanting to get to know me better, come to Montana and see me in my natural habitat."

Brooke leaned back with mischief in her eyes. "Tell me about your natural habitat."

★★★★

"This is it," Gwynn said as the black awning with The Mills House in white lettering came into view. It was a venerable historic building made of stucco, Palladian windows, and cypress timber, with an iron fence made of vertical spires separating it from the sidewalk. Terry stopped the car and turned to Gwynn as if waiting for her to get out.

She sat in the dark without speaking as the car idled, its headlights shining on the street, the dashboard instruments casting a faint blue light on the interior.

Terry reached across the space between them and took Gwynn's small, warm hand off the plastic container filled with her uneaten meal. He sandwiched her hand between his two large ones.

He squeezed her hand tightly, then released it. "Gwynn, it's normal to want to go after what you want. But remember that the only thing you can control in the process is yourself," he said, his voice sincere, and waited. Gwynn said nothing. It was as if what he'd said didn't mean anything or that she wasn't listening to him.

"Look, none of us had a say in whether we wanted to be born. We didn't get to pick our parents, our sex, how we'd look, or whether we'd be smart or dumb. All of that was decided by two people we may or may not have trusted to make the decision for us in the roll of the genetic dice. We then spend our lives from the moment we arrive on this planet trying to control the environment we find ourselves in," he continued as though she had asked him to.

"What?" she said coldly, looking at him for the first time since they'd stopped. Her face seemed impenetrable as if he were an Uber driver who'd said something inappropriately familiar.

Terry thought better of repeating himself. Handing her his card, he said resolutely, "Gwynn, call me tomorrow after you book your flight. I'll take you to the airport."

Sorrowfully, she took his card as if she couldn't help agreeing and said, "OK."

★★★★

Alex sensed Brooke was waiting for him to say something as they arrived at the front door of the carriage house. This was the time; with other women, he'd ask them to come inside with the hope of having sex. But his feelings for Brooke were different. He bowed his head like a penitent, knowing with her it wasn't the right thing to do. As he pondered what the right thing to say was, it occurred to him that a gesture would show her that something out of the ordinary had occurred tonight —something they both could think about later.

He reached both of his hands to her face and gently put his lips against hers.

Brooke didn't resist him. Her acquiescence led Alex to imagine the two of them were entering into new and uncharted territory. When he pressed his lips more completely onto hers, she slightly parted them.

Stepping back from her, he looked into her eyes. In them he thought he knew what she was thinking. He *had* kissed her, but then *they* had kissed each other, and that made all the difference. It wasn't either's first kiss, but he felt as if they both knew it was the first kiss with someone who mattered. And now they wanted to spend every minute they could with each other to discover what there was to discover between them.

He wanted to tell her how different he felt with her, that his relationship with Gwynn had been all about physical and sexual attraction. Although he knew these were the kinds of thoughts he should share, they weren't things that should be said in a rushed goodbye.

Alex saw she was looking at him with large, soft eyes. It was the kind of eye contact that felt like she was touching him with her fingertips. "Well, I'd better go. I have an early meeting with my adviser tomorrow," she said somberly.

Taking her hand, he walked her to her car. Opening the door, he said, "Can I see you tomorrow?"

"I'd like that," she said, sliding onto the driver's seat.

He leaned in and gave her a brief, soft kiss. "Great. Call me after your meeting."

Nodding, she whispered, "Sleep well."

Alex followed next to her car as she backed out of the driveway. He watched from the street until her taillights disappeared from view.

# Chapter 23

Love looks not with the eyes, but with the mind.

—*William Shakespeare*

At one o'clock in the morning, the nightstand light was on, and Alex was propped against the bed's headboard, sipping a glass of beer and feeling revitalized. He was in his boxers on top of the covers, staring across the room at his image reflected in the black HDTV screen on the opposite wall.

If he'd had his way, Brooke would be in bed beside him right now, but it wasn't as if nothing insignificant had happened. Things had. Things expressed when they kissed. When their lips touched, it had felt electric and pulsing—something he'd never felt before. The novelty of it excited him.

All the secrets that slept deep within him were coming awake. For most of his life, *he* hadn't had to make major decisions. His life had been pretty much decided by virtue of his family's wealth and position. Certain things were expected of the Whitgates, and he was the only one left to fulfill them. And the biggest decision of his life, who to marry—he'd been a whisker away from making it out of duty rather than out of the depth of feeling he felt now.

There were times when he'd thought Gwynn could sense something was wrong between them, but she'd acted as if whatever was bothering him was simply out of her control and that eventually, whatever it was, he'd resolve himself or it would be resolved by the flow of the happy life she'd envisioned for them. At least that's what he thought she thought. How would he know because they'd never talked about it? He couldn't remember them ever talking about anything substantial. He had no intention of making the same mistake with Brooke.

He thought back to returning to Montana after his discharge from the army and concentrated on pulling out feelings he'd hidden in a place deep inside. Was it the pain he'd seen in war, the loss of his father, or resentment for a life he hadn't chosen that mounted up and lay a sobering weight on the present? He sipped the beer as he thought about how he'd changed in small and subtle ways, in ways he hadn't thought about until now. Until his decision to break up with Gwynn, it was as if he had been standing by and watching life happen to him. Placing the beer bottle on the nightstand, he turned out the light. He wasn't going to find the answers he was looking for in one bout of introspection. As he slid under the covers, he heard a noise from the basement.

Alex jumped out of bed, grabbed his cell phone, and headed for the kitchen. He thought he saw a flash of light sweep against the wall by the basement door. His first thought was that it must be from the headlights of a passing car. But there was no sound of street traffic, and the main house would have blocked any light. He grabbed a butcher knife from the kitchen when he heard another noise. He was sure it was coming from the basement. As he walked to the basement door, his training kicked in, and he prepared himself to confront an intruder. Flipping on the light at the top of the landing, he called, "Who's down there?" At first, there was only silence; then he thought he heard the sound of a child crying.

Raising his voice as he descended the stairs, he said, "Hello, whoever you are, I'm coming down there." On the last tread, Alex thought he heard a child's whimper. "Come out. I won't hurt you."

Silence. The light from the landing lit only a small area of the room. With the light from his cell phone, he could see a brick wall only a few feet in front of him and a door in the middle of it. He opened the door. Metal shelves holding labeled boxes lined the walls. Alex remembered Donovan telling him the building doubled as a guest house and was used for storage. Then he thought, *Maybe the sound was an animal.* After a thorough search, he found nothing.

# Chapter 24

My mind is like a piece of steel, very
hard to scratch anything on it
and almost impossible after you get it there to rub it out.
—*Abraham Lincoln*

Leaving Alex in Charleston was all Gwynn could think of as her plane ascended high above the city. She glanced out the cabin window as inlets and streams of the blue-and-green shoreline below disappeared and mounds of the endless white clouds came into view. Over and over, she relived seeing Alex with another woman. How could he be with someone else so soon after their breakup? Had she meant so little to him? The shock of it caused a lump in her throat she'd yet to swallow.

"Try not to think about it," Terry had told her as they drove to the airport, which at first Gwynn had thought was the stupidest piece of advice she'd ever heard.

"How do I *not* think about it?" she'd snapped.

"You have to hack into your brain when a thought about Alex pops up. Close your eyes, take a deep breath, and follow the air as you inhale it into your nostrils. As it fills up your chest, follow it as it leaves your body. Do this for five breaths. Then focus on what you hear around you."

She closed her eyes and leaned back. She thought about all the articles she'd read about Charleston being a destination wedding venue in the bridal magazines she'd scoured while planning her wedding. Now, having been there, for the life of her she wondered why anyone would prefer the Lowcountry to the beauty of Montana or the excitement of New York City. *Now that's a destination venue,* she thought as she began to tick off the things she'd loved about the city where she'd lived before the move to Montana. In every minute of the day or night, something was happening. The lights never went off on Broadway, where thousands of hearts were lifted with each performance. At Lincoln Center, ballet dancers took flight, and sopranos hit inconceivably high notes. She thought about the Metropolitan Museum of Art and the famous painting by Jacques-Louis David, *The Death of Socrates*, and about the Frick Museum, which housed Rembrandt's self-portrait, art just hanging there and waiting for visitors to stand in awe of the artist's genius. She thought of the symphony concerts she'd attended at Carnegie Hall. She visualized a clock with the second hand and knew even as she sat in a plane thousands of miles away from there, people were falling in love, getting married, and being born.

Gwynn suddenly realized she was thinking about something other than Alex. She thought about what Terry had said about none of us having a choice about being born. She thought about what he'd said about control and knew control was how she navigated her world.

And then, jarred by the plane's turbulence, she thought about why she'd left New York. Hired right after college by a commercial real estate company, she'd met and fallen for one of the partners, Blake Weston. Blake had looked like a Nordic god, and Gwynn was all too happy to be his goddess. After two years of living together, she came home one night to an empty apartment and a note on the kitchen counter. He was sorry, but he'd met someone else.

Of course, her mother was only too happy to come to the rescue of her daughter with a U-Haul in tow. Gwynn remembered lying on the back seat in a fetal position during the entire trip back to Montana, with her mother constantly asking her to sit up and put a seat belt on.

Her mother's other mantra was, "It'll be all right, precious. I've been praying on it. Everything happens for a reason." Then she'd rattle on about how it was she and Gwynn against the world.

Gwynn remembered looking through the crack between the seats and seeing her mother's mouth moving and thought the only prayer she wanted to offer to God was to ask him to strike her mother mute. But then she remembered dismissing it, thinking He was probably working on more important things.

Gwynn thought about what her mother had done to control her life, like moving with Gwynn from Massachusetts, where the intact O'Brien family had lived, to Montana to make it even more difficult for Gwynn's father to have custodial visits with Gwynn. They had first moved to Fort Benton, where Diedre got her Realtor's license. After Gwynn went off to college at Northwestern, Deidre moved to Mountainville to start her own residential and commercial real estate company. When Gwynn returned to Montana, she joined her mother's real estate company. A few months later, she bumped into Alex while on her way to the ladies' room at The Cedar Tavern. She remembered his strikingly handsome face, muscular body, and square jaw. She remembered staring at him so intensely that she was afraid her look might leave a mark on his forehead. When he said through a lopsided grin, "Excuse me, ma'am. Have we met?" that was it. She'd set her cap for him.

*Fuck*, she thought. *I'm thinking about him again*. She closed her eyes, inhaled deeply, and began to follow her breath.

Diedre was waiting in baggage claim. It wasn't until Gwynn was standing right in front of her that she recognized her daughter. "Oh my God, Gwynn. What have you done to your hair?" she exclaimed.

Gwynn narrowed her eyes and pursed her lips. "Seriously, Mother. Your eyes are so wide that you look as if you have an ocular disorder."

Gwynn turned and walked toward the baggage carousel. Diedre hustled to catch up with her. Sneering at her mother, Gwynn barked, "Relax. It's a wig. I didn't want anyone on the plane to recognize me. That's all."

# Chapter 25

One of the most sublime things in
the world is plain truth.
—*E. G. Bulwer*

The sunbeams streaming into the room slowly took shape through Alex's bleary eyes. He sat up and threw his legs over the side of the bed. He heard chirping birds and the tinny noise of an animal scampering along the gutter on the side of the carriage house. He walked to the doorway and surveyed the wall where he'd thought he saw a flash of light last night.

On the wall was a large antique map behind glass of the Charleston peninsula. Maybe, he thought, the light had been a reflection from the nightstand lamp. But he was sure the lamp had been off. He walked to the basement door, opened it, flipped on the light, and went down the steps. He stood in the doorway to the storage room and looked around. Nothing was out of order, and there were no sounds like the ones he'd heard the night before.

Alex turned to climb the stairs when the dehumidifier tucked under the staircase clicked on, filling the room with its hum. *That must have been it*, he thought.

Alex heard the front door open as he reached the landing. "Hey," he called.

"Hey, yourself," Donovan said.

"What's up?" Alex said as he entered the living room.

"Not much. Just work. And the usual fuckups. The plumber never showed, and the tile man who finally did was stoned. So I've had to do some of the work myself to keep the project on time."

"Anything I can do to help?" Alex asked, lifting the coffeepot off the drainboard. As he filled the coffee maker with water, he glanced over his shoulder at Donovan.

Donovan placed a white paper bag on the kitchen table. "You already are. Brooke told me she saw the restaurant's program yesterday."

Alex turned on the coffee maker. He walked to the kitchen table and turned the computer around to face Donovan, who'd taken a seat.

Before Donovan looked at the screen, he unpacked biscuits from the bag and handed Alex one wrapped in a napkin. "Here. Try this."

Alex took a bite and raised both eyebrows, then closed his eyes while savoring the soft, flaky sensation as it melted slowly in his mouth.

Donovan smiled as he bit into his.

Alex poured them each a cup of coffee and sat down. "Let me know what you think," he said, pointing to the computer.

While swallowing the last bit of his biscuit, Donovan took a few minutes to scroll through the program and looked up at Alex. "This is great. It's exactly what my mom needs. Especially the whole inventory tracking. You won't believe the problems she's had with that."

"What's wrong, Donovan?" Alex said.

Donovan looked up from the screen and said, "What makes you think anything's wrong?"

"You may be a ringer at pool, but you suck at poker. The depth of the crease between your eyes gives you away every time."

Donovan laughed, sat back in his chair, and pressed his index and middle fingers against his lips.

"Well?" Alex said.

Donovan cleared his throat. "I spoke to Brooke on the way over here to see if she'd had a chance to show you around the city." He moved his left hand to his chin and rubbed at the stubble. "And" — he paused — "her voice sounded sort of dreamy like. She never sounds like that." He continued, "Is there something going on between the two of you?"

Alex let out the breath he'd been holding. "No. Not yet. I don't know how Brooke feels about me, but I've never felt this way about a woman. I'd like to spend as much time as I can with her while I'm here."

"To what point?" Donovan said, looking at him coldly.

Alex leaned in toward him. "The point? The point would be to get to know Brooke better."

"And then what? I saw you in Montana. You love everything about the place. And your mother is there. It's the same way Brooke feels about Charleston. And *her* mother is here. And I am too." His brow furrowed. "Let's say you guys do have a definite spark between you. And assume you take it to the next level and fall in love. How could it possibly work out?"

Alex stood up, intending to put his fingers through his belt loops, and suddenly realized he was still in his boxers. He sat back down. "Weren't you the one who said, *'Love is the thing around which all things bend?'*"

"Alex, that was different. It wasn't distance that threatened to keep my parents apart. It was prejudice."

"Distance is a lot easier to overcome than that. Are you saying you don't want me to see Brooke?" Alex asked.

"I'm saying that though I love you like a brother, Brooke is my sister, and I don't want to see her hurt."

"I can't believe what I'm hearing. Do you really think I intend to hurt Brooke?"

Donovan stood up and walked to the kitchen counter. He seemed to be mulling something over by the way he delayed answering. He turned and in a low voice said, "No. I'm sure you have no intention of hurting Brooke. Just like you had no intention of hurting Gwynn."

"Ouch," Alex said.

"I could tell from Brooke's voice this morning, just as I can tell by the look on your face now, that something is up with you two. The truth is, I don't want either of you getting hurt. Think about it. Both you and she are just coming off recent breakups. Rebound relationships don't tend to work out."

He knew from the deep breath and the time it took for Donovan to exhale it; he was finished saying his piece. Alex ran his fingers through his hair while summoning the right words. After a minute Alex said, "Look, I understand your concern. And I appreciate you being honest with me about it. If I had a sister, I'd probably be saying the same thing. I *get* it." Alex took his time and paused to collect his thoughts. "You're right about Gwynn. I did a terrible thing to her, and I will always regret it. And I've been thinking that when I get back, I have to go to her and apologize again, when she's not so upset. She deserves that. No question I was wrong. But as far as being on a rebound, I long for a relationship I never had with her, not for the person I was in it with." Alex stood and grabbed the back of the chair. "And you said yourself, Brooke wasn't really into the guy she broke up with."

The room grew quiet when Donovan didn't respond. He sat straight up in the chair, shoulders back, chest out, jaw clenched and his eyes remaining laser focused on Alex.

"Look, ever since we all got together at Cloudlands and since I've been here, I have this feeling that there must be a reason why we all met. Why we survived. For me, I think it was so I'd meet Brooke. I mean what were the chances I'd even come to Charleston. But if you object, I won't pursue a relationship with her."

The crease between Donovan's eyes deepened. He crossed his arms and said flatly, "What are you saying?"

Alex said, "I'm saying if you don't approve, I won't see your sister anymore."

"I know you, Alex. You don't give up that easily. What's up with that?"

"Nothing. I'm not up to anything. Because you're the one who's going to tell your sister you don't approve of her seeing me. And if she agrees, then I'll know I'm wrong about how she feels, and we aren't meant for each other. But if she doesn't," Alex said as he sat down and crossed his arms with a smirk, "you know all too well 'that mule kicks.'"

Donovan began to shake his head as he laughed. "Well, I intend to talk to her. I'm meeting her for lunch today."

"OK then. Are we good?" Alex asked, extending his hand.

Donovan's eyes shined with affection as he stood and the two shook hands. "We're good."

# Chapter 26

Advice is like snow; the softer it falls,
the longer it dwells upon,
and the deeper it sinks into the mind.

*—Samuel Taylor Coleridge*

Brooke met Donovan at Blossom on East Bay Street at noon. He was sitting in a booth and sipping a beer when she arrived. "What's going on?" she asked. "You never drink during the day when you're working."

He looked up from the napkin he'd been spinning with his finger. "I'm making an exception."

Bernice, the waitress, appeared. Her body art began with a caterpillar cocoon on her right shoulder, which became a swarm of butterflies fluttering down to her wrist. Brooke ordered an iced tea with lemon. After the waitress left, Brooke said, "Donovan, look at me. What's going on?"

He thought, *Are you kidding me, I'd have to be a cinder block not to have felt the electrical charge in the air between you and Alex when you first met.* He knew she had to have felt it. He had all but seen the sparks. But all he said very softly was, "Well, that's what I want to know. What's going on between you and Alex?"

"At the moment, nothing. I was going to try to see him at lunch today, but when you called and sounded weird, I thought I'd call him this afternoon. Is that what this is about? My seeing Alex?"

The butterflied arm appeared. "Are you ready to order?"

"I'll have the Blossom burger with fries," Donovan said.

"And I'll have the Caesar salad with shrimp and the dressing on the side," Brooke said, looking up at Bernice. Then, turning to her brother, she said, "Are you concerned about me seeing Alex? I thought you loved him like a brother, and aren't you the one who told me he was 'good people'?"

"I do, and he is. But how would your relationship work with him in Montana and you here? I'm worried that you'll fall for him, and then he'll be gone. I'm trying to do damage control before there's a need for it. Alex is handsome, charming, wealthy, and shit, I'd fall for him if that was my thing."

"I love you, Donovan. You are the best brother a girl could ever have. And I know how much you love me and that you would do anything to prevent me from being hurt. But Donovan, it's my heart, and it's my life. And it's time for you to trust that I know what I'm doing and respect I'm old enough to decide who I want to do it with." She sat back and smiled at him. "Besides, we've already discussed the geographical divide, and you don't get to Montana in a covered wagon anymore. And he invited me to go to his ranch after I finish my dissertation."

"Yeah, and what about that? After you get your PhD, I thought you had a job lined up at the VA clinic over on Bee Street."

"I do. And?" Brooke said.

"And your life is here. His life is there."

"I don't know, big brother. The therapist in me thinks you're afraid that if my heart gets broken, you'll have to kill Alex, and then you'd lose a friend," she said smugly but with a nice tone. "Or you're afraid that if I fall in love with him, you may lose a sister to Montana."

"Would you go out and live there?"

Bernice returned with their order. After she left, Brooke said, "No." She took a sip of tea and cleared her throat. "Look. I like Alex. I like him very much, and I want to get to know him better. At the moment, that's all there is. OK?" She reached over and tapped his hand, making a pouting face. "OK?"

Donovan couldn't help himself. He chuckled at the face she'd made just the way he had when they were little. It had worked then, just as it did now. His demeanor relaxed. "Look, I just want you to be happy. I don't want you hurt. So, I'll mention the same thing to you that I mentioned to Alex. I'm also wondering if maybe there might be some rebound here with the two of you just breaking up with people."

"I've studied that in my psychology classes. To put your mind at ease, and in a nutshell, a rebound is when you really don't like the person you're dating right after a breakup, but you're just using them to fill time or distract from the pain of the breakup. I don't feel that way about Alex at all. And from what I've observed, Alex is relieved he broke up with Gwynn. He feels terrible about the circumstances, but he's hardly pining after her."

After that, they interspersed bites of their meals with small talk.

Bernice returned and said, "Would y'all like dessert?"

"Just the check," Donovan said.

"You know, brother dearest, I'd like you to think about something," said Brooke.

"What?"

"About how neither mom nor I tried to stop you when you enlisted. We knew it was something you had to do for you. We missed you terribly and shed a lot of tears when you were deployed, and constantly prayed for your safe return. I don't think either of us took a deep breath until you came back for good."

"Yeah, I know. But I think this is different," Donovan said solemnly.

"Is it? You were drawn to do something you felt you needed to do. And getting to know Alex is something I feel I need to do. Try to think about it that way."

They slid out of the booth. Then Donovan put his arm around Brooke's shoulders and whispered, "You do know that if he hurts you, friend or no friend, I *will* have to kill him."

# Chapter 27

The first symptom of love in a young man,
is timidity; in a girl, it is boldness.
— *Victor Hugo*

Alex's phone pinged with an incoming text. He looked up from the program he'd been working on. He'd done what he'd been trained to do; he pushed his conversation with Donovan, although upsetting, out of his mind and concentrated on his mission. He wanted to get the program finished and scheduled for a trial run at Serenity. Alex winced, glancing at the clock on the wall. It was a little after two, and he hadn't heard from Brooke.

He read the incoming text:

> *I THOUGHT YOU WERE GOING TO CALL TO ARRANGE A TIME FOR US TO GET TOGETHER.*
> *I'M FREE TONIGHT.*
> *LOOK FORWARD TO HEARING FROM YOU.*
> *XO Hollis*

"Oh, damn," Alex said. "I forgot about her."

He sat back in the chair and stared at the text. *Maybe Donovan convinced Brooke not to see me. I might as well get this over with. I did promise*, he thought. He texted:

*TONIGHT. OK, WHERE?*

Her response:

*MAGNOLIAS 6:30. I'LL MEET YOU IN THE BAR. LOOKING FORWARD TO SEEING YOU!*

Almost as soon as he'd made plans with Hollis, Brooke called. "How's it going?" she asked.

Trying to hide his delight in hearing her voice, he said, "Just tweaking the program."

"Do you want to get together when you're finished?"

"Um. Well, it's sort of complicated."

"How so?"

"I'm sure you know about your brother coming to talk to me about you. He told me he was going to speak to you also."

"Yes, he did. We met for lunch."

"When I didn't hear from you, I wasn't sure I would. Then Hollis texted about meeting her, and I planned with her."

"I understand. I meant to call earlier, but my meeting this morning ran late. And I had to meet Donovan."

"Since you're calling now, I take it that …" his voice trailed off.

"I told him I want to get to know you better."

"I'm relieved to hear that. And I'm upset that I made plans with Hollis, I'd much prefer to be with you. But I did promise to meet up with her when she took me clothes shopping. I'm sort of stuck."

"Actually, I'm happy you're keeping your promise to Hollis. It's important to keep promises."

He felt a stab of disappointment flavored with annoyance. She sounded so clinical and not the least bit jealous about him meeting

Hollis. *Is that what I want?* he thought. *Brooke to be jealous? No. Definitely not.* If his experience with Gwynn had taught him anything, it was that jealousy isn't a sign of love. It's a sign the other person wants to possess you.

Brooke's voice almost startled him. "Tell me," she said. "Did you promise it would just be the two of you?"

"Uh, no. Actually, I didn't. Want to join us?"

"Yes, I would. Why don't I come over around six and we can walk to Magnolias together?"

"Great. That will give me time to finish working on this and get cleaned up." Then his voice dropped an octave. "Thank you, Brooke."

"For what?"

"For whatever you said to Donovan."

She chuckled. "Seriously, it's not like we're the Montagues and you're the Capulets. Donovan is just suffering from a chronic case of 'overprotective sibling syndrome.' It often happens when children lose a parent through death or divorce. I'm as protective of him as he is of me."

"I see. Are you going to diagnose me?" Alex asked.

"I have a working diagnosis, but I'll have to do a more thorough exam since I'm still ruling out a few things."

"As long as you don't rule me out. See you at six," Alex said. He smiled, wondering whether any part of her exam was physical and spent the next few minutes fantasizing about making love to Brooke. Rising from his chair to shower and dress for the evening, he looked below his belt and said, "Down, boy."

# Chapter 28

Friendships are fragile things and require as much care in handling as any other fragile thing.

— *Randolph S. Bourne*

When Alex heard the crunch of the driveway pebbles, he walked toward the front door. As he did he thought he heard something that sounded like a child's whimper coming from the basement. He opened the basement door, flipped on the light, descended the stairs, and once again found the room empty. He returned to the living room as Brooke walked in.

"Hi, there, cowboy."

"You look beautiful, Brooke."

"You're looking pretty nice yourself. I must compliment Hollis. She did well picking out that shirt and jacket."

"Hollis insisted I buy these. What do you think? Will I be overdressed for the place we're going to?" Alex said, opening his coat jacket and looking down at himself.

"No, you look … very handsome, and it's perfect for Magnolias."

"OK, then." Motioning a slight bow and holding his arm out for her, he said, "Please, allow me to escort you to dinner, my lady."

Brooke broke into a smile and slipped her arm through his. The heat of the day had broken, and the sun was making its way to the western sky, where it would throw off vibrant splashes of purple, gold, and yellow, the color of an egg yolk. They walked slowly up East Bay and were passing Rainbow Row when Alex said, "Oh, dang. I should have called Hollis and told her I had invited you to join us. I don't want her to be embarrassed when we walk in together."

"That's very considerate of you, but I called her and told her that I had invited myself. She was good with it. She said she was actually a little relieved because she thought you were the quiet type," Brooke said, turning to him with an impish smile.

"Is that right?" he said. "And what do you think?"

"I think you're careful," she replied.

"Careful?"

"You measure your words."

Alex smiled. "Is that your professional opinion?"

Brooke shook her head. "N-n-o. I'd need to spend more time observing you."

"That can be arranged." Alex leaned over and whispered in her ear.

They arrived at Magnolias to find Hollis looking beautiful in a low-cut bandage dress while conversing with a handsome young man, who was gazing at Hollis in that wistful way that has the launching power to send a girl right over the moon. The anxiety Alex had felt about how to end the evening with Hollis, so he'd have more time to spend with Brooke drained from him.

Brooke caught Hollis's eye, and Hollis waved them over. "Hi, guys. This is Blake Hudders. He just moved here from Virginia to do an orthopedic residency at MUSC, where I work. Isn't that a coincidence? I can introduce him to everyone at the hospital," Hollis said excitedly.

Brooke glanced at the cocktail napkin next to Hollis's drink and was relieved she hadn't begun practicing writing "Hollis Hudders" on it.

Blake stood as Alex and Brooke introduced themselves to him and Alex shook Blake's hand.

"Nice to meet you," Blake said.

"Would you like to join us for dinner?" Alex asked.

Blake cast an eye at Hollis, who appeared giddy at the thought.

"Yes, that would be great as long as I'm not intruding," Blake said.

*Are you kidding?* Alex thought. *You just saved my fucking night.* "Oh, you're not intruding, not at all. I insist," Alex said more forcefully than he meant to.

Hollis told the bartender that there would be four for dinner, and a hostess appeared a few minutes later to show them to their table.

"So, you're from Virginia?" Brooke asked Blake once they'd placed their drink order.

"Yes. Born and raised. I went to undergrad and med school at the University of Virginia," Blake said. A short pause. "And you? Are you from Charleston?"

"Born and bred," Brooke said. Smirking, she added, "Yes, sir, Hollis and I are regular southern belles. Aren't we, Hollis?"

Hollis's eyes narrowed at her. Brooke winked at her and leaned back in her chair, studying the menu.

Hollis jumped in. "Alex is from Montana. He's just visiting for the week."

Blake turned to Alex. "Montana. I've always wanted to go there. I hear it's spectacular. What do you do there?"

The word *spectacular* triggered in Alex's mind the majestic mountains looming high above the valleys, the sky that went on forever, the animals grazing on the plains. And then his thoughts settled on what Donovan had said about his heart being as synchronized with Montana as Brooke's was with Charleston.

Nudging him, Brooke said, "Earth to Alex."

"Oh. Sorry. I'm a rancher. I just remembered something I have to call my ranch manager about," he said.

Hollis quickly jumped in and said, "Brooke told me you invited her to go to Montana, and she's going to go."

Alex gave Brooke a broad smile, and she squeezed his hand.

Soon the four were engaged in lively conversation while laughing and exchanging life stories. When the check came, Alex reached for it, but Blake grabbed it first. Hollis's eyes widened at Blake's gesture.

"I've got this," Blake said.

As the group rose from their table, someone at the table behind them screamed, "He's choking. He's choking!"

Without a word between them, Hollis and Blake rushed to the table. Blake lifted a slumped-over man from his seat and, standing to his side, gave him five blows between his shoulders with the heel of his hand. Getting no result, he wrapped his arms around the man's waist and tipped him slightly forward, positioning his fist slightly above the man's navel. He grasped his fist with his other hand and pressed hard into the man's abdomen with quick upward thrusts.

After Hollis called 9-1-1 in a low, even tone Brooke had never heard emanate from Hollis's her throat, Hollis consoled the onlookers, whose faces were filled with fear. Blake glided the unresponsive man to the floor and checked for a pulse and the began performing chest compressions as Hollis knelt next to the man's head, giving intermittent rescue breaths.

A woman at the table where the man had been seated sobbed hysterically and kept calling, "Bob, Bob! Oh, dear God. No. No! I can't lose him. That man is my life. Please, God, please God, help him. Don't let him die." The other couple from the table put their arms around her and were trying to calm her when suddenly, Blake said, "We've got a pulse."

Within three minutes, the paramedics arrived and took over. They quickly started an IV, placed a heart monitor on him, and proceeded to "load and go." The sobbing woman repeated, "That's my husband! That's my husband. Help him! Help him. I have to go with him."

After the man was loaded in the ambulance the restaurant onlookers returned to their tables and settled in to resume their meals as the previous din of conversation filled the air.

Blake had helped Hollis to her feet and put his arms around her, pulling her into him. She seemed to melt into his body. After a minute or so, he released her and, looking into her eyes, said, "You were amazing. I didn't have to say a word to you. You knew exactly what I needed."

Hollis, who'd kicked off her heels when she knelt, stood on her tiptoes, and whispered something in Blake's ear. His eyes widened as did the smile on his lips, and he put his arm around her waist, guiding her to where Brooke and Alex stood.

"You were awesome, both of you," Brooke said. "Oh, my God, Hollis. I've never seen that side of you. And I've known you since the sandbox. And Blake. Charleston is so fortunate to gain a doctor like you."

Alex extended his hand to Blake and said, "Whenever you want, you have an open invitation to Montana to stay at my ranch. By the way, when you've finished your residency, we could sure use a doctor like you in our town."

Blake shook his head. "You're all giving me way too much credit. Anyone who knows first aid could have done what I did. Although," he said, pausing, "I suspect that whatever difficulty he had breathing may not have been from choking. He may have had a heart attack. I'll look in on him tomorrow."

Brooke said, "What do you say we all go to Mom's restaurant for a port?"

Blake and Hollis exchanged looks. "Thanks, but do you mind if we take a rain check? We have plans," Hollis said.

"OK, but the next time is my treat," Alex said.

"Aren't you leaving in a few days?" Hollis said.

"I'm extending my stay. Call with a few dates," Alex said as Brooke grinned.

After saying good night on the sidewalk, Hollis and Blake held hands and walked quickly to Hollis's car parked at the corner.

"What do you think that's all about?" Alex asked as he put his arm around Brooke and looked into her eyes.

"If I know my friend, it's about what she whispered in Blake's ear. She'd going to engage in carnal pleasures with him such as that poor, unsuspecting man never knew. And after she's through with him, he'll not be able to live without her," Brooke said, shaking her head.

He placed his hands on Brooke's shoulders and said, "Really? She didn't happen to teach you any of them, did she?"

"Wouldn't you like to know?" Brooke laughed. "So, tell me, when did you decide to extend your stay?"

Alex pulled her to him. "When I saw that woman's face and heard her sobbing at the thought of losing her husband."

"What struck you about it?" she asked as he pulled her back and tucked her hand into the crook of his elbow.

"When I wondered about the last time that woman told her husband how she felt about him. What if she'd missed the chance? Right then and there, I decided that I wasn't going to miss the chance to spend more time with you. And tell you that I have never felt this way before."

"And what way is that?"

"Well, first I realize the reason why no one has ever broken my heart is because I've never let anyone get close enough to touch it. But last night when we kissed, you may have thought it was my lips you touched, but it was the very soul of me."

# Chapter 29

Sex is an emotion in motion.

*—Mae West*

The question was out of his mouth before he realized it. "Want to come in?" Alex asked as they walked down the driveway. As he said it, he felt the air turn electric with possibility.

She looked into his eyes and ran the back of her index finger down the side of his cheek. He said nothing because all he could feel, all he could think about, was his racing heart.

"Yes," she said.

He held the door open for her and, once inside, kicked it shut with his foot. Alex took her hand in his and laid a soft kiss on her palm. Brooke's breath hitched in her throat as she felt his hands cup her cheeks and draw her closer. A heartbeat later, his lips met hers. All the longing of the past few days surged inside him in an all-consuming rush of heat.

Alex found himself drowning in the softness of her mouth against his. As Brooke traced her finger down the center of his chest, Alex felt his flesh tighten. Then she ran her fingers along his belt line as she grasped his hand, drawing it to her mouth. She licked his fingers very slowly as she watched a glassy gleam cover his eyes.

He squeezed her hand and gently tugged her into the bedroom. Reaching around her back, he unzipped her dress and let it fall to the floor. Brooke was naked when she slipped into bed.

Alex pulled at his jacket and shirt, scattering a button, dropping his clothes, and kicked out of his boxers. He approached the bed and saw her long, auburn hair fanned out on the pillow, her body a long S shape under the white sheet. She reached out for him and softly whispered his name. When he touched her, he felt electricity that seemed to spark down his spine. Trembling with excitement, he got under the sheet.

Brooke folded her arms around him as her warm mouth found his, and her tongue darted between his lips. Then she scissored her legs around his hips, creating more heat between them, as the sound of hurried breathing filled the air. Brooke summoned him deeper and deeper until Alex was about to explode; then she made him stop and lie motionless. After a few seconds, she sat astride him. Her head thrown back, her mouth open as if to receive rain, she began to ride him with varying rhythms, from hard to slow, to long, to lingering until he exploded inside her.

Then she took his fingers and kissed them as she lay on her back. At first, he circled her nipples with his tongue, then her navel, then her soft belly, then down into the valley between her legs, where her thighs pressed against the sides of his head. As she gripped his hair, churning her hips, she moaned softly at first, then louder and louder until he thought she might break the sound barrier. As her thighs released his head and her hands his hair, she fell back against the bed.

Alex pulled her close to him as if she were his second skin. As she ran her fingers through his hair, he said, "I wish you didn't have to go home tonight."

She kissed him deeply and sweetly. "I don't have to. On a hunch, I brought an overnight bag. It's in my car."

He kissed the top of her head. "Do you want me to get it?"

"It'll wait until the morning," she whispered. "I brought a change of clothes for after we take a nice hot shower. A very soapy and slippery one."

"Oh, stop. How do you expect me to go to sleep now? I'll be up all night counting the seconds."

"Well, if you're not tired, you don't have to wait until the morning," she whispered licking his ear.

Alex slid on top of her. Brooke could feel the heat turning up in her body and felt each breast gathering up into pointed peaks. He ran a finger gently around her nipples until she reached for him guiding him inside her. He was as hard as the first time. And as he filled her with himself, she felt as if his cock had been designed just for her. Brooke clutched at him, feeling him pound into her as if he would drive right through her. Then she felt his explosion as she became lost in her own.

# Chapter 30

True love is like ghosts, which everyone
talks about, and few have seen.
—*Francois de La Rochefoucaud*

Alex woke the next morning with a smile on his face and thought, *I made love last night to the woman I'm going to make love to for the rest of my life.* He rolled onto his side and, leaning on his elbow, studied Brooke's profile. *She has the most exquisite bone structure in her face,* he thought. *She'll be beautiful when she's ninety. But it's what's inside that head that attracts me the most.*

Brooke stirred, and he kissed her softly on the forehead.

She rolled to her side and, searching his eyes, said, "If you keep staring at me like that, you're gonna burn a hole in me."

His eyes traveled the full length of her body, and he said through a stifled laugh, "Yeah, well, your beauty is burning my corneas."

"My goodness," she said, her tone feigning worry, as she reached over slowly, guiding the tips of his fingers over her breasts, abdomen, and between her legs. "I guess then I'll have to teach you braille."

As they made love for the third time in less than twelve hours, Alex's heart was beating so hard, he worried he might die of a heart attack. Deciding he was too young and in too good a shape, he proceeded with all the gusto he had, which included a lot of rolling around and repositioning until he heard her moan loud enough that he was sure she'd felt the rocket ship lift off that he was aiming to launch her into.

They rested just as a sound came from the basement. Alex scratched his head and pushed his fingers through his hair. "Did you hear that?"

"Yes. It's probably the dehumidifier," she said dismissively.

Alex swung his legs over the edge of the bed, sat up, and slipped on his boxers. "I keep hearing that noise, and it's not the dehumidifier. It is almost like a cat mewing or a child crying, but there's nothing down there. And the other morning I thought I saw some flash of light by the basement door, and then it disappeared."

Brooke pulled the sheet up to her chin and sat against the headboard.

"You look preoccupied. What are you thinking?" he asked.

"I was wondering." She looked at Alex pensively. "It may be a ghost."

"I thought your father got rid of them."

"The ones that made themselves known at the time. But through the years, there have been others from time to time."

"And what do you do when that happens?" he asked.

"We help them pass on."

"We? You mean, you help with it, too?" he said.

"Well, Donovan and Calvin do mostly."

"What's it like?"

"It's a lot like helping the living get over bad memories that haunt them."

"I think I'm gonna need some coffee for this."

Brooke slipped out of bed and into the clothes on the floor next to it. "I'll make it. And some breakfast while I explain my theory about ghosts to you."

After Alex dressed in a T-shirt and khaki pants, he sat at the kitchen table and watched as Brooke busied herself.

*The other thing I want to do with her,* he thought, *is watch her for the rest of my life.*

A few minutes later, she placed a mug of steaming coffee in front of him. "Brooke, how about sitting down and telling me your theory?"

"Aren't you hungry?"

"I don't need to eat. I've been filling up on your beauty."

Brooke leaned over and whispered in his ear. "OK, you sweet-talkin' man." Sitting across from him, she placed her hands in her lap. "This is my theory, which by the way I could *not* defend in a dissertation. Ghosts are like the bad memories that haunt people. Ghosts hang around because of unresolved issues on earth, and bad memories hang on because of unresolved issues in a person's mind. If you can help a ghost resolve the issue that keeps them here, they can be at peace and move on to the afterlife, whatever that is for them. If you can help someone resolve the issues that haunt them, then they can be at peace and get on with their life, whatever that may be for them."

"Interesting way to look at it," he said.

"Ever since I was a little girl, if I wanted something explained, it was best if I could figure it out myself. For me, ghosts have always been a factor in my life, and so has the traumatic memory of my father's death."

"I can understand that."

"I mostly leave exorcising ghosts to others. I've worked on exorcising my traumatic memories by studying psychology and helping others get rid of what haunts them."

Alex nodded. "That seems like a healthy way to deal with what you went through." Placing the cup down in front of him, he waited a beat before asking, "But why now would a ghost suddenly show up?"

Brooke turned and leaned against the counter. Looking into his eyes, she said, "My guess is that whoever it is, it senses that she or he has company in you." She cracked eggs into a bowl and began to stir them with a fork.

"But why do you think they're still here?"

"This property was originally owned by Sarah Burroughs, an abolitionist. She was a widow who freed the slaves her husband owned after his death. Then she set about to smuggle slaves out of Charleston to the Underground Railroad. Some of them must have died here before they could start the journey."

"Good Lord. That woman must have had some courage."

"You can say that again. If caught, the slaves would have been viciously beaten or hanged. And for her the cost of helping them meant huge fines, which would have taken all her property—and then she'd been run out of town. Penniless."

"Why do you think she took the risk?" he asked.

Brooke placed her mug on the counter and said, "Why does anyone do the right thing? There's a voice in your head and feeling in your gut that will haunt you, so to speak, if you don't do it."

Alex shifted in his chair. "Umm, I can testify to that."

Brook chuckled and turned to the stove. "Well, in answer to your question about why some spirits may still be here, it goes back to July 14, 1822, when there was a slave uprising. It was spearheaded by Denmark Vesey, a literate freeman. He organized it after he was denied the right to buy his wife and children out of slavery by their owner."

Alex furrowed his brow. "Jesus."

"Interesting that you called on the Lord. That's what Denmark did in his despair. He turned to God and the Mother Emmanuel Church, which was the only place Blacks were permitted to congregate. From the pulpit, Denmark gave messages of hope for freedom using Bible passages, but in the church's backroom under the guise of giving religious instruction, he was organizing a revolt. His plan was patterned from the Haitian revolution. They would overcome the guards at the Charleston Meeting Street Arsenal, secure the weapons necessary to kill White slaveholders, liberate slaves, and commandeer ships from the harbor to sail to Haiti, where Blacks were free from the threat of enslavement. But the White militia was ready for them, and the revolt was thwarted."

"How'd they find out about it?" he asked.

"Apparently one of Denmark's confidants told his master, thinking he'd be rewarded with his own freedom." She turned from the stove and looked at him. "There's always a Judas Iscariot somewhere, isn't there?"

"Yup, there is. What happened after the revolt?" he asked.

Brooke placed a platter of scrambled eggs on the table and returned with plates and utensils.

"Slaves were randomly rounded up for questioning. According to recorded accounts, if a slave 'exhibited energy, excitement, activity, or agitation' while being questioned, he was automatically charged, tried in secret, and hanged," she said.

Alex's brows knitted. "Not much has changed since then, has it?"

Brooke looked down. "No, actually I mean today. When a Black man is stopped and shows those same signs as energy, excitement, or agitation, chances are high that some superego with a badge, a gun, and a grudge will make a snap decision and shoot them."

"But what does the revolt have to do with the ghosts on this property?"

She sat down across from him. After taking a sip of coffee, she said, "You can imagine how the militia quelled the revolt. The slaves who weren't shot or beaten ran for their lives. The city was in chaos. Many ran here, hoping Sarah would hide them. Which she did."

Alex pushed some eggs onto a fork and then put the fork down. "Where'd she hide them?"

"At first in the basement of the main house. The revolt was many months in the planning. As soon as she heard about it from her freedman, she had them dig a tunnel between the main house and the basement here. The brick wall down there hides a holding room. The door in it was installed a century later during the carriage house's renovation."

Alex set his fork on the plate. "This looks great, Brooke, but I'm sorry. I think I've lost my appetite."

Brook smiled at him and put her fork down. "Me too."

"Tell me something. How did she get them out of here?"

"Well, apparently there's another tunnel Sarah had built from the holding room to the harbor. That's where slaves would be picked up by boat under cover of night and taken up the river to the Underground Railroad." She paused and looked pensive.

"What's wrong?" Alex asked as he took her hand and squeezed it.

"It drove my father crazy that he never found the tunnel. Or the one from the main house to the holding room." She gave a slight laugh. "It bedeviled him."

Alex said, "But I still don't understand. Why now? Why appear now?"

Brooke smiled and said casually, "The problem with ghosts is that they're dead. They can't tell us why they appear. Or why they do what they do."

# Chapter 31

Our doubts are traitors and make us lose the
good we oft might win by fearing attempt.

—*William Shakespeare*

After agreeing that neither was up to breakfast, Brooke and Alex took a very steamy shower—together. They were drying off when there was a rap at the door.

"Are you expecting anyone?" Brooke asked Alex as she wrapped a towel around her body.

"No," Alex said, pulling on his pants and shrugging into his T-shirt.

Alex opened the door to see a rather piqued-looking Lotte standing there, peering at him from behind oversized sunglasses. "I saw my daughter's car here and wondered if she'd had a breakdown," Lotte said, pushing her glasses into her hair.

"No, Mom, I haven't, and you shouldn't have one either," Brooke said from behind Alex.

Lotte stepped past Alex. She raised her eyebrows as she appraised the towel wrapped around Brooke's body. When her eyes reached Brooke's face, she whispered, "The glow of your complexion tells me all I need to know."

With a disgruntled turn on her heel, Lotte walked out the door and toward the staircase leading to the back entrance to the restaurant.

Alex stood, his hand on the doorknob, watching Lotte until Brooke took his hand off it, closed the door, and said, "I think Donovan got to her."

"What do you mean?"

"I mean, he tried to sow doubt in me about you, but my mom is more susceptible to his opinions."

"Tell me the truth." Alex took her hands to his chest and rested them over his heart. "Do you have doubts about us?"

Brooke looked down. It wasn't until Alex took his finger to lift her chin so she was looking into his eyes that he could see hers were beginning to tear up.

"What is it?" Alex insisted.

After a few sobs, Brooke said, "No. I don't, but they do. They're afraid I'll get hurt."

Alex began to laugh. A moment passed before he could control himself. "They're afraid *you'll get hurt.* I'm scared to death that I'll get eviscerated. I've never been this vulnerable to anyone in my life."

Brooke kissed his lips softly and whispered, "Me too."

"Come on, you said it. It's not like the Montagues and Capulets revisited."

Brooke managed a smile. "No," she said, shaking her head. "It's the Lowcountry versus Big Sky Country. They're afraid I'll leave Charleston."

"Isn't everyone jumping the gun? We've only just met. What if you decide you can't stand me?" Alex said.

She kissed him on the cheek. "I think you've passed that hurdle already. I've got to get dressed and go talk to my mother before she has an apoplectic stroke."

"I'm coming with you," Alex said, catching her wrist as Brooke turned toward the bedroom.

"What are you going to say?" she asked.

"I won't know until I find out what's really upsetting her. One thing for sure, I'm not going to hide from her or have you go over there without me. If we're in this together, we go and talk to her together. Come on, that's what a good partner does," he said, pulling her into him.

Intertwining her hands with his, she asked, "Is this the steely inner strength I've heard cowboys have?"

"It's the steely inner strength anyone has for someone they care deeply about."

When Brooke and Alex appeared in the doorway of Lotte's office, she looked up from the computer and, crossing her arms over her chest, shoved the office chair back and swiveled it to face them.

"Calvin is meeting me here in a few minutes, so if you have anything to say for yourselves, please say it," Lotte said.

Alex was about to speak, but his throat tightened, and as he coughed to clear it, Brooke jumped in. "Mom, I don't know why you're acting like this. I'm over twenty-one, and you know enough about Alex to know he isn't a pathological liar, someone in huge debt, someone with a drinking problem, or a drug addict."

Brooke turned quickly to Alex. "You're not a registered sex offender, are you?"

Alex's head recoiled "What?"

"I'll take that as a no. OK, then. What is it, Mom? Out with it. What's your problem?"

Lotte looked at the ceiling and uncrossed her arms, placing her hands in her lap. She tapped her foot a few times before with rushed speech she blurted out, "He left his ex-fiancée standing at the altar. And while he seems burdened by it, at the same time he's already involved with *you*. And he's leaving as soon as he finishes the computer program. How could this possibly work out?"

Brooke walked over to her mother and knelt in front of her. Taking Lotte's hands into her own, she said softly, "Mom, I understand how this might look to you. But to me, it looks like a chance for me to find the kind of happiness you had with Dad. We know it takes a lot of effort for a long-distance relationship to work. Think about it this way. If our relationship can't stand the test of distance, then it will fail the test of our love. Isn't it better that we find out before we even think about 'foreverland'?"

The room was quiet for a few long moments before Lotte spoke. "Well, I want you to be happy. I just don't want you to be hurt."

Brooke stood and kissed her mother on the cheek. "I know that. I love you, Mom. I love you for all you've done for me. You've been my role model and the person I want to be. You've taught me so much. 'You *grow* through what you *go* through.' Remember that one?"

Lotte looked up at Brooke, smiled, and squeezed Brooke's hand.

"I expect that I'll grow through my relationship with Alex, and what would hurt me right now is not to have your support as I go through and grow through it. It would hurt me enormously not to be able to talk to you about it and get your sage advice as I have always done," Brooke said, wiping a tear from her eye.

Lotte stood and wrapped her arms around her daughter.

# Chapter 32

It's not what you look at that matters, it's what you see.

*—Henry David Thoreau*

When Alex opened the door to the carriage house, he heard a sound coming from the basement. "There it goes again," he said aloud.

"What?" Brooke asked from behind him.

He turned and reached for her, holding her in a tight embrace. "Are you okay?" he whispered.

She nodded into his chest. "Yes. She's okay, and it'll be okay."

Stepping back, she asked, "I heard you say something about 'There it goes again.' What were you talking about?"

"The sound in the basement."

"I'm going to ask Calvin to come over and check this out. See what he thinks," Brooke said.

"Good idea. Want me to go with you?"

"No, thanks. Calvin is a Gullah. And he doesn't like discussing the spiritual world with those he doesn't know well."

"What's a Gullah?"

"Very special African Americans who live in the Lowcountry regions of southern states. The word comes from the language they developed called 'creole.'"

"I thought creole was from around New Orleans."

"Duh. Louisiana is a Lowcountry region in a southern state."

"Ah, yeah. Sorry, you know I actually passed the Mensa test, but next to you I feel like a dummy."

Brooke threw her head back and laughed. "Really? Mensa? Have you ever taken the common sense test?"

"That's a trick question. There's no such thing."

"Oh, really? How much do you want to bet? Google it."

Alex studied her face. She was looking at him from under her eyelashes, and on her mouth was a slight side smile that seemed to be holding back a cackle.

"OK. I believe you. Go on, tell me the rest of the story about Gullahs."

"As I was saying, because the slave traders separated the kidnapped Africans from tribal members who spoke the same language to prevent them from speaking to each other and planning an escape, the enslaved Africans developed a unified language that preserved much of their African linguistics. It also absorbed the cultural heritage of various tribes, preserving spiritual beliefs in the afterlife, and included in their belief was that curses and spells placed on doers of evil in this life are justified."

"You are a wealth of knowledge. You know that? And I want you to know that I love that about you."

"Oh, and here, I thought it wasn't my gray matter that mattered but all things south of my cranium."

Alex looked at her with a wide grin and shook his head. It was a look that said, *No, south of your navel.* Followed by, "When can I see that part of you again?"

"Do you have to help my mom tonight?"

"She didn't say anything just now, but I don't think she was thinking about me staffing the restaurant. I think she was thinking about me staffing you," Alex said, smirking.

"Ha ha. You're such a card."

"Card-carrying crazy about you."

She stopped and turned, kissing him softly. "And I'm crazy about you, too, cowboy."

Alex took her overnight case from the back seat and watched as Brooke entered the back door of the restaurant. He walked into the carriage house and stopped at the basement door. He thought better of going down there until he heard from Brooke about what Calvin thought. Instead, he decided he'd clean up the kitchen from breakfast since they'd left the dishes on the table in their haste to get into the shower.

Alex loaded the dishwasher and smiled broadly, remembering bathing Brooke under the hot shower, and lathering her breasts with soap that smelled of lavender. He was remembering how she had pulled him close and clasped her feet around his buttocks when there was a knock on the door. He opened it to see Calvin standing there with furrowed brows and pursed lips.

"I hear we may have a spirit in the basement," Calvin said.

"I don't know what's down there. I hope you do. Come in."

Calvin nodded and stepped into the room, walking right to the basement door. Turning to Alex, he said in his all-business way, "You can come with me, if you want."

Alex smiled and followed Calvin down the stairs. When they reached the basement floor, the faint, reedy sound of a child crying came from behind the door in the middle of the brick wall. Calvin pressed the light on his phone and turned the doorknob slowly. The room was once again empty. But at the far end of it, the gossamer form of a young girl, no older than five or six, stood next to shelves lining the far wall.

"Who are you, child?" Calvin asked in a soothing voice. "We're not going to hurt you. We want to help you."

Without a response, the figure turned and passed through the brick wall.

"Holy shit!" Alex exclaimed.

"Yeah, ghosts do that," Calvin said, following it and shining his light behind the shelving. "You want to help me move these out?"

Calvin nodded and said, "The story is that there's an entrance door in here someplace leading to a tunnel that runs to the river. I think the spirit is showing us where it is."

They moved the shelving away from the wall to find that the brick wall ran the entire length of the room without a visible door or opening anywhere on the back wall.

"Look," Alex said, pointing to some grout protruding in between the bricks. He took off his shoe and, placing it on the grout, hit it with all his strength. Suddenly, a loud, creaking sound reverberated throughout the room, and a three-by-two-foot door popped open.

Calvin examined the front of the door. Alex saw Calvin's eyes grow wide. "Genius," he said, turning to Alex. "It's brick veneer."

Pulling open the door, Calvin knelt down to look inside the opening. "Let's see where this takes us."

"I'm right behind you."

# Chapter 33

Now I know what a ghost is. Unfinished business, that's what.

—*Salman Rushdie, The Satanic Verses*

Calvin's phone's light illuminated the entrance to the tunnel. "Whoever built this used palmetto logs to support it," he said, rotating the light to study the walls and floor. He turned and looked at Alex. "Let's see where this goes."

Calvin squeezed through the tunnel's opening, followed by Alex, who began to take pictures with his iPhone.

"I can't believe how dry the air is. The palmettos must soak up the moisture," Calvin called back to Alex.

The four-foot-wide tunnel took several turns and then steadily inclined for two hundred yards. "Hey, be careful. The cedar roots grew through the tunnel's roof," Calvin said. There was silence for a minute. Then Alex heard Calvin exclaim, "Holy Lord!"

Crawling while holding out his phone for light and taking pictures, Alex struggled to peer around Calvin. "What is it?"

"The cedar roots become a ladder to climb down into a room," Calvin said as he disappeared through the roots. Alex pushed the vertical roots aside and peered into the opening of a cave ten feet below the floor of the tunnel. "This is fucking unbelievable," Alex said as he climbed down the root ladder.

The ladder's rungs were supported by tightly woven sea grass. The cave looked to be about twelve by ten and had bunk beds three high on either side, a stove, and a table in the center. On one wall there was an open-shelved cupboard with all types of sweetgrass containers, cookware, and eating utensils.

"Look," Calvin said, pointing at the ten-foot ceiling.

Above them was a pipe fashioned as a vent.

"How come the ladder didn't rot after all those years?" Alex said, taking more pictures.

"Ever hear of cedar shingles?"

"Yeah," Alex said.

"If left to dry before weaving it with the sea grass, it doesn't rot."

"And by using the palmetto logs to line the tunnel, they kept this room dry. The same slaves who built Charleston built this," Calvin said with an air of solemnity.

They stood at the base of the vent and suddenly heard something that sounded like seagulls.

At the other end of the cave was another ladder. Calvin headed toward it and climbed up. Suddenly, Alex heard the creak of a door and a whoosh as the room was lit from above by a flash of daylight and a gust of sea air filled the room.

As Alex climbed up the ladder, his eyes adjusted to the daylight. Calvin was perched before him on a ledge.

"Hold up, Alex," Calvin called. "I think I found a rope ladder. I'm going to climb down." After Calvin maneuvered himself from the ledge, Alex moved onto it.

Alex looked out over the Ashley River. He climbed down the ladder and found himself standing in a grotto tucked into the west end of the battery wall. Calvin sat on a large boulder near the wall.

"This must have been the pickup point," Calvin said solemnly.

"Who picked them up, and where did they take them?" Alex asked.

Calvin lowered his eyes, studying the oyster shells that lined the beach. Then he slid his hands from his pockets, paused, and stood, breathing deeply. "Probably other abolitionists who were friends with Miss Sarah. They would take the slaves to safe houses that were part of the Underground Railroad."

Alex nodded and stood silently next to Calvin, who seemed to be studying the horizon. After a few minutes, Calvin said, "I think whoever that little girl is, she got separated from her mother or family, and she's still waiting for them to come for her."

Alex immediately thought of Clarissa still waiting for her Irishman.

"I think to help the child, I need to call my cousin, Alberytha. She's a medium, and she can help the child pass over. She says a child's brain has more plasticity and is more open than an adult's. That's why they're far more susceptible to a medium," Calvin said. Turning back toward the ladder, he added, "No way to get out of here except how we came. Let's go. I need to call Alberytha. I know she's going north soon to see her new grandchild."

They climbed out of the tunnel to find Lotte standing in the holding room.

"Where have you two been?" she said.

"You know all the stories about there being a tunnel in here that leads to the river? It's true. You should crawl through it and see for yourself. It's somethin' to behold," Calvin said.

"I'll take your word for it, thank you very much," Lotte said. "Did you take any pictures?"

Alex handed her his phone, and her face lit up as she scrolled through the photos. "Good heavens. This is unbelievable." She handed the phone back to Alex. "My husband looked but never found the tunnel. He'd be thrilled."

"That he'd be," Calvin said.

“I’ll have to let the historical society know about this. Their theory has always been there had to be a tunnel.” She paused. “How did you find it?”

“We saw the figure of a little girl go through the wall, and Alex noticed an irregularity in the brick mortar. He hit it, and the opening appeared,” Calvin said.

“What about the little girl?” Lotte asked.

“We weren’t able to contact her. I’m going to call my cousin.”

“Alberytha?” Lotte asked.

“Yes,” Calvin said.

“I like her. James used her several times to help him with some ghosts he couldn’t get to pass over. He placed great stock in her,” Lotte said.

“I’m going to go home, clean up, and call her,” Calvin said, heading for the staircase.

As they climbed the stairs, the sound of a child whimpering came from the holding room. Calvin turned and called, “Don’t cry, little one. We’re going for help. We’ll be back.”

After Calvin left, Lotte turned to Alex and said, “How is the computer program coming?”

Relieved she had asked about that and not about his love life, he said a little too excitedly, “Oh, I think you’re going to really like it. Want to see a preview?”

Lotte grimaced. “Guess I’ll have to rip the Band-Aid off sometime.”

Alex smiled. “Really, learning technology isn’t that painful.”

Grimacing, she said, “Ugh.”

# Chapter 34

Let friendship creep gently to a height; if it rushes to it,
it may soon run itself out of breath.

—*Thomas Fuller*

Calvin told Alex the only time Alberytha would be able to come was later that evening. Since Calvin had to work, he said he asked Donovan to attend in his stead.

*I'd better let Brooke know,* Alex thought. "Brooke, it looks like there's going to be a séance tonight in the holding room," Alex explained.

"What time? I'll come over."

"Seven thirty. What should I do to get ready? Find a crystal ball? Candles? A table that levitates?"

"Tell you what. I'll come a little early and bring a few things, but there's a card table and chairs in the basement under the stairs by the dehumidifier. You can set it up and put four chairs around it. Listen, I have to go, but I'll see you around six."

"I'll count the minutes," Alex said.

After he hung up, he took his computer and walked over to the restaurant.

"Where's Lotte?" Alex asked Calvin, dressed in his chef's clothes, and he was barking directions to his sous-chef.

"Lotte's in the basement checking inventory. I hope you got something to help her with that. Inventory drives her crazy," Calvin said. He looked Alex square in the face and said with deliberateness, "I don't like to see her get upset."

Alex tucked the computer under his arm and went to the open basement door. "Hey, Lotte, it's Alex. I'm coming down."

Alex found her with a notebook and calculator; she was bending down and counting wine bottles on the lower racks. "Hi, there," he said.

"Hi, there, yourself."

"I have something to show you that will make your life a lot easier," Alex said, putting the computer on the barrel in the corner. After a few clicks, a 3D picture of wine racks appeared on the screen. "Now watch this," he said, scrolling the mouse over a small sensor on the bottom of the rack. It lit up as the name of the bottle of wine and the number of bottles removed from the rack appeared in the bottom corner of the screen, making it look like an inventory sheet.

"You mean, if I put those little sensors in the bottoms of the wine racks, I'll know every time someone takes a bottle out of that rack?"

"Yup. No more inventory hell. I'm also gonna get a few cameras and install them throughout the restaurant. If someone ever steals anything, you'll catch them in the act."

"Well, I don't know any restaurant that hasn't had that problem. It's probably a good deterrent. Now, let's go upstairs, and you can show me what else you've done with the program."

As they climbed the stairs, Alex asked, "Did Brooke tell you about what happened at Magnolias the other night?"

"Yes. I called Hollis and told her how proud I am of her. Frankly, I've always wondered what kind of nurse she was. Don't get me wrong. I love her like my own daughter, but she can act a little ditzy sometimes, especially around boys."

"Let me tell you, she sprang into action during the emergency as if it were second nature to her. And sprang into action when she met this guy, Blake. Hollis looked at him like a cat about to devour a canary."

Lotte laughed. "I heard. Anyway, since I'm going to get all teched up, I decided to invest in an AED and train the staff in its use. I already require them to go for CPR and learn the Heimlich maneuver." She hesitated. "Although I recently read that calling it the Heimlich is no longer politically correct. I guess it turns out Dr. Heimlich was a bit of a charlatan. Now it's referred to as the 'abdominal thrust.'"

"I heard that, too. Well, my aunt requires the same from her staff, and I'm going to tell her she should get an AED too."

"Does she have cameras in her restaurant? I've always worried about it infringing on the guests' privacy."

"You bet she does. She's had problems with missing inventory, and once the cameras were installed, it stopped. And as far as privacy goes, there's no expectation of privacy in a public place, and your restaurant is a *very* public place."

As they walked into the kitchen, Calvin nodded toward the computer under Alex's arm. "When are you gonna show me what you've been working on?"

"Do you have time now? I was just going to go over it with Lotte."

"Yup," Calvin said, wiping his hands on a towel tucked into his apron's pocket.

Alex said, "Why don't we go into the dining room and sit at one of the tables?"

It took Alex forty-five minutes to explain the programs and answer the questions they had about them. Then he sat back and watched as Calvin and Lotte exchanged looks. Alex eavesdropped on the telepathic message they were sending each other. He folded his arms across his chest. "It will work. Trust me," he said.

Calvin just shook his head and sighed. "I don't know. It looks complicated. When are you gonna set it up for a dry run?"

"Once the equipment comes," Alex said, "I'll install it when the restaurant is closed."

Lotte was looking at Calvin as she touched Calvin's arm and said through a resigned smile, "Cal, I'm trusting him with my daughter's heart, so I guess compared to that, this isn't much of a gamble."

Calvin broke into a smile so big the pink of his gums showed. Standing up from the table, he put his hands on his hips. "Is that right? You and Miss Brooke? I'll be. It's about time she let that heart of hers out of its cage." Then he leaned in a few inches from Alex's face and said in a whisper, "But if that child gets so much as the slightest hurt to that heart of hers, you'll have to answer to me."

Smiling, Alex said without missing a beat, "My goal is to protect her from ever being hurt."

"Okay, just so we understand each other," Calvin said.

"Yes, sir, we do."

"Can you give me a list of the equipment I'll need to order to get the program up and running soon?" Lotte said.

"I took the liberty of ordering it. I thought it would be easier since I know the exact specifications and the vendors who have it in stock. It should be here in a day or two."

"Oh. Thank you. Please give me the receipt, and I'll pay you for it," Lotte said.

"Let's see how you like it first," Alex said.

"That's a deal," she said, glancing at her watch. "I have to get back to tracking inventory."

"Can I help?" Alex asked.

"No. Thank you for asking, but I have to do this myself." She hesitated a moment and added, "Anyway, I hear you have a séance to get ready for."

"Brooke's coming to help me with that."

"Is she?" Lotte chuckled. "If you got her to attend one of Alberytha's séance's, something is definitely in the air." Looking down, she muttered under her breath, "Like pheromones enough to lift a hot air balloon." Then, clearing her throat, she said, "Let me know when you get the equipment. We can run the program one morning, and then if it all works, I'll have the staff come in early so we can practice."

"Sounds like a plan. Will you need my help serving this week?" Alex asked.

"No, I have a full staff." She smiled at Alex and said, "By the way, Brooke told me you're staying for another week."

Alex furrowed his brow. "Do you object to that?"

Lotte pursed her lips. "Only a selfish mother would object to something that makes her child so obviously happy." She winked at Alex. "And you so obviously do."

# Chapter 35

I shall not commit the fashionable
stupidity of regrading everything
I cannot explain as a fraud.
—*C. G. Jung*

At six o'clock Alex heard Brooke pull into the driveway. He went to the door and leaned against the doorframe as she parked the car.

Brooke was about to open the car door when she saw Alex's hand on the handle. As she slipped out from the driver's seat, he kissed her.

"Miss me?" she asked with a smirk.

He brought her hand to his lips. "Every time you leave me, it's as if an hourglass is turned upside down in my heart, and I feel each grain of sand passing slowly until I see you again."

Brooke squinted as a ray of the setting sun caught her eyes. She stepped into the shade, looking at him oddly.

"What's with the weird look?" he asked.

"Come on. Let's take the packages in, and I'll tell you."

Alex grabbed two plastic bags from the back seat and carried them to the kitchen table. He turned to her and said, "OK, spill it."

"It's just odd that you would use the metaphor of an hourglass. An hourglass has a lot of spiritual meanings. I mean, with the séance and with everything that's been happening."

"If you ask me, there are a lot of weird things going on around here."

"Take a look around. You're in Charleston, the home of many unexplained things."

"So, what's spiritual about the hourglass?"

Brooke opened the refrigerator, handed Alex a beer, and poured herself a glass of wine. Sitting opposite him at the kitchen table, she began. "The hourglass is the symbol that existence is fleeting, and the 'sands of time' will run out for all forms of life. An hourglass was used on pirate flags to let their victims know that their time was up." Brooke sat back and sipped some wine, then put down her glass. "I'd be remiss if I left out that for a woman it symbolizes that she passes with time from a maiden to a mother, and I'm not wild about this one, but as the story goes, she turns into a crone."

"I dated a girl once who was into new age stuff, which by the way is why it wasn't for very long. Anyway, she said that a crone was someone who passed with age into a zone of wisdom, freedom, and personal power."

"Hmm," Brooke mused. "I like that interpretation."

"Well, my money's on that's the type of crone you'll be."

Their eyes met, and they looked at each other for a long moment until the sound of a car in the driveway interrupted them. "That must be Donovan," Brooke said. "Oops. I'd better set this stuff up on the table."

Picking up the plastic bags from the table, Alex said, "I'll help you."

By the time Donovan walked into the holding room, the table had a white cloth over it, a large pillar candle burned in the middle, and tea lights flickered all over the room.

"Hey, you two. This looks great. Alberytha will be pleased," Donovan said.

"As long as you are, big brother," Brooke said, planting a kiss on his cheek.

"Have you two attended one of these before?" Alex asked.

"Yes. A few years ago, after my mother bought her house," Donovan said. "She asked Alberytha to help Clarissa pass over. But despite everything Alberytha tried, Clarissa didn't want to leave her tree or her belief that her lover would return for her."

"Why do you think some people hang on like that?" Alex said.

"Ask the shrink," Donovan said, hooking his finger toward Brooke.

"Let's go upstairs and wait for Alberytha. I have an unfinished glass of wine I hear calling my name," Brooke said.

"And I hear a beer calling mine," Donovan said.

The three sat down in the living room, and Alex asked, "Okay, Brooke, why do you think some people refuse to want to let go of something that keeps them stuck from passing into the afterlife?"

She inhaled deeply. Then in her clinical voice, said, "My theory is that whether the person is living or dead, it's out of fear."

"Fear? Fear of what?" Alex asked.

"Fear of change. They've built up such a comfort level with the defenses they have around whatever they're dealing with that in order to let go of it, they'd have to go through a very uncomfortable and unsettling period of change. I mean, it's not like peeling bark from a tree. It's more like peeling layers of skin off. It can be very painful." She lifted her shoulder in a half-hearted shrug. "Sometimes people prefer the stability of their current beliefs than the painful process of the unknown that change brings."

"How does that work with ghosts?" Alex asked.

"As my father explained it, when a person dies with unfinished business on earth, they can't pass on until they've resolved it. Some ghosts, like some of those living, prefer to hang onto what they know."

Just then, there was a knock on the door. Donovan rose to open it, and Alberytha entered the room.

# Chapter 36

Joy's recollection is no longer joy, while
sorrow's memory is still sorrow.
—*George Byron*

The genetic code of Calvin's family played out on Alberytha's face and frame. She was close to six feet tall and had a broad jaw, high cheekbones, and a wide set of twinkling caramel eyes. She wore a brightly colored kaftan and a matching scarf wrapped her head, and she carried a large canvas bag over her shoulder.

"Hello, y'all. I know you two," she said, smiling at Donovan and Brooke. "And you must be the one Calvin calls the 'cowboy,'" she said, extending her hand to Alex.

"Alex Whitgate," he said, clasping her hand. "I've heard a lot about you."

"Is that right? And Calvin's told me a lot about you. You're from Montana, ay. I hear you have your share of spirits out there."

"Yes. Mostly in the Native Indian burial grounds," Alex said.

"Where they were slaughtered," she said dolefully. "Just like my people were during the Vesey uprising." She paused and said, "Calvin thinks there's a child here who died during it."

"Yes, ma'am. And we think it's a little girl. We saw her form in what looks to be a holding room for slaves Miss Sarah helped escape to the Underground Railroad," Donovan said.

"I see. Alex, have you ever been to a séance before?" she asked.

"No, ma'am," he said respectfully.

"Then let me explain what I'm going to do," she said, placing her canvas bag on the end table next to the couch. She took out a bottle filled with a thick greenish fluid. "This is olive oil. It's been used for centuries in religious ceremonies for healing and strength. We use it for protection from evil spirits that may be lurking here." Alberytha made the sign of the cross three times after pouring a little on her fingertips. As she crossed herself, she closed her eyes and began to recite the Twenty-Third Psalm. Upon saying, "I shall dwell in the house of the Lord forever," she opened her eyes to see the three had closed theirs and bowed their heads. She smiled.

"You see, Alex, I inherited an ability to conjure and hoodoo from my mother's side. And so you understand, emotion is what allows a ghost to break through and connect with the living. It can be anything from passion, anger, or concern, but whatever it is, it *must* be very, very intense."

Alex nodded.

"Since I understand this ghost appeared when you did, I will be asking for your help."

"Now, Donovan, please lead the way to the room where Alex saw her," she said.

Donovan showed the way to the basement stairs.

As they entered the holding room, Alberytha took salt from her canvas bag and sprinkled it in a circle around the table. Then, taking the seat in the chair facing the tunnel entrance, Alberytha motioned Alex to take the seat opposite her.

Brooke and Donovan sat opposite each other. After everyone was seated, she said, "Calvin told me that you found the entrance to the tunnel this afternoon. I always wondered how Miss Sarah got our people out of here." She paused and harrumphed. "And how she got them in here."

Pulling his cell phone from his pocket, Alex asked, "Would you like to see the pictures of the tunnel?"

Alberytha reached, taking the phone from him. Scrolling through the pictures, she sighed and shook her head. Her eyes widened as she seemed to focus on one of the pictures. "Good Lord, what an incredible feat to build ladders like that. And what incredible courage to build the tunnel under the noses of White people."

As she handed the phone back to Alex, Donovan said, "Tells you how much they were willing to risk for their freedom. If they'd been caught, they knew they'd be tortured and killed."

Alberytha pulled out a large ashtray and some wooden sticks from her bag. "Now, I will burn some palo santo wood for our protection." She lit the wood, and soon the room became permeated with an incredible meditative smell. After inhaling a few deep breaths, she said, "Let's join hands." Once they were joined, she said, "Alex, I'd like you to summon her."

"Um, look, ma'am, I mean no disrespect to you or this séance, but my knowledge about time travel comes from Harry Potter. And I don't have a time turner. And I have no idea how to do that," Alex said, his tone meant to bring an end to any further discussion.

"This isn't time travel. It's mind travel. You close your eyes and think of the brilliant blue of the ocean. Concentrate on what looks like the thousands of glittering sequins scattered on its surface. Put yourself there at the water's edge. Look up at the blue sky. Think about the sounds that drew you to this room. Picture a child who is stuck between two worlds, crying out for you to help her. She's reaching out to *you*. Tell her we're here to help her."

The encouraging looks Brooke and Donovan gave him made Alex feel as if they were converging on him like members of a support group. Brooke nodded at him under her long, black lashes and smiled, and Donovan gave him an eyebrow flash and a triple nod. Alex took a deep breath and closed his eyes, then did another deep inhale, but his mind didn't clear. Inhaling the sweet, woodsy scent of the palo santo, he thought that if this were a movie, this was the part when the eerie music would start, and he'd be laughing until his side hurt at how fake the whole thing was—except it wasn't a movie, and it didn't feel fake.

"You have to summon her, Alex," Alberytha repeated. "It's you she reached out to." She stared at him and after a long stretch of silence said, "Close your eyes and speak to her in your mind. Ask whatever the voice in your head tells you to say."

What the voice in his head said was, *Good one, Alex. What are you going to do now? Say you can't do it?* Much as the idea appealed to him, he was the one who always ran toward danger when others ran in the other direction. And he'd never run from a challenge. Besides, he had a feeling that whatever was unfolding here wasn't by accident. He was meant to witness this. To be a part of it.

"The child may speak through me. If she does, Alex, ask her name and what happened to her. Ask the questions that come to mind," Alberytha said. "They *will* come to mind."

Glancing at Brooke and Donovan again, Alex took a deep breath, exhaled, and took another. He closed his eyes and focused on the surface of the ocean. Concentrating on its glittering surface, he fell under the spell of chromatic visualization. Slowly and imperceptibly, he thought he could actually hear the operational chatter in his mind grow quiet. At first he could see light and dark streaking, and then he saw himself walking through the tunnel and stepping into the grotto just as he had earlier in the day.

And then there was an outer body vision of him as he saw himself walking toward a little girl dressed in a white cotton dress with plaited black hair standing at the river's edge. He saw it not like in a fuzzy snapshot but in vivid detail. He touched her shoulder and felt the warmth of her pallid skin. She looked at him with piercing amber eyes. He heard himself explain that he was there with some other people, and one of them had special powers to help her. As she reached for his hand, he felt a gust of arctic air. He opened his eyes to find he was back in the room, sitting at the table.

Alberytha's eyes were closed. "I feel the presence of a child's spirit here. Are you here, child?" When there was no reply, she said softly, "Child, we invite you into our circle. Be guided by the light. If you can hear me, make your presence known. We are here to help you."

For a moment everything was still. But then Alberytha's eyelids fluttered and drooped, her chin slumped to her chest, and her hands fell into her lap. Suddenly, her head flew back, and her eyes opened slowly as she stared fixedly at the dark mouth of the tunnel. Her thick, full lips parted, and she began to speak in the voice of a confused and angry child. "I want to go to my mamma. Where is she? I want to see her now."

Alex felt an eerie sensation as he stared at Alberytha's mouth. The marionette lines around it made the words of the young child seem as if they were coming from a puppet. Before coming to Charleston and seeing the ghostly vision of Clarissa, Alex had been around lucid and intelligent people, most of whom didn't believe in ghosts, so he would have concluded that Alberytha was faking it. But tonight, the thought didn't even cross his mind.

And then what to ask her came to him. "What is your name, little girl?" Alex asked softly.

"Ruby," the voice said. "When can I see my mamma?" Ruby said in the reedy, whiny voice that had initially brought Alex to this room in the middle of the night.

"What's your mother's name?"

"Cecilia. My mother's name is Cecilia. When can I see her?" Ruby said, sounding eerily real.

"Soon. But first, tell me how you got separated from her," Alex asked.

"When I first came here, I was with my mother, but then she went with Miss Sarah to bring other slaves here to escape. I was very mad. Mad at her for leaving me. But I'm not mad anymore. I'm sad.

I want to see my mamma now. I want to see her now," the child's voice screeched as Alberytha's head jerked up.

Alex imagined the child stamping her feet or hitting something. "Ruby, we want to help you go to her. That's why we're here. It may help us to know how you got separated from her."

Sounding high pitched and distressed, the child's voice said, "I wasn't supposed to leave until she came back, but then there was a lot of shoutin' and screamin' outside, and a woman waitin' in the room grabbed me by the arm and dragged me through the tunnel. She put me in a boat." Then the child's whimpering sound began again.

"Ruby," Alex said in a gentle, quiet voice. "Tell me what happened when you got in the boat."

"There were too many. I fell outta the boat. The water rushed into my nose and mouth so fast I couldn't breathe. I waved my arms and kicked my legs, but I sank under the water. My eyes burned, and I couldn't see. I tried to breathe, but I couldn't. I think someone tried to grab me, but I sank under the water again. Then I saw a bright light, but I didn't go to it. I had to wait for my mamma, so I came back here. Where is she?" Ruby asked in an increasingly agitated voice.

Alex swallowed. "Ruby, she's on the other side, looking for you. To see her, you have to leave here." He had surprised himself. *Where did that come from?* he thought. It hadn't even felt like he was speaking.

There was a deafening silence in the room. Then the candle on the table flickered as if a wind had blown through the room, and with it, a small, pulsating orb of light hovered over the table.

After a long pause, the ghost child said, "How do I find her?"

Suddenly, Alex saw the grotto in his head and said softly, "Go back to the grotto and wait. You will see the light you saw under the water. Follow it, and it will take you to your mamma."

The orb grew brighter but remained hovering over the table.

"It's time to go, Ruby," Alex said. "It's time to go. She's been waiting for you."

The orb moved slowly toward the tunnel entrance. As it vanished into it, the room's air filled with the scent of an electrical charge.

Suddenly, Alberytha slumped forward onto the table. She was still for a few seconds before she opened her eyes and lifted her head. Then she sat back and closed her eyes. Suddenly, she began to shake her head as if someone were doing it for her.

Looks passed between the others at the table.

After a few minutes, Alberytha closed her eyes again, leaned forward, put her arms around her wide girth, and began to rock back and forth. In a voice that was barely a whisper, she said, "The child is gone. She's passed over."

The room was silent for a long moment before Alberytha leaned forward and focused on Alex's eyes as if she were looking for something. "How do you feel?"

"I felt her presence, and now I don't," Alex said, shooting Brooke and Donovan a look.

"Good. Then it's done. Now she's at peace because of you Alex and soon you will be too." She hesitated a moment and turned to Alex. "Now you know there's a place to go after mortal life." With that, she abruptly stood, collected her things, and walked to the stairs with Donovan at her side.

# Chapter 37

Those that cannot change their minds,
cannot change anything.
—*George Bernard Shaw*

While Donovan assisted Alberytha up the stairs, Alex and Brooke sat staring at each other.

Alex opened his mouth and then closed it again.

"What are you thinking about?" Brooke asked.

"That was unbelievable. Before what just happened, I always thought our bodies were like a computer, which stops working when its components fail. And that's it. The end. I didn't believe there was a heaven, a hell, or anything else."

"Well, I've always been biased in favor of ghosts and an afterlife by my father. And from a psychological perspective, when people who claim they don't believe in ghosts yelp in fright when they see something eerie in the corner, they're acting in contradiction to their belief. While there is some disagreement in the field, I believe behavior is the means by which a person's beliefs and emotions are represented."

Alex leaned his elbow on the table and held his chin in his hand. "Um, so you're saying if people react fearfully to something they know doesn't exist, they may have to reconsider what they believe in the first place." He sighed and sat back in the chair. "Like I've done."

"Yes. Exactly."

"And what about the afterlife?"

"There have been some studies in evolutionary psychology that propose a psychological adaptation or evolved cognitive mechanism designed to help humans survive. But I think the issue is more philosophical and rests on a person's belief in God or a supernatural being."

Before they could discuss the matter further, Donovan returned. He sat down, and the three passed looks between them.

"I can't believe I spoke to a ghost. I felt like I was wading into the River Styx without a life raft."

Brooke smiled.

"From where I sat, it didn't look like you needed any help staying afloat," Donovan said. Rubbing his temples, he stood up. "Let's get a drink and some food. How about Pearlz?"

"What's Pearlz?" Alex asked.

"It's an oyster place where the patrons are mostly locals," Brooke said. "You like oysters, don't you?"

"Sure do. Love 'em," Alex said, as a bright smile appeared on Brooke's face.

As they walked up East Bay, Brooke and Alex held hands while Donovan walked in front of them. When they arrived at Pearlz, there was a line. Alex recognized the twenty-something woman at the hostess stand from the Boll Weevil. She seemed to be writing something down. When she looked up, she smiled at them and waved them to her. She crooked her finger for Donovan to bend so she could whisper in his ear.

Alex watched as the hostess's layered shoulder-length blonde hair swished back and forth every time she tossed her pretty head. He also noticed Donovan's eyes were riveted on the silky camisole that barely covered the girl's ample goods. Alex overheard what the woman said and whispered into Donovan's ear, "I think she'd like you to squeeze her in. Who is she?"

"Bridgit," he said, raising an eyebrow.

Alex studied the blackboard with the evening's special written on it. And then he surveyed the restaurant's old brick walls covered with various paintings of people slurping down a gelatinous blob from a liquid-filled half shell and realized these weren't the oysters he was expecting. The twenty-foot-high ceiling made the small interior look larger than it was. The low-cut tops and short skirts on the female wait staff made Alex think of the poultry section of the grocery store: breast, thigh, leg. He had time for only one carnal thought about Brooke before he slid into the booth next to her. He put his arm around her and said, "These are not Rocky Mountain oysters, are they?"

Brooke's head spun around to look at him bewildered. "Rocky Mountain oysters? What's that?"

"Um, they're actually not oysters. They're deep-fried bull testicles," Alex said.

Brooke's head jerked back. "Bull testicles? Seriously. Eck," she exclaimed.

"They're good," Donovan said. "I had one at Alex's aunt's restaurant."

Through a laugh, Alex said, "They're cowboy caviar. And there's a five-day extravaganza every August in a town near my ranch that attracts thousands of people every year. And fifty thousand pounds of fried balls are devoured during the event."

Brooke made a face as if she'd just tasted something disgusting and it had returned to the back of her throat.

"There's even a contest," he said. "Like the one in *Funny Farm* when Chevy Chase beats the record and eats thirty lamb fries."

"I remember that," Donovan said. "And he threw up when he found out they were lamb testicles."

"Yeah, he didn't get a trophy. But you should see the one you get at the contest I'm talking about." Using Alex's hands to demonstrate the size, he said, "The winner gets a huge silver bull testicle on a pedestal with their name and the number of balls they've devoured on it."

"Hi, you guys. I'm Laurel. I'll be your server," she said. Laurel's eyes never left Donovan's when she asked, "What can I get y'all?"

Donovan answered, "I'll have a Charleston ale."

"Chardonnay for me," Brooke said.

"I'll have what he's having," Alex said.

"I'll get that right out for you," Laurel said, her lips slipping in a grin at Donovan.

Linking her fingers together and looking into Donovan's eyes, Brooke said, "I see you have a new conquest."

Donovan shrugged.

"What did you think about what Alberytha said at the end?" Brooke said.

"As my mind cleared … I don't know how to describe it. She said I'd be at peace. Like she knew something was going to happen." Alex hesitated.

Laurel's breasts strained against her blouse as she bent to place the beer bottles and frosted glasses in front of Alex and Donovan and the wine glass in front of Brooke.

Donovan watched intently, smiled, and asked, "I didn't read the blackboard. What's your special?"

"You mean, on the menu?" said Laurel, her tone sultry, her eyes fixed on his.

"Umm, he means on the menu," Brooke interjected, meeting Laurel's narrowed eyes with her own. "I think we're good with four dozen PEI oysters and a cup of clam chowder for each of us."

Laurel jotted down the order and focused on Donovan. "If you want anything, just let me know," she said and walked toward the computer behind the bar.

"It's obvious what she wants from you, Donovan," Alex said, chuckling.

Brooke nudged Alex in the side and laughed as Donovan shrugged and poured beer into his glass.

Alex noticed Donovan was studying the inside of the glass as if the answer to whatever he was thinking about was in it. He put his hand on Brooke's knee and nodded toward Donovan.

"What are you thinking about, Donovan?" asked Brooke.

"Dad," said Donovan.

Brooke reached for his hand.

"Whenever I'm involved in a séance, thoughts of him flood my mind. I hope he knows how right he was," he said.

"What about?" asked Brooke in a soft, sympathetic tone.

"About what he used to say. 'The dead never die, they only change forms,'" Donovan said, then took a long draw of beer.

"I remember that. And he always added, 'It's the same with love. If you truly love someone with all your heart, that love never dies. It just changes forms,'" Brooke said.

# Chapter 38

The treasures of the deep are not so precious
as are the concealed comforts
of a man locked up in a woman's love.
—*Conyers Middleton*

After two more rounds of drinks and three more dozen oysters, they walked back to the carriage house three across. Donovan was walking on the street side and at times had to step off the curb when the narrow sidewalk couldn't accommodate them. Brooke's left arm was looped around Donovan's elbow and her right arm around Alex's.

When they arrived at the carriage house, Brooke said, "Donovan, I think you should sleep here tonight."

"No, thanks. I'm fine," he said.

"No, you're not," Brooke insisted.

"I think he is," Alex said. Then, noticing the hostile stare Brooke was giving him, he turned to Donovan and said, "Prove it. Close your eyes and touch your finger to your nose."

"See," Donovan said after he'd completed the exercise. "I'm fine."

"How about walking in a straight line," Brooke said, unconvinced.

Donovan proceeded to do a heel-to-toe walk in a straight line without wavering. "I'm good. Really, I am."

Brooke emitted a reluctant, "If you say so."

Alex and Brooke watched Donovan back out of the driveway. When he reached the road, they turned and walked to the front door.

"I think he's sober enough to drive. But I think he's just sad," said Alex.

"You'd better be right. I shouldn't have let him drink so much. Alcohol is a depressant and screws with your brain chemistry. Especially your decision making."

He opened the front door and stood aside to let Brooke pass. As she did, he put his hand around her wrist and gently pulled her into him.

"Speaking of screwing," he said.

Closing the door with his foot, his hands moved over the curve of her hips, and he leaned in, placing a soft kiss on her lips and then another on the tender spot under her ear. He guided her to the bedroom without taking his eyes from her. He noticed her trembling in anticipation. Without a word, Brooke slipped out of her dress and climbed into bed, patting the spot next to her.

He quickly unbuckled his belt, his pants falling to his ankles, and almost fell while kicking off his shoes. He yanked his shirt off, slipped under the covers, and took her into his arms. He reached for her hair, his fingers releasing its fasteners. Her silky hair fell, brushing her shoulders and breasts. Picking up a fistful of her hair, he took a deep breath and buried his face in it. He heard Brooke's breath catch and felt her shiver.

Then slowly he began stroking, touching her body with his fingertips before moving to explore inside her. He was circling, rubbing gently, caressing her as her back arched, bringing her closer to him. He could feel her urging him on, taking his hands and moving them between her legs. She stretched upward to rub herself against the full length of his body. She moved her hands to the back of his neck, down his spine, and clutched him closer. "Now," she said. "Oh, God, now."

Unleashed, he covered her with his body and thrust deep and then deeper inside her with such passion that he thought he felt steam rising off them.

His face was strained with urgency and tension, and then he moaned loudly, and there was relief as he rolled to his back.

She turned her head to look at him, and he reached for her, pulling her to him and then wrapping his arms tightly around her.

"I never want to let you go," he whispered.

"I never want you to," she said softly.

# Chapter 39

Every man's life is a fairy tale, written by God's fingers.
*—Hans Christian Andersen*

The sun was barely over the ancient oaks, and the birds were just beginning to call to each other when Alex opened his eyes. He lay on his side, facing Brooke. He inhaled a breath louder than he'd meant, and Brooke's eyelids fluttered. As she opened her eyes, she let out a satiated smile.

"Good morning, cowboy," she said, smiling. After a yawn and a stretch, she raised herself on her elbow and looked at him quizzically.

"What?" he asked.

"I was just thinking," she hesitated.

"Thinking what?"

She sat up, leaning against the headboard. There was a long pause before she spoke. "Thinking you're leaving in a few days, and I mean, I'm already missing you. How is this going to work?"

Alex sat up next to her, leaned over slowly, and kissed her on the forehead. "How it's going to work is that I will fly back here to see you until you can come to Montana. And as I told you before, we actually have cell service and Wi-Fi out in the western part of the states."

She looked down and pulled at the bedspread, fumbling with it between her fingers. "But even if I come to visit you in Montana, I'm not going to stay there."

"I wouldn't ask you to. Look, we don't have to live in a cookie-cutter world. We can design our own world. If *you* want us to work, it will work."

"Why did you say if *I* want us to work?"

"Because *I* know I want to make it work. It's up to you. I already know we're meant for each other," he said, pulling her into his arms. With her head on his chest and the crown of her head touching his chin, he said, "Coming here has given me the time for some serious analysis of my life."

"A change of scenery often does that."

"I've heard some parents write letters to their newborn baby, telling them they can be anything they want to be. Encouraging them to follow their passion in life. In my case, my parents wrote out a prescription no different than if I'd been born with some malady and a doctor had ordered an antibiotic. I was to follow in the footsteps of all the prior Whitgates, and that was supposed to be a proxy for my passion in life."

Brooke pulled away and sat up. Facing him, she wrapped the sheet around her, kissed her fingertips, and touched his cheek. She didn't say a word, but he understood from her look that she was urging him go on.

"And I was on the path to doing just that. Get married and have little Whitgates who'd be born into the same prescribed life I'd been born into. But then something inside me screamed, 'Don't do it.' And then Donovan showed up, and the servers at my aunt's restaurant didn't, and then Donovan asked me to come here."

Brooke's gaze remained fixed on him. "Sound almost like divine intervention."

"Sound like it was meant to be. Me meeting you."

Alex sat on his knees and took Brooke's hand. "I know this is going to be hard, being away from each other, but I know it would be harder for us not to work it out."

Brooke fell back onto the bed, looking at Alex longingly, and wet her lips. She raised the sheet for Alex to see her squirming body. "It sort of feels as if a portal opened for us. And something else is opening for you," she said, spreading her legs.

"You little minx," Alex said, about to get under the covers when he heard a vehicle pull into the driveway. "Crap, crap, crap," he said, jumping out of bed and reaching for his pants. "Don't move," he commanded, winking at her as he closed the bedroom door.

A few minutes later, he opened the bedroom door to see Brooke sitting on the edge of her bed with her head in her hands. Kneeling in front of her, he gently pulled her hands away from her face and wiped the tears from her cheeks with the sheet. "Brooke, what's wrong?"

"Who was that?"

"The FedEx man. He delivered the equipment I ordered for the restaurant. Who did you think it was?"

She sighed and sighed again. "I was afraid it might be the police telling us Donovan had an accident. I worried when he left. We shouldn't have let him drive."

He took her hands and lifted her chin so they were eye to eye. "Listen to me. I've seen your brother drunk on more than one occasion. The man must have a liver that runs on warp speed filtering the alcohol he consumes. If I thought for a moment he shouldn't drive, I wouldn't have let him. I know your father died in a car accident and *never* would have taken the risk. He and Nick are the only brothers I have. I love him."

"But you did a sobriety test. You must have thought there was the possibility," she cried.

"I saw how worried you were and didn't want it to turn into an argument between us. I wanted to show you he was fine."

"So, were you trying to prove you were right?" She paused. "I mean, we're bound to have arguments. Are you going to have to be right all the time?"

Alex pulled her up from the bed and held her tightly. He stroked her hair and whispered, "No. Because I'd rather lose an argument to you than lose you to an argument."

# Chapter 40

Love is a thing to be *learned*. It is a difficult, complex maintenance of individual integrity throughout the incalculable processes of inter-human polarity.

—*D. H. Lawrence*

Alex was in the kitchen, making coffee, when his phone rang. "Good morning, Hollis," he said. "Mind if I put you on speaker? I'm making coffee."

"Of course. I tried Brooke's phone, but it went to voice mail."

"Oh, well, she's in the shower."

"Mmm, is she?" Hollis said, followed by the ubiquitous southern saying he'd heard these last few weeks. "Well, bless her heart."

Alex chuckled at how versatile the saying was. Sort of like "fuck you." It could be used as a noun, a verb, an adjective, in the past tense, the present tense, and the pluperfect subjunctive.

"Um, I'm calling because Blake and I would like to get together with you two before you leave, and we are both off tonight. Any chance we can meet you for dinner?" Hollis said.

"I'll have Brooke call you. That would be nice," Alex said.

"Great."

"Oh, wait a minute. The equipment came for the restaurant's computer system, and I need to be there tonight in case there are any glitches."

"Oh," Hollis said, sounding crestfallen. She paused and said, "What if we come to Serenity?"

"I'll have Brooke call you," Alex said.

"Well, good luck with the install."

"Thanks, Hollis."

Alex hung up and was turning to fill the coffee maker with water when he felt Brooke's arms slip around his waist, resting her head on the back of his shoulder. "That feels good. Hey, Hollis just called and asked about getting together tonight."

She extended her hand to take the coffee carafe. "What do you think?"

"I want to install the equipment today and do a dry run before the restaurant opens. I told her I'd need to be at Serenity tonight to make sure there are no problems. She said they'd come to Serenity. What do you think?"

"I'll have to check with Mom if there's a table, but if not, we can sit at the bar, since there aren't reservations for that. Would it be distracting for you?"

"I'm good with it."

"OK, your turn for the shower, and I'll fix something for breakfast."

He kissed her on the cheek and whispered, "Let's make it an early dinner. I'd like for us to have an early night."

Nudging him with her hip, she said. "Get goin'."

★★★★

As the coffee maker dripped coffee into the carafe, Brooke took out the ingredients for an omelet and phoned Hollis. "Hey, you, good morning."

"Hey, you, yourself. Have fun last night?" Hollis said.

"I'll tell you all about it later. I want to hear all about you and Blake. Alex said you're off today. Want to meet for lunch?"

"The short version is, I think I'm in love with Blake." She giggled. "Why don't I give you the long version at lunch? But what about tonight? Will it work?"

"I'll have to check. Let's talk details at lunch. Where do you want to meet?"

"How about 82 Queen? We haven't been there in a while, and they just renovated the dining area in the courtyard," Hollis said.

"Sounds good. What time is good for you?"

"Twelve thirty?"

"See you there," Hollis said.

Brooke heard the water in the shower turn off, poured a steaming cup of coffee, and took it into the bedroom. Peeking into the bathroom, she said, "I put a cup of coffee on the bedside table. Cheese and tomatoes OK for your omelet?"

"Anything. I'm living on love," he said softly as he dried himself off. "Be right out."

Brooke went back into the kitchen, and as she prepared the omelet, she wondered what it would be like to be married to this man. It was true that he seemed different from when he had first come to Charleston, but then as far as she was concerned, next to Paris, Charleston was the most romantic city on the planet. Her mother always said, "If you can't fall in love in Charleston, don't waste your time trying anywhere else." Right then, Brooke decided Alex had been right when he said she should come to Montana and see him in his natural habitat.

"Did you speak to Hollis?" he called.

Without turning from the stove, she said, "Yes. She's in love. Again … but this time she sounds different."

"How?"

"Remember me telling you her voice was so different when she was trying to console the people that night at Magnolias?"

Alex strolled in. "Yes."

Sliding the omelets onto plates, she said, "Like that. There was something new in her voice. It wouldn't surprise me if she wants to meet for lunch to show me a diamond engagement ring from Croghan's Jewel Box that it has its own zip code."

His head began bobbing like he was trying to shake something loose from his gray matter. "How do I know that name? I've seen it somewhere," he said, taking a seat at the table.

"What name?"

Lifting a fork to his mouth, he said, "Croghan's Jewel Box."

"Oh, you probably saw it when we've walked down King Street. That's where every proper Charlestonian bride gets an engagement ring."

"I see," he said with a smirk, thinking, And *that's where I'll get yours.*

"Anyway, Hollis and I are meeting for lunch, and I'm sure I'll get the Google Map directions to where she and Blake are headed."

"I hope it's the same place we are," he said over the coffee cup poised at his lips.

"You know, on that subject, I have to talk to you about something."

She saw his face become pinched and worried and quickly said, "I want to visit you in Montana sooner than later. I'm going to my dissertation adviser to see if we can have virtual meetings. I already emailed him the draft of my thesis."

"Are you serious?"

"Absolutely. You've seen me in my natural habitat, and I need to see you in yours."

Alex let out a rush of air that sounded as if it started in his toes. "That would be great. Really great," he said.

"Oh. And there's another thing I think we should do to see each other for who we are."

"What?"

"There's a test two psychologists, Elaine and Arthur Aron, made to measure closeness and compatibility in relationships. It's a list of thirty-six questions that's supposed to test whether you're falling in love with the *right* person and are the *right* person for the relationship."

"I'm game."

"Well, I don't have it with me. Maybe we can find some time tomorrow. We'll need to look into each other's eyes as we answer each question."

Alex touched her wrist and put his arm around her waist. Looking into her eyes, he said, "Sound like my kind of test."

# Chapter 41

We are not to lead events, but to follow them.

—*Epictetus*

After kissing Brooke goodbye, Alex texted Lotte to tell her the equipment had been delivered and that he was going over to install it. He checked the time. It was eight a.m. Mountain Time. His mother would have finished her swim by now.

Answering on the first ring, Mary said, "Good morning, son." After a pause, she added, "If it wasn't for caller ID, I wouldn't have been sure since I haven't heard your voice in so long."

"Oh, come on, Mom. I called you a couple of days ago."

"Yes, and I said then that I could tell by your voice something was going on that you weren't telling me."

"I met someone."

She laughed. "I already know. Nick called Donovan, and he told Nick you've fallen for his sister."

"Dang, they're like two old ladies."

"Watch it, Alex. I'm an old lady. And I'll have you know I just read an article that reported the results of a survey that found men gossip thirty percent more than women."

"Mom, you're not an old lady. I wanted to be the one to tell you about Brooke."

"Why didn't you?"

"I was afraid you would think it was too soon after breaking my engagement with Gwynn."

"Do you think it is?"

Without hesitation, he empathically said, "No."

"Then it doesn't matter what anyone else thinks. I thought we just went through this."

"Ahem. Guess we did."

"So, when are you coming home? And when do I get the chance to meet this girl?"

"Well, if things work out with the install at the restaurant, soon. I've invited her and two of her friends to come to the ranch."

"I hope it works out."

"Well, I'm installing the equipment today. It depends on how well the program runs and how well some people adjust to it."

"Just let me know so I can get things ready. And please tell Brooke I'm looking forward to meeting her."

"Mom, I was wondering. Have you heard anything about Gwynn?"

"No. Seems you and Gwynn are old news. The mayor is involved in a scandal. He's accused of sexual harassment by his secretary. And Jenna, his wife, is definitely not standing by her man. Rumor is, she's already filed for divorce. Why?"

"I've been doing a lot of thinking, and I maybe I should try to see Gwynn when I get back and apologize to her now that things have cooled off."

"Hmm, you may need to think hard about that."

"What do you mean?"

"I mean, think about whether you're apologizing to make yourself feel better or if it will make Gwynn feel better."

"Why do you say that?"

"Although time helps bad memories fade, contact may cause her to regress into anger if she isn't fully healed."

"Thanks, Mom. I'll give it more thought. I'd better go now. I love you."

"Love you, too, Alex."

Alex's next call was to Lotte to make sure she'd received his text. She said she'd be there in an hour or so and reminded him on how to disarm the alarm.

After installing the equipment on the first floor and loading the program, he moved to the basement. He looked around for a ladder to install the camera in the corner of the ceiling, but all he could find was a step stool. He glanced at his watch. Lotte would be here soon, and he was anxious to load the program. He pulled the step stool next to the barrel, placed the camera and screwdriver on top of it, and heaved himself up. He stood up and balanced himself, but when he bent over to pick up the camera, the barrel shifted and began to wobble. Alex jumped off, sticking the landing as he heard a grinding sound and saw the barrel slowly move away from the wall. He stood up and saw behind the barrel an opening to a tunnel. He'd crawled about one hundred feet before he heard Lotte calling his name.

"Holy shit," Alex exclaimed as he climbed out of the tunnel and saw her descending the staircase.

"I'm sure this leads to the holding room in the carriage house," he said. "The engineering is incredible. The palmetto logs they used here are better support than in the tunnel El Chapo used to escape from prison."

"I'll be damned," Lotte said, leaning in to inspect the tunnel's entrance. Standing up, she looked at Alex. "After all this time, *you* found it. James looked for it for years. He tried to move that barrel and said it must have been fixed into the floor. In the end, he just left it, saying the spirits must want it here for some reason. Who would have thought the reason would be you?"

"What makes you think it's me?"

"Because that's how the spirit world works. They pick us. We don't pick them. You saw Clarissa, Ruby, and now this. It may mean there's a spiritual reason you're here."

Alex shrugged. "Well, I sure don't know what that might be, but I do know the terrestrial reason. So, I'm gonna up and load the program now."

# Chapter 42

Self-reflection becomes self-torment
when learning doesn't occur.
—*Jeffrey G. Duarte*

Alex was climbing the stairs when his phone rang. It was Gwynn. Walking to the bar, he sat down on a stool and pressed "accept." While the call connected, he put his elbow on the bar and pressed his forehead into his palm.

"Hi, Gwynn. How are you?"

Silence.

Dropping his left arm to his side, he sat straight up. "Gwynn? Are you there?"

"Ah, yes. I wasn't sure you would answer, so I hadn't given it much thought. You know, about what to say if you did … I thought I'd just give it a try."

Alex looked at his watch. It was two o'clock there. He thought she sounded either drunk or drugged. After a long moment of air silence, he said, "I know you've called. I'm sorry I haven't been available. How have you been?"

"Oh, Alex, I'm so sorry for ruining everything. I should never have…" She sobbed.

"Gwynn, listen to me. This whole thing is my fault," he said as he heard her utter a high-pitched, prolonged mournful cry. "Gwynn," he said slowly, lowering his tone. "Gwynn," he repeated. No response. "I'm going to hang up now and call your mother. I'm coming back soon. We'll talk then."

When there was no response, Alex ended the call and dialed Diedre's number. She answered on the third ring. "Hello."

"Diedre, it's Alex."

"What do you want? Haven't you done enough to destroy my daughter?"

"I'm sorry. I truly am. I'm calling because I just had a disturbing call from Gwynn. I think she needs help."

"I know that. You're supposed to be so smart. What do you do when you know someone needs mental help and they say they're not sick? 'You're the one that's sick.'"

Alex began to rub his index finger over his lips so hard he thought he felt them swelling. "Since you asked me, I think she needs an intervention."

"And who do you suggest? Since you're so good at knowing what my daughter needs," she said so sarcastically that Alex felt his face burn and mouth turn dry.

Swallowing hard, he said, "If you're really looking for me to suggest someone, it'd be Cody. I know Gwynn likes him."

After a long silence, Alex heard Diedre blow her nose. Then she said, "Um, maybe Cody would be good."

"I'll call him right away."

"You know, Alex, this doesn't make up for a Goddamn thing you've done."

"I know."

There was another long moment of silence before Deidre spoke. "Go fuck yourself, Alex." Then the line went dead.

Alex sat staring at the phone until he felt a slap on the back. Looking up, he watched Donovan take a seat next to him. "So, what's goin' on?"

Alex pressed his fingertips against his eyelids.

Donovan said, "Bad day?"

Alex eyed him through a half-closed lid.

"Aw, huh," Donovan said. "One of those. I know what will help what 'ails' you." Donovan began to chuckle to himself as he walked around the bar. He took two beers from the refrigerator and handed one to Alex. "My dad used to say that when guys came in here with their sad stories, he'd give them an 'ale' on the house for what ails them."

Alex gave a half-hearted laugh.

After a few moments of quietly looking at each other as they drank, Donovan said, "So, what's going on?"

After draining half the bottle, he told him about Gwynn and Diedre's call.

"Sounds like it's a good thing you're here."

"I feel so guilty about hurting Gwynn and her mother."

"My father used to say that guilt is a hungry emotion, and if you let it, it will eat you up. And then there'd be nothing left of you to be able to change whatever caused you to feel guilty in the first place." Donovan leaned on the bar and looked into Alex's eyes. "If my father were here, I think that's what he'd tell you."

"I feel like he *is* here—in you."

Donovan sucked in his lips as he took a deep breath. After a long moment, he said, "Thanks. That means a lot to me."

"Will you tell me the truth about something?"

"What?"

"Does your mother think I'm an asshole?"

"Has she ever said, 'Bless your heart' to you?"

"Yeah."

"That's southern for 'You're an asshole.'"

# Chapter 43

Never approach a bull from the
front, a horse from the rear,
or a fool from any direction.
—*Cowboy Wisdom*

Cody was climbing the stairs to Gwynn's front door when he heard loud voices. He stopped when he reached the porch and listened.

"Get out! Go home and stop bothering me!" Gwynn cried.

"You need help, Gwynn, I'm your mother. It's my job to take care of you."

"If you hadn't been such a fuckup as a mother, maybe I wouldn't need help. Anyway, I don't need yours," Gwynn yelled.

For a moment Cody thought of bounding back down the stairs, but the door opened, and he found himself face-to-face with Gwynn. She stood in the doorway with a fireplace poker in her hand, a snarl on her face, and a frightened-looking Diedre in the foyer behind her.

Cody touched the brim of his Stetson. "Howdy, Gwynn." Then, nodding to Diedre, he said, "Ma'am."

They just stood there, looking at him as if he'd just crawled out of a spaceship. "Um, I was on my way to the feedstore and thought

I'd stop by," he said. "But if this is a bad time, I can stop by some other time."

Suddenly, Gwynn burst out laughing as Deidre rushed by him, descended the stairs, and got into her car. Cody looked hard at Gwynn. Despite her blonde hair piled haphazardly on top of her head and the oversized T-shirt and frayed denim shorts that looked like she'd slept in them, there was no question about it—she was a beautiful woman. *But this one should come with a warning,* he thought.

"I guess I'd better be goin'," Cody said.

"No. Don't. I'm glad you stopped by. Come in," Gwynn said, stepping into the foyer.

Cody glared at the poker. Gwynn followed his eyes, looked down at it, and walked to the fireplace. Leaning it against the brick, she said, "Would you like something to drink?"

"Thanks. I'm good," Cody said.

"Well, I need something. Let's go to the kitchen."

She motioned for him to sit at the table as she poured herself a glass of wine. Turning toward him, she lifted the glass and said, "My mother is driving me crazy." Sitting across from him, she sighed. "So, tell me the truth. Why did you stop by?" She waited a moment before she added, "I know I'm not on the way to the feed store."

Cody took off his hat, leaned back in his chair, and smiled. "The truth is, Gwynn, I grew fond of you over these last few months, and I thought I'd stop by and see how you're doin'," he lied.

She took a long drink and snickered. "Why would you give a rat's ass about me?"

He began to shake his head. "Because you're worth caring about. Look, Gwynn, what happened to you stinks. Everyone thinks so. But we all get the stuffing knocked out of us from time to time. We fall down, and while we're lying there, stuck on our backs like a beetle, we see people walking over us and around us, trying to help us get back on our feet when all we want to do is be left alone and lie there." He watched as a slow smile grew on Gwynn's face.

She drained the glass and gave him a half laugh. "That's about how I feel. Like a beetle stuck on its back." She changed the subject with, "Why does that happen? How does it get stuck on its back?" Cody decided to go with it rather than redirect her.

"Usually when it comes in contact with a pesticide, it uncontrollably kicks up its legs and flips over," Cody said.

She got up and refilled her glass. Leaning against the counter, she said, "Men are like pesticides to me." She snorted a laugh and said, "What's the antidote to a pesticide?"

"Staying away from it," he said.

"Good advice. You know, if I had a big brother, I'd want him to be just like you," she said softly.

"And if I had a little sister, I'd want her to be just like you," he lied again.

She looked into her glass and was quiet for a moment. Then she looked up at him. "When I was a little girl, I thought I had the power to stop my father from leaving me. That was the first time I felt like a beetle flipped over on my back, kicking my legs up. Actually, I think that's exactly what I did. And as little as I was, I swore to myself that I was never going to feel that way again. But here I am … again … powerless to prevent people from leaving me."

"Look, Gwynn, power isn't a force you use to get your own way. Your power is in here," he said, pointing to his heart. "And in here," he said, pointing to his head.

"Maybe that's why my mother keeps saying I need a head doctor." Gwynn took a long drink. "Do you have any idea how exasperating it is to hear that over and over again? Especially since I'm not sick and I don't need help. But she does. She's the crazy one."

He rubbed the stubble on his chin and said in a low tone of voice, "I'm sure it's frustrating for you to hear that. But she's your mother, and she loves you. Maybe she thinks it's like if you broke your leg, you'd go to a bone doctor to get it fixed, and since it's your feelings that have been shattered, maybe … I don't know … maybe she's right. Maybe it would help."

Gwynn looked at him with narrowed eyes. "Do *you* think I need a head doctor? Because I don't."

He took in a deep breath and thought for a minute before he said anything. "Only you can answer whether you think you need one. I came here because I've been thinking about you ever since our last talk. You were pretty angry that day."

Her eyes trailed slowly from her penetrating gaze at Cody to elsewhere in her mind. She heaved a deep breath. "Yeah, I was." She hooked her thumb toward the knife block. "And you helped me not to do something very stupid."

"No one blames you for being angry *that* day. But it's been several weeks now, and the thing is, maybe you should think about whether you feel any less angry." He ran his fingers through his hair. "Look, little lady, I had to learn the hard way that it's best to explain your anger to someone rather than express it. It's the only way to open yourself up for solutions."

She crossed her arms across her chest, stared at him, and said nothing.

"Well, I have to get going," he said rising from the chair.

"Thank you for stopping by. I know you mean well, but really, I'm fine."

"Just thought I'd share some old cowboy wisdom."

They walked to the front door. Cody placed his Stetson on his head and, touching its brim, said, "Take care of yourself, little lady. And if you want to talk, call me." He walked down the stairs to his truck and turned to see her leaning against the doorway. The sun caught the glitter of tears as they rolled down her cheeks.

# Chapter 44

Mastering others is strength. Mastering
oneself makes you fearless.

*—Lao Tzu*

"Are you all right?" Brooke asked, climbing onto a bar stool next to Alex.

His brows were knitted with concern as he shook his head and said, "Let's go to the park. I need to talk to you about something."

"What's wrong?" she asked. "Is something wrong with the program?"

"No. It's not the program. It's Gwynne." Standing, he pulled Brooke into his arms. "I don't want to talk about it here."

With intertwined fingers, they crossed the street to the park. She guided him over to the bench they'd sat on the first day they spent together.

Alex put his elbows on his knees with his head in his hands. "Gwynn called me today. She sounded out of it. And I asked Cody to go over and see her. Cody said he was concerned Gwynn might harm herself or her mother. Gwynn insists she's not sick and doesn't need help."

Brooke looked from him out to the harbor. The sun was still burning white, not quite ready to drop into the horizon.

Alex nudged her. "Tell me what you're thinking."

She studied Alex for a moment and said, "Since I haven't met her, and all I'm going by is what you've told me, I'm thinking her personality has been pulverized by her mother's duplicity. I'm sure Gwynn's father didn't leave *her.* He left because of *her mother.* But her mother parleyed *her* anger at him for leaving *her* by telling Gwynn *he* left *them,* which included Gwynn. And that lie then and all the years since have created a perfect storm for her abandonment issues to come to the surface when she lost you. I mean, she may have other serious mental problems given her aggressive outbursts, but that's what I think."

Alex groaned. "So, I'm the catalyst for this mess."

"No, you're not. You're as much of a victim of her mother's decision to keep Gwynn from her father as Gwynn is. And the bad news is, abandonment issues don't spontaneously revert just because the person suffering from them finds someone to love. A child who experiences traumatic loss often fixates on finding fulfillment through objects rather than people. And often the person they 'fall in love with,'" Brooke said, using air quotes, "is the vehicle for obtaining the object. For example, you told me about the monogrammed toilet paper she bought. Understandably it didn't make sense to you, but she was looking for objects to fill her need to show you that you belonged to *her.*"

"Sheesh, it's like she was branding me the way I brand our cattle."

"Yes. Exactly. And her wanting your mom out of the house was her way of making sure you love her more than your mother. With your mother in the house, she was afraid she'd be pushed aside, and you'd place your mother's needs and opinions ahead of her."

Alex ran his hands through his hair. "Damned. It all makes sense. But what can I do? I don't want her to hurt herself. I'd like to get her help."

"Unfortunately, it sounds like she also suffers from anosognosia."

"From what? That sounds like cancer."

"No, it's not cancer the way cancer eats away at the body. But you could think of it like it's a cancer of rational thought. It's when a person is unable to recognize they have a mental health problem. When a person suffers from anosognosia, they're not being stubborn or in denial. It's just that their brain can't process the fact that their moods and thoughts don't reflect reality."

"How the hell do I help her?"

"First, no one should tell her she's mentally ill and needs help. There's a clinical psychologist, Dr. Xavier Amador, who has done extensive research on how to reach people with serious mental illness and make them understand they need help. He talks about it in terms of illnesses like schizophrenia and bipolar disorder. But I think it's just as applicable with people who have personality disorders. Anyway, the program is called LEAP. It stands for Listen, Empathize, Agree, and Partner. We can watch Dr. Amador's TED talk, and I'll get his book for you. The bottom line is, if you learn the LEAP program, you may be able to talk her into getting help."

"But if I talk to Gwynn, don't you think maybe that will give her the idea that if she gets help, she and I may get back together?"

"The whole point is, if she gets the help she seems to need, it will help her understand that you and she are not going to get back together again, and she'll be healthy enough for a new relationship."

Alex stood. Facing her, he held out his hands and pulled her to her feet. He wrapped his arms around her, gave her a soft hug, then stepped back and said, "I love you." Stepping back, he smiled and said, "I know it sounds so *Jerry Maguire*, but you complete me."

"I you love, too. And you complete me." She sighed and tugged at his shirt to bring his mouth to hers.

They were kissing passionately when someone in a passing car yelled out, "Get a room."

# Chapter 45

There are three kinds of people in the world,
the wills, the wont's, and the cant's. The first
accomplish everything; the second oppose
everything; and the third fail at everything.
—*Eclectic Magazine*

When they returned to the restaurant, Donovan was sitting at the bar and looking at the program. The staff meal was over, and Calvin was already barking orders in the kitchen.

"Holy shit," Alex breathed. "I missed the chance to show everyone the program. I'd intended to run it tonight."

"That's OK. I told Mom and Calvin that you had a ranch matter to deal with. They were relieved," Donovan said, swiveling around to look at them. "I think it's probably for the best. You're gonna need more time and dry runs before they're going to be comfortable with it."

"You're probably right," Alex said. "Have you had much time to look through it?"

"Just the inventory part. This is gonna help my mom a lot. Don't worry, I'll help them if they have problems when you leave. They're gonna love it," Donovan said.

"Did you get your ranch business taken care of, Alex?" Lotte asked from the doorway.

Brooke and Alex turned to see her smiling at them.

"Yes, ma'am. Sorry I missed the team meeting to explain and run the program," he said.

"I'm not. I've been nervous all day just thinking about it," Lotte said. "And Calvin took Pepto Bismol in preparation for it." Laughing, she added, "We open soon, so I have a few more instructions for the servers. They're in the kitchen. Calvin wanted to speak to them. There's been some slacking on cleaning the barware, the server hutch, and the barista station."

"Blake and Hollis are coming at five thirty, so we can get four seats at the bar. Is it still all right, Mom?" Brooke said. "I mean, since Alex doesn't have to stay, we can go somewhere else."

Alex whispered to Donovan, who was standing next to him, "Want to join us tonight?"

"Thanks, but I'm meeting a friend," Donovan said.

"Laurel?" Alex asked.

With narrowed eyes, Donovan rubbed his nose, giving Alex the middle finger.

Alex chuckled and refocused on what Lotte was saying.

"It's fine, Brooke," Lotte said. "In fact, Calvin made something special for the four of you. And since I told the staff about this new program, maybe, Alex, you could just talk to them for a few minutes and preview what it's all about."

"Yes, ma'am, I'd be happy to," Alex said, heading to the kitchen.

Alex crossed the room and strode into the kitchen just as Calvin finished lecturing the staff.

After Lotte introduced him, Alex said, "First, sorry that I missed the team meal, since now we won't have much time to talk about the computer program we're going to be trying out tomorrow. So, I have a question for you. Who here has ever thought of saying to a guest,

'You may see the smile on my face, but in my head, I just slapped your face and stabbed you with a fork about ten times'?"

Everyone laughed, even Lotte and Calvin as many in the group raised their hands.

"This program won't eliminate rude guests, but you'll find it will make them more tolerable because it should make your experience serving them less stressful," Alex said.

"We're in," the group chanted.

Lotte stepped forward. "OK, then, if y'all can be here at one tomorrow afternoon, we'll run through the program and get used to it before we open. Of course, you'll be paid overtime for your time." She smiled as they all confirmed they'd be.

A few minutes later, the back door opened, and Hollis and Blake appeared.

"Hey, you two," Brooke greeted.

Just then Alex realized he hadn't asked Brooke how her lunch with Hollis had gone. But judging by the radiant look on Hollis's face and the contented look on Blake's, Alex thought their relationship must be going well.

Blake walked over to Alex and extended his hand, while Brooke and Hollis giggled about something. "Nice to see you again, Alex," he said.

As they shook hands, Alex said, "What are those two up to?"

Blake shrugged. "Who knows? How have you been? Worked everything out with your program?"

"I think it's ready. We're going to meet tomorrow and give it a dry run," Alex said.

"I think it's great that you're doing it. Charleston may be steeped in tradition, but let's face it. The world is starting to transform from the physical to the digital. I mean, look at medicine. No patient charts to hold, no Merk manual or PRD in our pocket to look up diseases and the medicine. Everything is computerized." He paused. "The downside as I see it for medicine, at least, is that we're losing the human interaction physicians used to have with patients. That's what I try to keep alive when I care for a patient."

"I couldn't agree with you more. And I think many people are eating out more because they're looking for more of a human interaction," Alex said.

"What are you two talking about?" Hollis asked, hooking her arm around Blake's.

"About how lucky Alex and I are to have the two most beautiful women in the city at our sides," Blake said, winking at Alex.

"Yeah, Blake, aren't you worried that your nose is going to grow?" Hollis said, laughing.

Blake put his right hand up, "I swear, it's the truth."

"He's telling the truth. You two *are* the most beautiful women I've seen since I got here," Alex said, putting his arm around Brooke.

"I hate to break this up, but the door is opening, and the bar will be full before you know it," Lotte said.

Two hours later, the four had made plans to visit Alex at his ranch the week of Fourth of July. The restaurant was crowded, and since the bar didn't have orchestrated table turnaround time, there was a group of guests hovering behind them, waiting for the four stools to be vacated.

"Hey, y'all, why don't we go to the Vendue Rooftop Bar and have a drink?" Hollis said. "I've been wanting to take Blake there. Have you been, Alex?"

"No, I don't think so," he said.

"That's a great idea," Brooke said.

As they turned to get up, the group behind them all but jumped onto the vacated stools, ready to order drinks ten minutes ago.

"Let's go through the kitchen and thank Calvin for the special gumbo he prepared for us," Brooke said.

As they walked through the dining room and into the hall, Blake noticed the AED defibrillator hanging by the ladies' room. He tapped Alex on the shoulder. "Did you do that?"

"I just suggested it. Lotte took care of the rest," Alex said.

"There's no question in my mind that it will save somebody's life," Blake said.

"Come on," Hollis said, pulling Blake by the hand. "Let's get out of here before someone needs to use it."

When they walked into the kitchen, it was a blur of movement. The printer on a shelf to the right of Calvin was making a grinding noise as it spit out tickets Calvin caught and shoved under a stainless-steel ticket holder strip. It was mounted at Calvin's eye level and ran the length of the pickup window. As he lined up the tickets, he began to shout orders to the cooks on the line.

The line cooks were a chaos of motion. Their hands whirred, slicing, chopping, sautéing, pulling containers from the shelves above their station, and wiping the rim of each plate before passing it to Calvin.

Calvin's eyes remained focused on the sauté pan in his hand and yelled, "Pick up."

"Let's go. I'll thank him tomorrow," Brooke said, pointing to the back door.

# Chapter 46

You never close your lips to those whom
you have opened your heart.
—*Charles Dickens*

When they arrived at the Rooftop Bar at the Vendue, Brooke could tell Hollis was smiling, even though her back was to her, by the way Hollis held onto Blake.

"She's definitely in love," Brooke whispered to Alex, who held Brooke's hand.

Alex leaned over and whispered, "She's not the only one, is she?"

Laughing, Brooke jabbed Alex in the arm.

After they were shown to their table, Blake put his hand on Alex's shoulder and said quietly, "Is there something wrong, Alex?"

Alex glanced at Brooke, who he could tell had overheard the question. She nodded for him to share.

Once they were all seated and the waiter had taken their drink orders, Alex asked, "Blake, what makes you think something's wrong?"

Blake looked into Alex's eyes and said, "Because I saw sadness behind your eyes earlier. Like I said, I look at people."

Hollis and Brooke exchanged looks, and Alex took in a deep breath. "Since we've all been through a life-and-death event at Magnolias together, I guess it's OK to share what's eating me."

Alex walked Hollis and Blake through his history with Gwynn and his concern for her. He explained that he was struggling with how he wanted to help Gwynn with Brooke's suggestions.

Blake took a sip of his beer and leaned forward to engage Alex. "Look, man, we're human, and our humanness means we sometimes make mistakes, and the guilt we feel when the mistake hurts another human is a healthy response to owning our actions. But—and this is a huge but—you need to understand that you weren't the one who denied Gwynn the future she envisioned for herself. That happened way before you ever met her."

Alex began rubbing his forehead. "But like I asked Brooke this afternoon, how do you get someone help when they don't think anything's wrong with them?"

"We struggle with the same problem in medicine," Blake said.

"I'll vouch for that," Hollis said. "So many times a patient will be discharged from the hospital with a prescription for, say, high cholesterol or blood pressure meds to prevent heart disease. They may take the bottle until it's empty, but then they don't get a refill and end up with a readmission with a stroke or heart attack."

"With all due respect to psychologists, I don't think it's all that difficult to understand. I'm familiar with anosognosia. People who are ill focus on a certain point in time when they didn't have the problems they're facing now, and their brain can't accept a contrary view of themselves," Blake said.

"That's how Brooke explained it," Alex said, taking a long drink of beer.

"You have a recommendation of how to deal with it, Brooke?" Blake asked.

"Yes, but it's too heavy of a discussion tonight. I'll send you the link to it," Brooke said.

"OK, enough of that," Hollis said. "Let's celebrate our friendship and drink to going to Montana."

They lifted their drinks under a pale crescent moon that shone above them like a silvery symbol of their new beginning together, innocent to what they would soon face.

# Chapter 47

Ever has it been that love knows not its own
depth until the hour of separation.
—*Kahlil Gibran*

The sun rose slowly, looking like a fireball and sending searing bands of crimson over the entire horizon as Brooke and Alex stood at the railing in the park overlooking the harbor.

"I'm going to miss having morning coffee with you," Alex said, turning to look at her. "I'm going to miss waking up next to you and holding you in my arms." He cleared his throat. "I'm going to miss the smell of your hair and the softness of your skin." His voice cracked. "Brooke, I love you."

"Alex, I love you, too. And maybe we won't be physically together, but if we have what I think we do, there won't be any distance between our hearts."

They looked at each other. He put his finger under her chin, pushed away the windblown hair from her face, and said, "I'll carry your heart with me. I'll carry your heart in my heart."

Brooke blinked. Alex noticed her swallow hard before she spoke. "And I'll carry your heart in mine."

Alex pulled her close to him and wiped the tears from Brooke's eyes. "Let's go," he said.

"You know," Brooke said, "I feel like there's some unseen force at work."

"There *is* an unforeseen force. It's called *love*."

As they walked up the driveway to the carriage house, the front door opened, and Donovan called from the doorway, "Warm croissants and jelly are on the table."

"So," Donovan said, looking at Alex and then studying Brooke's eyes. "I stopped by to see if you'd need my help with anything today. I have to go to the construction site this morning, but I can come back midafternoon." Donovan put his arm around Brooke's shoulder. "What's wrong?"

"Just sad," Brooke said.

"Because the asshole is leaving?" Donovan said.

Elbowing Donovan in the side, she pushed away from him and walked toward the table. "Come on, you guys, these are getting cold," Brooke said.

After Donovan finished chewing a croissant he'd plopped into his mouth, he said, "So when do you think you will be leaving?"

"If things go well today, probably the day after tomorrow," Alex said, glancing at Brooke, who put down the croissant she'd been holding. He took her hand and squeezed it.

"Hey, Donovan," Alex said with a cheerful tone. "Why don't you come to the ranch Fourth of July week?"

Donovan pulled at his chin. "Thanks, I'll have to let you know. Like I've said, I'm in the middle of constructing the house for the owners from hell. The house itself is going to be the best advertising I could have for my business, but it's not without its price. Money makes some people real assholes."

"It's usually new money," Brooke interjected, narrowing her eyes at Donovan.

"Alex, you know I didn't mean you. There are exceptions, but these are private equity people who are building a multimillion-dollar house on a four-million-dollar lot on the ocean just to flaunt the fact that they can. It has four ovens, two dishwashers in the gourmet kitchen, a four-car garage, and an infinity pool overlooking the ocean that cost more than the average American family makes in a year. You get the picture. And they treat the workmen and me like they need a clothespin on their nose when they talk to us," Donovan said. "If our parents hadn't taught us how to deal with people like that, I'd have hauled off and socked the guy by now."

Brooke smiled. "Mom used to say, 'Be thankful for knowing some difficult people, they'll teach you who you don't want to be.'"

Donovan and Alex chuckled. Donovan stood and said, "I have to go. Good luck today, Alex."

Brooke looked at her watch and said, "Dang." Laughing, she said, "Now you have me saying it."

"*Y'all* be sounding like a Montanan," Alex said after Donovan had closed the front door. Taking Brooke's hands and pulling her to her feet, he said, "Any chance we have time for a roll in the hay?"

"Oh, cowboy, how I wish. But I have to go. I'm meeting my adviser about working virtually with him while I'm in Montana."

"Oh, in that case, get a move on. Daylight's burning," he said, kissing her. "Call me later about dinner plans."

"Good luck today," she said and was gone.

He sat down at the table and thought about the last few weeks. *I see a fork in the long road of following my family's expectations. It's like I got used to it just like a dog gets used to a leash. But now I can see all I was doing was checking off the next thing on life's to-do list.*

His cell chimed. "Shit," he said aloud. "Speaking of life's to-do list." It was Gwynn.

He felt his face get hot, and his throat turned dry. Thinking about what Brooke had said about talking to Gwynn, he knew he wasn't ready to speak to her and let the call go to voice mail. He walked into the bathroom. After standing under the hot shower for a few minutes, he crouched down and began to shake his head. But he couldn't shake the scenes of his life he had blocked for so long that now looped through his mind. The loss of his father, the lives of the fathers he took in Afghanistan, the faces of their wives and children, and Gwynn's rage-filled face.

As he was drying off, there was a rap at the front door. He wrapped a towel around himself and went to the door.

"I thought I'd see if you could go over this computer shit with me before the others get here," Calvin said.

"Sure, I'll get dressed and meet you over there."

Ten minutes later, Alex opened the restaurant's back door to find Calvin sitting at the counter with his head in his hands.

Calvin looked up. "Alex, I ain't scared of no ghost or nothin'. But I'm scared about if something goes wrong with this thing in the middle of a busy night. What do I do? I mean, I can handle the chaos now, but that's known chaos. I couldn't handle it if this thing went down."

Alex put his hand on Calvin's shoulder. "I get why you're worried. That was my aunt's biggest fear when I computerized her restaurant. I programmed a fail-safe if that should happen. Let me show you." Alex powered up the computer he'd installed on the shelf to the right of Calvin's station next the ticket printer. "You see this?" Alex asked, holding up a wire between the computer and the ticket printer.

"Yeah," Calvin said.

"Should something happen, like the program shuts down, freezes, or slows down longer than five minutes, the system will automatically revert to the ticket system, and the servers will see on their terminals to go back to handwriting the guest's orders," Alex said.

Calvin grunted. "You're asking me to take a huge leap of faith here," he said, eyeing the computer.

Alex patted Calvin on the shoulder. "I know. But I'm sure you've done harder things than this."

Calvin shot Alex a look and slowly broke into a smile. "You know I have."

# Chapter 48

We must be our own before we can be another's.

—*Ralph Waldo Emerson*

By the time everyone sat down for the team meal, Alex had run them through the program several times, and the consensus was that they were comfortable with it. While there had been a few groans from Calvin and Lotte, they seemed less nervous about the computer being demonically possessed.

Brooke would arrive soon, and Alex was anxious for her help to return Gwynn's call.

"What'll it be?" Shelly, the new bartender asked as Alex sat down at the bar.

"I'm gonna need something stronger than a beer. I've got to make a call I'm dreading."

"Ex-girlfriend?" she asked.

"Ex-fiancée," Alex said, looking up at her. "How'd you know?"

"I'm in premed. And I've recently studied the anatomy of the face. Mind if I go over the anatomy of a frown?" she asked.

"Be my guest."

"Your depressor angular fibers are bringing down the sides of your mouth, the orbicularis oris is pursing your lips, and the mentalis muscle is slightly lowering your lower lip at the same time. This combination of muscle movement often happens with the kind of tension that comes with an ex," Sherry said, pouring him a bourbon. "This will help trigger a release of endorphins."

Alex laughed and tipped the glass toward her. "Good to know."

"Good to know what?" Brooke said, rubbing the back of his neck.

"That feels so good," he said, turning to pull out a barstool for her.

She put her hand on his shoulder and kissed his cheek. Sliding onto the stool, she said, "Relax."

"What can I get you, Miss Brooke?" Shelly asked.

"The house chardonnay. Thanks, Shelly, and please call me 'Brooke.'"

Shelly placed a generous pour of wine in front of Brooke. Alex lifted his glass to Brooke, and they touched the rims of their glasses. "So, what's good to know?" Brooke asked.

Shelly made herself busy at the other end of the bar, buffing glasses.

"That for the first time in my life, apparently I'm wearing my emotions on my face," Alex said. "And I've always been a great poker player because no one could ever tell what I was thinking."

Brooke looked deep into his eyes. "You're not playing poker now. You're living life and feeling it."

Alex leaned over and kissed Brooke on the lips; he caught Shelly's smiling eyes as she turned toward a couple who had sat down at the end of the bar.

"I wanted to ask if you think I should return Gwynn's call from this morning."

"What did she say?" Brooke asked.

"I don't know. I didn't pick up and thought I'd wait until I saw you to listen to the voice mail," he said.

"Here, give me your phone, and we'll listen to it together."

Alex entered the code unlocking the phone and handed it to Brooke. She leaned into him, and he put it to their ears.

Gwynn's voice sounded shaky. "Um, Alex." There was a sigh, punctuated with silence, and then another sigh. "I was wondering"— sniff, sniff— "when are you coming back?" Her voice cracked, and she said, "I know I've been wrong about a lot of things. I mean, I need to talk to you. Please, Alex, call me back."

"What do you think?" Alex asked, his brows furrowed. "I mean, I never told her I was away."

Brooke sat back and took a long drink of her wine. "I think what you thought you saw you saw. It was no ghost. Gwynn was here."

"What do I do in the meantime?" Alex asked.

"Nothing right now. Not until you study the LEAP program information I sent to your email today.

"And then?"

"And then pray."

"That's not a very therapeutic answer."

"You'd be surprised. Sometimes the best thing a person who's struggling with feeling so overwhelmed that they don't know which way to turn is to give it to God."

# *Chapter 49*

The single biggest problem in communication
is the illusion it has taken place.
—*George Bernard Shaw*

Brooke and Alex were sitting at the bar for less than five minutes when Benita, one of the servers, tapped Alex on the shoulder. "Fire in the hole. Or I should say, in the kitchen."

"What's wrong?" Alex said.

"Calvin is yelling so loud Lotte came in and told him they could hear him in the dining room," Benita said.

"Why?" Alex said.

"He says the fucking computer doesn't work, and the doors just opened, and a party of twelve, who'd preordered their menu selections, arrived," Benita said. "I tried to see if I could troubleshoot the problem like you showed us this afternoon, but he won't let anyone near it." She put her hands in a prayer position and said, "I was sent for you."

Alex, followed by Brooke, walked to the kitchen with Benita.

The kitchen staff were silent, not like they were in a church but in a graveyard.

Calvin had his hands on his hips and was stomping his foot on the floor, shouting expletives at the computer, whose screen was black.

Whatever exhilaration Alex had felt about converting Calvin and Lotte into technological true believers churned in his stomach. Suddenly, he felt his heart race, his blood pressure increase, and his hands form fists. Then he caught Brooke's eye and thought of LEAP. Instead of yelling at Calvin to calm down, he just listened to him rant and walked over to Calvin's station. Alex examined the monitor's connection. He unplugged it from the outlet and plugged it back in again, but nothing happened.

"This isn't fucking goin' to work," Calvin blared.

Alex said nothing. Stepping back from Calvin's station, Alex spotted the problem. He pushed the power button, and the screen came to life. "OK. I'm not sure how this got turned off, but I'll look at the camera footage and find out. From now on, one of the servers will be assigned to check your station at least an hour before opening. That should be plenty of time to troubleshoot."

Addressing the group who had gathered around Calvin's station, Alex said calmy, "OK, you all know what to do. I'll be right here if you need me for anything. And I mean *anything*."

After the group dispersed, Alex turned to Calvin. "You're right. This is not getting off to a good start, and I'd feel the same way you do right now. But please, give it another chance. Let me help with the next few orders. After that, if you want me to disconnect it, I will."

Calvin glared at him. "I'll do it for Miss Lotte." Then he took his place at his station as the screen lit up with the orders for the table of twelve. The digital ticket showed what had been ordered along with the ingredients, special requests, add-ons, substitutes, food allergies, and the like. The screen permitted Calvin to assign the orders to the line chefs by the table number and seat of the guest who had ordered it. Each line chef studied his or her monitor and got to work.

Alex turned to Brooke. "I'm going to stay in here awhile. Why don't you go back and wait for me?"

"I'll wait here," she said, kissing his cheek. She walked to the small table against the back wall and sat down to watch.

Alex watched as servers appeared at the pickup window, retrieving orders without Calvin yelling "pick up" as if to the dead. He simply touched the screen, and a server would appear, check the screen mounted next to the pickup window, and take the order to the seat of the person who'd ordered it.

After a few more orders came in, Calvin seemed more comfortable with reading the screen. His furrowed brows softened. After an hour, there had been no double orders or send backs. The line cooks were scrambling to keep up with the orders, but it wasn't chaos; it was an organized effort to produce beautiful-looking and sumptuous-tasting food. Alex put his hand over his mouth, feigning a cough but hiding a smile.

Lotte waked through the swing door and stood next to Alex. Without looking at Alex, she said, "I didn't hear Calvin yelling and was worried he may have left."

Alex covered his mouth and chortled. "I covered that contingency. I put Gorilla Glue on the mat at his station."

Lotte giggled.

"You okay if I look at the camera footage on the computer in your office? I'd like to find out who turned your monitor off."

"Of course."

Alex waved Brooke over.

A few minutes later, Alex sat at Lotte's desk. Brooke and Lotte stood behind him as he scrolled through the kitchen's camera footage. They saw Calvin and the staff in the kitchen earlier when he was barking at them about cleaning the stations. When Calvin left for a few minutes, Zeek, the dishwasher, used a bar mop to wipe down Calvin's station. He sprayed germicide all around the stainless-steel work area and then took another towel and wiped down the monitor, apparently unaware that he'd hit the power button.

"I guess we know how that happened," Alex said. "You'll have to add to your list of instructions to make sure that if anyone wipes the computers or monitors, they must make sure they don't hit the power button."

He heard Brooke and Lotte sigh in tandem and swiveled around to look at them.

"Let's go tell Calvin what happened and see if he's OK at the moment," Alex said.

Lotte's eyes grew wide as they entered the kitchen. Calvin wasn't screaming, and the line cooks weren't looking as if they were about to walk the plank. Things seemed to be running smoothly as Calvin and the line cooks cranked out the orders from the monitors. The noise in the room was of china plates being placed on stainless steel and pans hitting the burners rather than Calvin's booming voice yelling barbs at the line cooks like, "Are you fucking kidding me? Where did you go to culinary school? McDonald's?"

"You OK in here, Calvin?" Alex asked.

"Yeah, getting the hang of it. And I'm making your dinner, so go on," Calvin replied, dismissing him with his hand.

As soon as Brooke and Alex sat down, Shelly brought them another round.

"How's it going in there?" she asked, leveling her eyes toward the kitchen.

"So far so good. Guardedly optimistic," Alex said.

Shelly smiled and whispered, "Frankly, it's going to be great. I worked at another restaurant that converted to a computer program, but it was shit. It wasn't customized like this is to Serenity, and we had a lot of glitches." She looked up at a couple seated a few seats away. "Duty calls."

Alex sat back, crossing his arms.

"What are you thinking?" Brooke asked.

"I'm thinking about what I'm learning."

"What's that?"

"How to communicate with a person you know doesn't want to hear what you're saying. I read about LEAP it this afternoon. When I heard Calvin yelling at the computer, my normal instinct was to yell back and say something like, 'Hold on and give me a fucking minute to find out what the problem is.' But then, I thought, *Wait, don't. If I do, we'll both be out of control. I'm not going to win this argument by raising my voice. I'll get through to him if he believes I'm listening to him.*"

Brooke leaned over and kissed him. "I find how smart you are to be such a turn-on."

"Dang it, girl. Now you got my motor running, and we can't leave until the end of the night."

"Look at it this way, cowboy. Even if Calvin throws another hissy fit about the program and wants to go back to the way things were at the end of the night, you'll still have something to look forward to."

"What do you think the problem is with him?"

"You have to understand. Calvin is very much invested in his culinary expertise. I mean, he's earned a position of respect among other chefs and the owners of other restaurants here in Charleston. He probably looks at some machine coming in and simplifying the steps he's always taken to produce an amazing meal as undermining his value."

"Makes sense. Chester, my aunt's chef, was sort of the same way until he started to feel less stressed. The line cooks became more productive, and since there were less mistakes, he made more money." Alex paused. "I'm going to make the rounds and check on how things are going."

"Good idea," she said, stroking his palm with her index finger.

He returned fifteen minutes later, followed by Benita carrying Brooke and Alex's dinner. After she placed the plates on the bar, she whispered, "Hey, Alex. Thanks. There were some nights I hated going into the kitchen to pick up. Compared to that, it's like Zen in there."

Brooke and Alex looked at each other, clinked their glasses, and devoured the corn bread and Calvin's legendary pulled pork and collard greens.

The rest of the night passed quickly. At eleven thirty everyone gathered in the bar.

"Everyone, get whatever you want to drink," Lotte said.

After Sherry and Benita served everyone and poured themselves a drink, Lotte stood next to Calvin, turned, and looked directly into his eyes. "I want to raise a glass to my dearest friend, Calvin, whom I learned something about tonight. He showed me that by doing something I knew he didn't want to do, what a true and loyal partner he'll be. So, I'd like to announce that as of this evening, Serenity is under new management. To my new partner, Calvin."

Calvin stood transfixed. It took him a minute to absorb what Lotte had said. "Partner?" he gasped. "Are you serious?"

"I couldn't be more serious. I know it took a lot for you to put what I thought was best for Serenity above what you thought best for *you.*" Lotte raised her glass and was joined by all of them raising their glasses. "To Calvin."

# Chapter 50

No cord or cable can draw so forcibly, or bind so fast,
as love can do with a single thread.

—*Richard E. Burton*

"What a night!" Brooke said as Alex opened the door to the carriage house.

"Did you have any idea your mom was going to do that?"

"Absolutely none. But I do know how she feels about loyalty. My mother is the quintessential businesswoman, and she keeps her business cards close to her vest. In the back of her mind, she probably thought that if Calvin could prove he was willing to put the restaurant above his ego, then it was time to give him what he's been asking some time for—and avoid the risk of him leaving and starting his own restaurant."

"I've been wondering why neither you nor Donovan went into the restaurant business."

"My mother would have loved it, but she said she saw it wasn't our passion. She said unless you have passion for what you do, you'll feel like Sisyphus rolling the same boulder up the hill every day."

Alex took her in his arms, laced his hand in hers, and with a glimmer in his eyes whispered, "I wouldn't mind if you were the boulder."

"And I wouldn't mind if you were a little 'bolder.'"

Instead of producing the laughter Alex expected at his pun, Brooke began to cry.

Alex cradled her, rocking her back and forth. "What's wrong?" he whispered.

"I'm going to miss your weird sense of humor and your stupid puns," she murmured through a sniffle.

He stroked her hair with his fingertips to calm her, but his gesture only made her cry harder.

She looked up at him, tears streaking her cheeks and sliding down her nose. "Ever since I met you, I've felt the coils that have held me together all my life loosen. And with you leaving, I feel as if I'm unraveling."

Cupping her chin, he lifted her face to look into her eyes. "Brooke, my love, you're not unraveling. You're unfolding and opening yourself up for possibilities you never imagined. I know because I feel the same way."

"Is there a possibility that making love is in the immediate future?"

As she leaned against him, he walked her into the bedroom. He gently laid her down on the bed and kissed her forehead. After helping her off with her clothes, he slipped out of his. She reached out for him and softly whispered his name. When he touched her, he felt their repressed desire from earlier in the evening jump like a spark between them. She folded her arms around him and pressed her warn mouth against his, her tongue darting between his lips.

An hour later, he felt his heart hammer against his chest as Brooke lay so close to him that he wasn't sure where his skin stopped and hers began. Pressing his lips against hers, he took her hands into his and kissed them, feeling her smile against his chest.

The next morning through the dim haze of sleep, Alex saw the sun's rays spread out in irregular patterns over the bed. He lay awake, listening to the sound of birds until Brooke stirred.

He tightened his hold on her and kissed the crown of her head. "I was just wondering. We never went through those questions you mentioned. The ones that are supposed to tell us if we're compatible." He paused. "I mean other than sexually."

"Oh," Brooke said, brightening. "Do you want to do it now?"

"Why not?"

"I'll get them," she said, slipping out of bed and into his T-shirt.

Alex turned to his side and, resting his head on his elbow, exhaled long and slow. "You look sexy in that."

She pulled the neck of the shirt down over her upper right arm and made a circle with her shoulder. "Be right back."

Brooke returned and sat cross-legged, facing Alex with a broad smile. She opened a small folder. "We're to look into each other's eyes when we answer a question, okay?"

"Got it," he replied, sitting up crossed-legged.

"First set. First question. If you had the chance to have anyone in the world as a dinner guest, who would it be?"

"Mmm. Dead or alive?"

"Either I guess."

"Then I'd have to say my father. Then I could tell him about *you*."

Brooke leaned over and kissed his lips. Before speaking, she took a deep breath and cleared her throat. "I don't think there's a more perfect answer."

Alex touched her cheek with the back of his hand, waited a moment, and said, "What about you?"

"My answer's the same. *My* father so I could tell him about *you*." She looked down at the folder and closed it.

"Are we done? I thought there were thirty-five more questions."

She began to pull off her T-shirt. "I don't know that there would be an answer to any of the other questions that could tell me any more about our compatibility as that one did. Besides, I don't want to waste the time we have left together."

Alex reached for her hand. "Come here, you minx."

# *Chapter 51*

Goodbye always makes my throat hurt.

—*Charlie Brown*

Thursday started out like any other day, with Brooke and Alex wrapped in each other's arms and opening their eyes to the dappled sunbeams slipping through the slats of the plantation shutters. But when they heard the rap on the front door, Alex knew it would be different from any other.

Alex opened the door to find Donovan holding sacks in one hand and balancing three coffees in a carrier in the other. "Mornin'," Donovan said sullenly. "I thought I'd stop by and see you since I can't make it to the airport."

Alex took the sacks. "I'm glad you came. I was going to call you to see if I could meet you somewhere before I left."

Brooke appeared in the bedroom doorway, wearing a Citadel T-shirt and white shorts. "Hey, big brother. What'd you bring?"

"Your skim milk latte and your favorite, croissants and jelly," Donovan said, kissing her on the cheek.

Brooke got plates as Alex and Donovan sat down at the table. "How'd it go last night?" Donovan asked.

Brooke carried the plates to the table. "Oh, you'll never guess what happened."

"Mom made Calvin a partner," Donovan said, taking a sip of coffee.

With her hand on her hip, Brooke stood next to her brother and said, "How did you know? It was after eleven last night when she made the announcement."

"I know what time the restaurant closes, and I texted her and asked how the program worked out," Donovan said. "She called me and told me all about it."

"What do you think?" she asked.

"I think it was a smart move. Calvin's been getting itchy lately, and if Mom didn't give him an ownership interest in the business, as much as he loves her, I think he would have gone out on his own. He's going to have his twins in college next year. Even with scholarships, you know that doesn't cover everything. And he's still paying alimony to two ex-wives."

Brooke nodded as she bit into the croissant. "I agree. Now she has someone she can share the load with."

"What time is your plane?" Donovan asked Alex.

Brooke looked down at the croissant on her plate.

"One this afternoon. I fly to Charlotte, then to Detroit, and take the puddle jumper to Mountainville," Alex said, reaching for Brooke's hand and giving it a squeeze. "Do you know yet if you can come to the ranch the week of the Fourth of July?"

"Wish I could. But the house should be ready for the kitchen install then, and I have to be here for that. But I'll come out as soon as it's finished. I'll need a break before I start to build another McMansion," Donovan said.

"Do you think people are building these huge houses so they can live together without killing each other?" Brooke said.

"Maybe. You should see how some of them don't even try to hide the contempt they have for each other," Donovan said.

"Life's too short. Why suffer like that?" Alex said.

"Because they're suffering in comfort. Remember what I said about people being fearful of change?" Brooke said.

There was a knock on the front door. Opening it, Alex was surprised to see both Lotte and Calvin standing there. "Come in," Alex said.

"We came to offer you breakfast before you go and to say goodbye," Lotte said, her voice catching. She walked over to her children and kissed their cheeks. "Hey, you two."

"Hey, Mom," Brooke said as Donovan stood to give his mother his seat.

"That's OK, Son. We're not staying. Calvin has something very special waiting for y'all. Do you have time for breakfast, Donovan?" Lotte asked.

"Wish I could, but I have to meet a sub at the construction site," Donovan said, turning to Alex. "Walk me out to my truck, will you?"

The sun was already heating the air to scorching, and sweat dripped down Alex's shirt, sticking to his back. "One thing I'm not going to miss is this heat," he said.

Rubbing the side of his neck, Donovan said, "I don't know how to thank you for everything you've done."

Without hesitation, Alex said, "Give me some dates when you can come to the ranch."

Donovan chuckled. "I promise I will. Ya know, I never would have imagined that the installation of a computer system would be the impetus for my mom to make Calvin a partner. You have no idea how relieved I am she has him to share the work with."

Placing his hands on Alex's shoulders, he pulled him in for a bear hug. Then Donovan climbed into the driver's seat of his truck and powered down the window as he backed out of the driveway. "Have a safe trip. And tell that asshole, Nick, I said hi."

Alex waved as Donovan's truck pulled into the street. He turned to walk back into the carriage house when the door opened and Lotte and Calvin emerged.

"Brooke is changing and said y'all will be right over. See you in a few," Lotte said.

When Alex and Brooke walked into the dining room, there was a table set for four, draped with a white damask tablecloth. The teardrop-shaped flames flickering from a silver candelabra gave the room an ethereal feeling. A bottle of Dom Pérignon chilled in a silver ice bucket. The table was set with Herend china, Orrefors water glasses, and champagne flutes. Soft music played in the background as Calvin pulled out a chair for Lotte and Alex did the same for Brooke.

"Thank you so much. This looks beautiful," Brooke said.

Calvin poured the champagne and remained standing. He lifted his glass and said, "I'm not a sentimental man, or at least that's what my ex-wives say. But today my heart is as full as this glass when I think of all you've done for us, Alex, and how happy you've made Miss Brooke. To you, cowboy. Happy trails home." Calvin raised his glass, followed by the others; as they clinked glasses, Alex noticed Calvin's eyes were glistening.

After a breakfast of biscuits with gravy and jam, sweet milk waffles, fried chicken, kolaches, and grits, followed by a chocolate tart, Alex pushed himself away from the table and stood. "Unfortunately, it's time for me to mosey on home. I want to thank y'all for your southern hospitality." He began to choke up and wiped his eyes with the back of his hand. "Um, I'm not a poetic man, but I'm a grateful one. When I came here, I was going along to get along, although I didn't know it. Thanks to y'all, especially Brooke, I do now."

Lotte dabbed at her eyes with her napkin and stood to hug him. "I'm going to miss you. Come back soon."

Calvin walked around the table and stood in front of him for a long moment. He gave Alex a hug and a pat on the back. Stepping back, he said, "I'm gonna miss you, cowboy."

Brooke began to cry, and Lotte went to her, motioning Brooke to stand. She wiped away Brooke's tears with her napkin and put her arms around her. "It's OK, baby. It's OK."

Alex took a deep breath, motioned a salute, bowed his head, turned, and left.

# Chapter 52

Life takes you unexpected places. Love takes you home.

—*Melissa McClone*

They walked into the Charleston International Airport terminal at eleven thirty. After Alex checked his suitcase, they walked to the security checkpoint. They hugged and kissed, and Brooke's eyes began tearing up.

"Brooke, it's only two weeks until you come to Montana. You'll have all the time now to work on your dissertation. And I'll be busy cutting the herd. It'll go by so fast that it will seem like tomorrow."

"I love you, Alex," she said, bursting into tears.

Choking back his own, he said, "Me, too. You."

She laughed at his lack of articulation and with a tissue wiped her eyes and then dabbed at his.

Alex took an audibly deep breath. He swung his backpack over his shoulder. "I'll call you tonight."

She watched him snake through the security line, and after he retrieved his things from the conveyer belt, he placed his Stetson on his head and walked a few feet up the concourse. He turned and looked for her. Catching her eye, he touched the brim of his hat and tipped his head.

★★★★

Something in Brooke's heart hitched, and tears began running down her cheeks as she watched until he was out of sight. As she drove back to Charleston, she suddenly felt a veil of fatigue shrouding her. When she saw the signage for Sullivan's Island, she took the exit from I-526 to 703 and went over the causeway, continuing on East Ben Sawyer Highway. She noticed that new palmetto trees between overgrown oleanders lined the road.

She rolled down her window and breathed in the scent of plough mud and salty air. Her father's parents had a beach cottage on the island. Although it had long since been demolished and replaced by a multimillion-dollar testament to someone's ego, she had loved coming here and reliving her childhood memories. Her grandmother, Aoife Donovan, had been a stately woman with high cheekbones and fine facial features, who was proud of her mixed Gullah and Irish heritage. Brooke shook her head and thought about her grandmother's belief in the Green Man, leprechauns, and the Gullah spirit world. No wonder her father hadn't been afraid of ghosts. *And neither is Alex*, she thought, smiling to herself.

Brooke's first memories of her grandmother were tied to the aromas of her okra soup, corn bread, and fried chicken. Although there was always corn beef and cabbage on St. Patrick's Day, every time she visited there were homemade cookies and a generous showering of love. Her father was often in the kitchen, cooking with his mother, the love between them palpable. Her grandfather, Booker Bryant, spent hours with Donovan in his woodworking shop and took him crabbing or fishing.

Brooke continued to Station 18 at the end of the island near the lighthouse, which she knew would be less crowded. She parked her car and climbed the walkway protecting the dunes to the beach. On the horizon she saw several shrimp boats, their nets down, followed by a flock of seagulls. The beach was empty except for a couple holding hands and strolling on the water's edge.

Brooke took off her shoes and left them on the side of the walkway. She headed toward the lighthouse and saw a washed-up palmetto log lying at the base of the dunes. She sat down and burrowed her feet into the sand. Throwing her head back, she searched the sky for Alex's plane. The tide was going out, and there was so much blue sky that she wondered how Montana's sky could compare to this.

She picked up a handful of sand and let the fine, white particles run through her fingers, remembering what Alex had said about the hourglass. She wondered what her grandmother would say about Alex. She closed her eyes and pictured her. A breeze came up from nowhere, and on it she could see her grandmother as clear as if she were sitting next to her. Then she thought she heard her grandmother's voice say, *"Child, no need to ask me what I think of your young man. No need to measure my opinion against your judgment. When you love someone, it's only your opinion that matters and no one else's. You have to trust your judgment because love is the ultimate test of trust. You see, girl, you're risking the chance they'll break your heart, but you're trustin' they won't."*

Brooke heard a plane overhead and saw its jet stream in the sky. She stood and said, "Until we're together again, I will carry your heart in my heart."

★★★★

Alex's could feel the thrum of the engine and the vibration of the plane as it lifted off the tarmac and banked right. He looked out the window for the last glimpse of the shimmering blue water of the Atlantic before the plane flew into the clouds and out of the mysterious bubble he'd been living in for the past few weeks. He thought about how he'd grown to love the scent of salt water and the odd smell of rotting marsh life in the plough mud. He thought about the dolphins and the sound of the ocean roaring in and pulling away. He thought about the southern food, the city's charm, and the civility of those who lived there. He closed his eyes and thought about

Brooke. He thought of what his father had told him. *"It's not how long a person has stayed in your life. It's about what you've learned from them."*

He'd taken off more than his clothes when he was with her; she'd stripped away the cloak of tedium that came with being born into inherited wealth and a life predetermined by family expectations. He thought about how much she was a part of her beloved Lowcountry and as committed to her life in Charleston as he was to the ranch. He closed his eyes, and with a knot in his stomach, he worried about how the relationship could actually work out.

# Chapter 53

Love is friendship that has caught fire. It is quiet understanding, mutual confidence, sharing and forgiving. It is loyalty through good times and bad times. It settles for less than perfection and makes allowances for human weaknesses.

—*Ann Landers*

Standing fifty feet back from security, Mary sighed with relief as the arrival of Alex's plane was announced. It was a half an hour overdue. The plane hadn't crashed, nor had it been hijacked; those were always her first thoughts when a plane was late in arriving.

Mary looked around at the others standing near them. One group in particular caught her eye. It was a family standing a few feet away. The mother seemed nervous as she rubbed her hands together and checked and rechecked her watch. The father standing next to her appeared stiff and uncomfortable as he repeatedly leaned down to quiet a small blond-haired boy, around four or five, who bounced excitedly from foot to foot. A little girl around ten stretched her neck, searching the faces of the passengers who began to emerge from beyond the checkpoint as they streamed by.

When a soldier who didn't look old enough to drive, no less fight in a war, appeared carrying a duffel, the shrieking started. The small boy charged at the young soldier and tackled him at the waist. The soldier guarded himself against the charge and picked up the boy. The mother began to cry as she and the little girl rushed to the soldier, hugging and kissing him. The young soldier put down his duffel, guided his little brother to the ground, and walked slowly to his father. The soldier put out his hand, but in what appeared to be an unnatural motion, the man opened his arms, and the soldier fell into them. Guiding his son's head onto his shoulder with his left hand, the father gripped his son's head tightly with his right. The mother and two children moved closer and wrapped their arms around the two, melting into a family hug.

Overcome with emotion, Mary wiped a tear from her eye. Suddenly, she felt a tap on her shoulder and turned to see Alex standing there with a look of concern.

"What's wrong, Mom?" he asked.

She motioned to the soldier and his family, who were walking toward the exit.

Alex nodded, glancing at them. "I sat next to him on the plane. He's just getting back from Iraq. This is his leave before he deploys to Afghanistan."

"I thought we were out of Iraq," she said.

"Sort of. We still have a surveillance presence. He's a drone operator. He'll be OK. He's not going to be in a combat situation."

She scoffed. "Tell that to his mother." She waited a beat and asked, "Did you get his name?"

"Drew Smyth. Why?" Alex asked.

"I'll say a prayer for him," Mary said, slipping her arm around Alex. "Come on. Cody drove me. He's waiting in the cell lot."

After stopping at baggage, Mary called Cody to pick them up at arrivals.

"I'm anxious to hear all about what's been happening here since I've been gone," Alex said.

"I'm anxious to hear all about Brooke," Mary said.

As Alex climbed into the back seat, Cody said, "Hey, partner, how are ya?"

"Good. It was a good trip," Alex said as Cody and Mary exchanged looks.

Once they were on the highway, Alex said, "So, what's going on with moving the herd to the summer pasture?"

"Well, now that the calving is over," Cody said, looking in the rearview mirror at Alex, "we're gonna have to pack in for a week or two to improve the line camps, corrals, and springs."

"And brand the spring calves and thin the herd to make sure there's enough grass for grazing up there," Alex said.

"That's for sure. The summer pasture can't feed the growing herd," Cody said.

"I think we'll take the Piper up and look over the pastures to take stock of what needs to be done," Alex said.

"OK, enough about the ranch. So, what's going on with you and Brooke?" Mary asked, turning to look at Alex.

Alex leaned forward, put his hand on his mother's shoulder, and gently squeezed it. "Well, truth is, I think I'm love."

"Don't you think it's a little too soon?" Mary said.

"Mom," Alex said quietly, "my whole life has been planned. Brooke is the best thing I never planned on." After a moment passed, he added, "Besides, you don't get to pick the right time to fall in love. It picks you."

There was silence for a few minutes before Mary spoke. "Well, you're right about that. There is no timeline for love. I'm looking forward to meeting Brooke," Mary said as they pulled into the parking lot at The Cedar Tavern.

"Why are we stopping here?" Alex asked.

"You know your aunt. She has to make a party out of every occasion. It's a welcome home dinner," Mary said.

The lot was full, and several people sat outside on rustic wooden benches, drinking beer while waiting for a table. Alex thought of the difference between this scene and that of Serenity. "You know, I never gave much thought to cowboy traditions. In Charleston, people talk a lot about all of their traditions, but here we live them."

Cody and Mary exchanged a look.

"Cody can regale your friends with cowboy stories about the 'old times,' can't you?" Mary said.

"Be happy to," Cody said.

They walked into the restaurant and were met by Peg, who was standing next to the hostess station. "Well, look what critter the cayote dragged in?" she said, reaching out to embrace Alex. She kissed him on the cheek, and he kissed her back. After hugs all around, Peg said, "Follow me." She led them toward the side room.

As they passed the bar, Alex saw Nick, whose back was turned toward him. "Hey, you all go ahead. I want to say hi to Nick."

Alex sat on a barstool and waited for Nick to spot him, which he did almost immediately.

"Hey, you varmint," Alex said as Nick approached him. "I heard you've become quite the bartender."

Nick walked around the bar. "I'm the employee of the month. How the hell are you? How was Charleston?"

In his peripheral vision, Alex saw a woman sitting on a barstool a few seats away from him. She turned in his direction, then quickly turned back to study the drink in front of her.

"Nick, you haven't been here for a full month, you asshole."

"Well, your aunt told me if I stick around for a month, I will be, and I have no intention of leaving."

"That's good to hear. Let's catch up later. Mom and Cody are waiting for me," Alex said.

"OK, what do you want to drink?" Nick asked.

"What do you think?" Alex said.

"I wasn't sure if all that high-falutin' living in Charleston had changed your taste buds to a mint julip," Nick said.

Alex put his hand on Nick's shoulder and said in a low voice, "No, it just changed my heart."

"Christ, Alex," Nick said. "You drank the Kool-Aid." He stood back, scanning Alex from head to toe. "A whole fucking gallon."

"What can I say? It was smooth going down, and there's been no bitter aftertaste," Alex said. "Just a hankering for more."

"Alex," Mary called softly. "Come on. We're ordering."

"Let's catch up later," Alex said.

When Alex entered the side room, he saw there was a table set for six. He looked to the right and saw Jake and Jesse deep in conversation, standing in front of the bookcase that featured the rodeo buckles of famous cowboys. Alex walked over and said, "Howdy, you two. What are you talking about?"

"Welcome home, cous'," Jesse and Jake said in unison. "We hear you had a good time in Charleston."

Alex felt his cheeks burn. "Is there anyone in this town who doesn't think my business is theirs?"

"Can't think of anyone," Jake said, punching Alex in the shoulder. "Anyway, we also heard that you're going to the summer pasture and culling the herd. We'd like to go with you."

"Yeah, we haven't been on a drive since last summer," Jake said.

"Sure, you're always welcome. But the one you were on was in the flatlands. The summer pasture is way up there, just below the ponderosa pine forest. We can only get there on horseback, and we'll be gone the better part of a week or longer," Alex said. "Um, I've got to make sure Cody approves. I'll be right back."

"Cody, can I have a word with you?" Alex said, nodding toward the French doors leading to the patio.

"What's up?" asked Cody.

"Jake and Jesse want to go on the drive to the summer pasture. I don't want them thinking I don't want them to come, but I also don't want them thinking this drive is going to be easy, like the last one they were on."

Cody nodded and walked with Alex to Jake and Jesse. "I hear you two want to come on the cattle drive."

"We sure do," Jake said.

"We can use you, but I need to warn you. It's treacherous," Cody said.

"We know," Jesse said.

"Do you? The only way down from the rim is a steep trail ride. It's very dangerous because we don't know what happened over the winter," Cody said.

"We understand. We're up for it," Jake said.

"You'll be in a saddle for hours. You'll get tired to the point that you'll think it's intolerable and impossible to stay in the saddle. It gets real cold up there at night, and although there's a cabin, it's been unoccupied since last fall and has no electricity or heat. And the smell will be of sweaty horses, stinking men, and whatever dead wild animals we come across," Cody added.

Cody glanced at Alex as Jake and Jesse looked at each other.

"Thanks for the warning, Cody," Jesse said. "We're okay with it. When do we leave?"

"Well, Alex and I have to take the Piper up and fly over the valley to see where the cattle are located and then get all the provisions together. Maybe in three or four days. I'll let you know. I'm curious. Why do you want to come?"

Jake put his thumb in a belt loop and rubbed his chin. "I just finished my student teaching. I was going to teach biology. But I don't think it's for me."

"Why not?" Alex asked.

"Too much time inside. I also majored in animal husbandry, and I'd rather do that," Jake said.

Alex turned to Jesse. "What about you?"

"After I graduate next spring in aeronautical science, I think I'd like to start a business offering to fly over the farms and ranches, checking fences and the herds for those who don't have a plane," Jesse said.

"How'd you get that idea?" Alex asked.

"From you. Remember you taking me up with you last winter when old man Vreeland called you during a snowstorm and asked you to fly over his land because his prize bull was missing?"

Alex laughed. "Yeah, I do. We spotted him standing in the middle of Vreeland's upper the pasture."

"Does your mother know about this?" Cody asked.

"Yes," Jake said. "She's all for it. She wants us to do what we want."

Cody nodded and walked back to the table.

"OK, now it's time for the download about Charleston and why you look so happy, Alex," Peg said.

Alex filled everyone in on the salient points of the trip and ended by explaining that Brooke and some friends would be coming in two weeks in time for the Fourth of July.

"Great. I'll arrange a real western night for them with square dancing and a western-themed menu—and fireworks."

"I have a feeling the only fireworks Alex is interested in is between him and Brooke," Cody said, slapping Alex on the back.

# Chapter 54

The heart has reasons that reason does not understand.

*—Jacques Bossuet*

Alex went onto the terrace to call Brooke, who answered on the first ring.

"Hey, cowboy," she said. "Home safe and sound?"

"We stopped at Aunt Peg's restaurant for dinner and an inquisition about you."

"What did you tell them?"

"The truth."

"And what's that?"

"That I never believed in love at first sight until the first time I saw you. I could barely breathe, and it was as if time stood still. And then I had this warm feeling in my heart and in my pants."

"You're a bad boy," she said, laughing. "Naughty, naughty."

"I've never felt comfortable enough with anyone else to say exactly what's on my mind and not be afraid of being judged in some way."

"I feel as if somehow our hearts have been shrink-wrapped together."

"Shrink-wrapped, huh?"

"Hermetically sealed."

Alex looked up. The sun was beginning to go behind Blue Ridge Mountain, and the sky was taking on a navy blue background for the constellation of stars that were beginning to peek through. "I miss you."

"I miss you, too. But I'll be there soon. I can't wait."

"Neither can I."

Jake stuck his head out and said, "Mom's getting ready to have the dessert served."

Alex nodded. "Brooke, I have to go, but I'll call you tomorrow. I love you."

"I love you, too."

★★★★

An hour later, they pulled into the driveway to Cloudlands.

Cody parked the truck near the back door of the house. Alex opened the door for his mother and helped her out as Cody grabbed Alex's backpack and luggage.

When they entered the kitchen, Mary said, "We'd like to talk to you about something, Alex."

"Want a beer?" Cody asked, looking at Alex.

"I don't know. Am I going to need one?" he said.

"Maybe," Cody said.

"OK, then," Alex said.

"I'll have a glass of wine," Mary said.

"Come, let's sit outside on the lanai," Mary said.

She flipped a switch next to the French doors to the patio, and the large hurricane lanterns flickered on. She walked to the sofa and sat down. Cody and Alex sat across from her.

"OK," Alex said. "What's going on?"

Cody leaned over, his grip tightening around the neck of the beer bottle and placed it between his knees. "Um, it's Gwynn."

Alex put his beer down on the table, leaned back, and ran both hands through his hair before intertwining his fingers. "Now what?"

"Your mother and I are worried about her mental health. And we're worried that she'll … she'll hurt herself, her mother, or … you," Cody said gravely. "I didn't tell you everything about my visit with her. There was nothing you could do from Charleston. But I had a bad feeling about her mental state after I spoke to her."

Alex put his elbows on his knees and held his head in his hands. Then he looked up and said, "I'm not worried about myself, but I am worried about Gwynn and Diedre."

Mary shivered. "Well, that's what we want to talk to you about. What can we do to help her? What should we do?"

The three sat there for a few minutes before Alex said, "I talked to Brooke about it, and she told me about a method called LEAP to use when talking to someone who needs mental help but doesn't think they do."

"Brooke sounds like a smart girl," Mary said.

"She is. Very. Well, I told her all about what happened with Gwynn, and she helped me understand a lot about Gwynn and how I might be able to talk to her about getting help."

"Do you think maybe you should talk to Diedre about it?"

"Trust me, Diedre doesn't want to talk to me about anything," Alex said. "Well, Gwynn called me when I was in Charleston, and I told her I'd talk to her when I got back. One way or the other, I risk setting her off. But I think talking to her is less of a risk."

Cody nodded thoughtfully. "I agree with you, Alex. Either is a risk. I trust your judgment, but if you're going to talk to her, I think you need to come up with a plan just in case she goes off on you."

"I do have a plan," Alex said. He explained anosognosia and the LEAP approach to get someone to accept treatment and answered their questions. They were talking about a plan when the headlights of Nick's truck spread light over the cobblestoned courtyard. Nick waved and climbed the stairs to the lanai, taking a seat next to Alex.

"Want something to drink, Nick?" Mary asked.

"No, thanks. I'm good. Just stopped by to see Alex," Nick said.

"Well, you boys catch up. I'm exhausted," Mary said as Alex and Cody stood.

"Good night, Mom," Alex said and kissed her on the cheek.

"Night, Mary," Cody said. Then, turning to Alex and Nick, he nodded and said, "I'm turning in myself. Good night, boys."

Nick waited until they were alone, turned to Alex, and said, "What the hell happened in Charleston? I've never seen you look this happy."

# Chapter 55

Where everything is bad, it must be
good to know the worst.
*—F. H. Bradley*

The level of Gwynn's excitement when Alex asked her to meet him at a coffee shop in town caused him to have second thoughts. The first thought after he hung up with Gwynn was to call Brooke.

"Good morning, beautiful," Alex said.

"Good morning, cowboy. How's it going out there?"

"Good, I think. I just called Gwynn. I'm supposed to meet her today at eleven. I've been going over the information you sent me. I want to go over it with you and practice what I should say."

Over the next hour, they rehearsed various scenarios. "OK, I think I've got a good grasp on this," he said.

"Just promise me that if Gwynn starts to get excited, has rapid speech, or gets a raged look on her face like the one you told me about, you'll get up and leave."

"Trust me," Alex said. "I know how to duck and make a quick exit. Cody will be nearby. The coffee shop is next to the feed store, so if she sees him, he won't look out of place."

"I'm glad Cody will be close by. He seems to have a calming effect on her."

Alex heard her sigh. "He'll be just outside the coffee shop."

"Good." There was a long pause before she said, "Call me as soon as you finish talking to her. I'll be worrying about you."

A little after eleven, Alex entered Mocha Mama Coffee Shop.

Gwynn sat at the table next to the large brick walk-in fireplace. While Alex had always found Gwynn to be so beautiful, he saw her differently now. The allure she'd once had over him was gone. And the tight, low-cut shirt she wore that accentuated the rise and fall of her breasts had no effect on him, and neither did the perfume anyone within walking distance of the store could smell.

When she saw him, she smiled broadly and stood. "Good to see you, Alex."

If he didn't know better, he may have been fooled into thinking she was fine. But he was on high alert for an ambush.

After she took a seat, Alex said, "Thanks for seeing me. How have you been?"

"OK, I guess. Obviously, as you saw the last time we were together, I was overwrought that things didn't work out between us."

"Hi, folks, I'm Tony. What can I get you?"

"I'll have a double espresso Chiaro and a scone," Gwynn said.

"Just a coffee, black," Alex said.

After the waiter left, Alex looked directly at Gwynn and said, "I'm so sorry I hurt you. I never meant to."

Her eyes narrowed. "Then tell me, why did you?"

"I've done a lot of self-examination about that."

"Have you?" Gwynn said in a slightly caustic tone."

Alex sat back in his chair. "Yeah, well, I wanted to talk to you about something that's helped me a lot, and I was thinking that it may be something you may want to consider."

Gwynn cocked her head. "What's that?"

Tony appeared, placed their order on the table, and left.

"I've been seeing a psychologist."

"You have? When? I thought you just got back," Gwynn said, sounding suspicious.

"While I was away. The guy I was visiting has a sister who is a psychologist, and she helped me see some things more clearly. Like what is wrong with me to have done what I did to you."

Gwynn's eyes grew wide.

*Alex, get to the fucking point,* he thought.

"Look, Gwynn, I saw how much I hurt you that day. And I wanted to tell you how much talking to someone about things that hurt can help."

"Humph. My mother has been trying to get me to go talk to someone, but it's because she keeps telling me I'm acting crazy."

"We all act crazy sometimes."

Gwynn recrossed her legs. "Yeah, well, I have felt my share of crazy lately."

*Christ, this is hard,* Alex thought. *Why aren't there five top things to say to an ex to heal the hurt you caused them?*

"Well, I'm not telling you what to do, but I thought maybe it would help you if I shared what I'd done."

Suddenly, Gwynn's face grew tight. Her eyes narrowed, and her voice grew loud and high pitched. "Well, I'm happy for *you.* So happy *you* got over it."

*Listen, empathize, agree, partner,* Alex thought. He waited a long beat before saying, "I'll never get over hurting you, Gwynn. What I am saying is that talking to a professional helped me to learn to live with what I've done, and it may help *you* live with what I did to *you.*"

"Howdy, Gwynn," Cody said, tipping his hat. Turning to Alex, he said, "The truck's loaded. We'd better get movin'."

Gwynn sat back and stared at Alex with something that looked between a scowl and a smile.

"Oh, we're leaving for a cattle drive," Alex said. "I wanted to talk to you before I left. Cody and I are picking up our order from the feed store. I didn't realize it would be ready so soon. Maybe we could talk when I get back."

"I see. Well, I'll think about what you said. If nothing else, it would get my mother off my back."

Alex combed his fingers through his hair, stood, and put money on the table. "Thank you for talking with me. Take care of yourself, Gwynn."

"I came in because I heard Gwynn's voice when a customer opened the door," Cody said as they walked to the truck.

"She was upset because I said talking to someone helped me. It pissed her off that I felt good about anything."

Alex called Brooke and told her about his conversation with Gwynn on the way to Cloudlands. When he ended the call with "I love you," Cody laughed and said, "Dang it. There might be little Whitgates in the future after all."

# Chapter 56

Love many things, therein lies the true strength,
and whosoever loves much performs much,
and can accomplish much, and what
is done in love is done well.

—*Vincent van Gogh*

The next few days went quickly while Alex and Cody worked on the plan to brand and vaccinate the calves and drive the herd up to the summer pasture. First, they flew over the ranch by quadrants in the Piper, the video camera mounted on the underbelly of the plane recording the areas. Alex would later use a DJI Zenmuse XT drone for pasture surveillance, mapping the exact location of the cows and calves. The drone would also see strays under forest canopies and could detect predators.

They counted the number of calves to be branded and vaccinated from the ear tags put in shortly after they were born. They studied the video, looking closely at each cow, and gave her a score on how she was mothering the calf and whether her calf had a good disposition or was wild and snorty. Alex's father had instilled in him a laundry list of culling criteria. Alex could still remember his father explaining why culling was so important to building a top-quality herd. *"I'm not in the ranching business for a tax write-off. I'm in it for a profit. And knowing how and when to cull is key."*

The older Alex got, the more he realized that his father's guidance and commitment to doing things the right way come "hell or high water" was what had made Alex a good soldier and rancher.

They decided they needed ten cowboys bedsides themselves, Jake, and Jesse. Six would drive the culled heifers down to holding pens, where they would wait to be trailered to market, while six would drive the remaining herd up to the summer pasture.

Alex and Cody went over the list of twenty-five candidates. "What do you think, Cody?" Alex asked.

"I think we'll need two good ropers and four on the ground. Slim Maynard and Carlos Banderas are the best ropers, and Javier Lopez, Raul Martinez, Dalton Garrison, and Josh Kessler are the best on the ground for branding and administering the vaccinations. If you agree."

They were sitting in Alex's office in one of the converted stables off the courtyard where Alex stored and worked on the drones. He was at his desk, and Cody was sitting at a large table covered with pictures the drone had taken. Cody stood up and walked over to the chair in front of Alex's desk.

"I've been thinking that maybe it would be best after this drive for me to take a job running old man's Vreeland's Circle V Ranch. He's been asking me for years."

Alex's mouth hung open. He swallowed, cleared his throat, and said, "Why? Why would you even think about leaving? I mean, if it's the money, let's talk about it."

Alex started to laugh as if he'd just heard a joke.

"What's so funny?" Cody asked as his eyes narrowed.

Alex stood and walked around the desk. Sitting on its edge, he said, "That's just great. That's just great. Just when you think things are going well, shit hits the fan."

"What are you talking about?" Cody asked, rubbing the back of his neck.

"I'm talking about the fact that I feel like I'm finally getting my shit together. I'm going to live the life I want to live, not what generations of Whitgates have preordained."

There was silence for a moment.

"And now you leave?" Alex said, throwing up his hands. He began to rub his jaw and looked up at Cody, who was also rubbing his jaw.

"Look, Alex, it just seems to me that Jake and Jesse want to be part of this ranch."

"Yeah, but you are *this* ranch, Cody," Alex exclaimed. "My father always said that the smartest thing he ever did, other than marrying my mother, was hiring you to manage the ranch."

"I just feel as if it may be time for me to move on."

"Well, it's not. It couldn't be the worst time. How could I possibly go to Charleston to see Brooke if you weren't here?"

Something changed in Cody's face. His voice rose. "It may be all well and good for you if I stay, but how could I possibly ask your mother out for a date while I work for her?"

Alex stared at Cody, remembering a few random comments he'd made after Alex was discharged and permanently returned to the ranch. Something about handing over the reins to Alex. And something about how lonely his mother had been while Alex was away. What a beautiful woman his mother was.

"What makes you think you can't date my mother if you work for her?" Alex asked calmly.

"For the same reason the armed service doesn't permit an enlisted person to date their commanding officer."

"I understand what you are saying, but even the military recognizes the Married Couples Program exceptions. And if you don't know by now that my mother would never allow her personal feelings about anyone to undermine her interests in keeping Cloudlands the best ranch in the state ... Jesus, she all but nagged me into marrying Gwynn just so there would be future heirs to leave the ranch to."

"You have a point there," Cody said, grinning.

"Look, I don't want you to go, and I'm *sure* that my mother doesn't either. But I also don't want to be selfish and stand in your way if there is a reason other than wanting to date my mother." Alex hesitated, then said, "Do you mind if I ask you something?"

"Go ahead."

"Why now? After all these years, why suddenly now?"

"Because as you just said, you are getting your shit together. I was going to leave when you got back, but you seemed detached, um, distracted. I didn't think you were ready to take on the full responsibility of running the ranch."

"And now you do?"

"I do.

"But you haven't answered my question. Why now?"

"Because I'm sitting here, watching everyone pair up. You. Nick. A couple of the ranch hands are getting married. The sun is beginning to set for me. I'm not getting any younger, and this is not the dress rehearsal. I'm not going to be moseying by this way again. It's time for me to tell your mother that I'm in love with her."

"Mmm. I have a news flash for you, Cody. I think she knows and feels the same way."

"You think she does?"

"I do," Alex said emphatically.

Cody stood up and hugged Alex so hard that it felt like a chiropractic adjustment.

# Chapter 57

The expectations of life depend upon
diligence; the mechanic that would
perfect his trade must first sharpen his tools.
—*Confucius*

Two days later, when the sun was first introducing itself to the day, fourteen cowboys met at the ranch's barn, where the heavily muscled quarter horses bred specifically for cattle drives were stabled. Cody had carefully chosen twenty brood mares and two stallions for strength, endurance, rough trails, cow sense, and cooperation to annually provide the ranch with foals of superior bloodlines.

Although the cowboys were there for their horse assignments, the horses would be trailered for the first fifteen miles to the lower pasture. The cowboys would follow in the ranch's trucks driven by ranch hands, who would drop the cowboys off, trailer the horses, and return to the ranch. Two other trucks would caravan to the pasture. There was a custom super-duty "King Ranch" edition Ford F-150 towing a paneled trailer with supplies and a custom-made Ford F-450 Cutaway serving as the modern mobile chuck wagon on all-terrain tires. It was manned by Duane Baxter and his seventeen-year-old son, Danny. Duane, who was referred to as "Doc," had been a medic in Iraq and had gone to culinary school on the GI Bill. But he suffered from PTSD and found he couldn't tolerate the loud kitchen noises of slamming pots or dropping plates. When the ranch wasn't using the Cutaway, Alex let Duane hire it out to smaller ranches as a site cook for cattle drives and rodeos.

By the time they reached the herd, unloaded the horses, and saddled up, the sun and the temperature were rising. They branded and vaccinated fifty calves before they heard the distinct sound of the triangular-shaped dinner bell Danny had bought on Amazon for his father.

Alex glanced at his watch. It was a little past noon. Looking up at the herd ahead of him, he saw a hawk make a kill on the edge of the tree line and lift off with a white-tailed jackrabbit as the rabbit's companion took shelter under the grass. Alex felt overwhelmed as if suddenly something inside of him had shifted. He pulled up on the horse's reins.

Cody trotted up to him. "Something wrong? You okay?"

"I'm fine. Just feeling conflicted. I love this land, I love ranching, I love Montana, and I love Brooke. How the fuck is it going to work out with her?"

"Well, if you remember, it's the same dilemma I had trying to work out asking your mother out."

"Yeah, but you're here, and she is too. What if Brooke has her practice in Charleston? I know how much she loves it there. With you staying and managing the ranch, I've been thinking maybe I could live in Charleston and raise our family there, and then I could come out here in the summer."

Cody shifted in his saddle. "Take it from an old cowboy who's learned a thing or two about worry. It's like a thin stream that trickles through your head, and if you let it, it can cut a deep channel that will drain all the good thoughts from your mind." Cody's horse, Diablo, pawed at the ground and put his ears back. Cody held up the reins and said, "Whoa, boy, hold on there," and Diablo's ears went forward, and he stood still. "He loves being out here almost as much as we do.

But he can't be out here all of the time, and neither can we. Alex, think about it. If you want it to, it will work out with Brooke. And I have to tell ya, I can't wait to meet this gal. She must be somethin'. Now let's get some lunch. Daylights burnin', and we've got a lot to do before nightfall."

After lunch the branding resumed. Suddenly, Alex noticed Jake was chasing after a timid calf, which was heading for the trees. Jake hunched over the saddle horn to avoid tree limbs as he entered the wooded area. Just as Jake was about to rope the calf, a cougar jumped down from a low-hanging limb directly in front of Jake's horse, Lass.

Lass reared, and Jake hit his head on a tree limb, falling to the ground. Lass's hooves hit the cougar's head, and it faltered and fell to its side. Lass nudged Jake with her muzzle. After trying several more times to rouse Jake, Lass galloped out of the woods to the clearing.

Alex saw a riderless Lass as she broke through the tree line and yelled at the top of his voice, "Rider down!" He galloped to the tree line where Lass had emerged, with Cody right behind him.

A hundred feet in, Alex saw Jake lying on the ground with the cougar ten feet away from him. Pulling his rifle from the saddle holder, Alex yelled to Cody, "Get Duane." Alex sighted the rifle on the cougar's head, took aim, and shot. The momentum of the blast to the animal's head made it shudder, but then it lay still—and so did Jake. Alex dismounted in one movement with his rifle in hand, ran to Jake's side, and knelt beside him. He felt for a pulse and said, "Thank God." Alex's biggest fear was that Jake may have a cervical fracture and didn't want to move him until Cody and Duane could assist in stabilizing Jake's neck.

When Alex heard sounds behind him, he stood and aimed the rifle in case it was the cougar's mate.

"It's us," Cody called before they came into Alex's view. "I called for an air rescue, but we have to get him to the upper hay pasture so the helicopter doesn't start a stampede."

Duane dismounted from behind Cody and knelt next to Jake. "We need to roll him over and check his airway," Duane said.

Alex and Cody knelt on opposite sides of Jake.

"I'll stabilize his neck, and at the count of three, we'll roll him toward me," Duane said.

With Jake on his back, they could see the gash on his forehead was still bleeding. Duane dug into the leather bag slung over his shoulder, pulled out a four-by-four gauze pad, and applied pressure to the wound. "This is deep. He's going to need stiches." Duane used his middle and forefinger to open Jake's eyelids. "Well, he's breathing all right. His eyes react to light. They aren't dilated or swollen, and there's no blood from his nose or ears. His head must have hit something before he fell off. Let's get him out of here."

Alex and Cody moved their arms under Jake, grabbing each other's forearms. Duane held Jake's head as they lifted him off the ground. They carried him to the clearing and loaded him into the back seat of the waiting Ford King Rancher. Jesse stood next to the truck with tears in his eyes.

Getting into the truck's driver's seat, Alex rattled off orders as if getting ready for an assault on a target. "Duane, you tend to Jake in the back. I'll drive the truck. Jesse, get in. Cody, take charge until I get back," Alex commanded.

# Chapter 58

Train your mind to be calm in every situation.

*—Buddha*

Alex and Duane watched as the air-rescue helicopter lifted off, then looked at each other for a long moment.

Alex's phone rang, and he glanced at the caller ID.

"Alex, what's going on? I heard a helicopter," Mary said. "Did someone get hurt on the drive?"

Alex took a breath. "Yes. Jake."

He heard her gasp.

"They're taking him to St. Vincent's. He fell off his horse and hit his head."

"Oh, my God," she cried.

"Mom, listen to me. You need to stay calm for Aunt Peg. Don't call her. Go over and tell her. I sent Jesse with Jake. Have one of the ranch hands drive you and Aunt Peg to the hospital. I have to go back to the drive, but I'll be there as soon as I can."

"Where's Cody?" she asked. "Is he OK?"

"He's with the drive. He's fine. He has to stay with it. Look, Mom, the best thing you can do is go to your sister and be strong for her. I'll be there as soon as I can."

Alex hung up and said, "Let's go."

They were both quiet for a few minutes; then Alex said, "Thanks, Duane, you were great."

Duane didn't respond. He just looked out the passenger window. Alex glanced over and left him to his thoughts. But after a few more minutes, Alex said, "What do you think Jake's chances are?"

Duane's face was somber. "If he doesn't have a cervical injury and his head injury isn't too bad, he should be OK. But those are two big ifs." He paused and said, "That boy was sure lucky not to have been mauled by that cougar."

Alex's jaw tightened, and he felt emotion building in his chest. Wiping his eyes with his sleeve, he said, "Um, are you OK to continue with the drive?"

Without hesitation, Duane said, "Yup. Danny loves these drives, and so do I. Why do you ask?"

Alex swallowed the stone he felt in his throat. "You told me you have PTSD when I hired you. I want you to take care of yourself if you're having any flashbacks because of what happened to Jake."

He turned and stared at Alex. "I've just been sittin' here, thinkin' I didn't have one. Out here, I'm not preoccupied with intrusive thoughts." Duane rubbed his temples and said, "Do you ever have them? I mean, you were in combat. Do you ever feel like you're in a waking nightmare?"

Alex rubbed the side of his neck. "No, not like that, but I have some really *bad* memories, and sometimes I have nightmares."

"Danny's mother ran out on us," Duane blurted out. "She said she couldn't take it anymore. She said she didn't sign up to be a nurse and a purse." He looked over at Alex, then back at the passenger window. "I couldn't work for a while until you gave me this job, and she had to work double shifts at Walmart. She said she was tired of working like a dog to support me and sick of taking care of me. She said she needed to take care of herself."

Alex took in a deep breath and didn't know what to say. He suddenly thought about LEAP and realized he didn't have to say anything; all he had to do was listen.

A minute later Duane broke the silence. "I never should have married her. I knew in my gut Jen was wrong for me, but she was pregnant with Danny," he said, his voice trailing off.

They rode in silence for a few minutes. Then Duane said, "I enlisted right after high school. My father was an abusive drunk, and I knew if I didn't get out of there, I might kill him. I met Jen in basic training. She was what the guys called a 'townie.'" He paused.

Alex didn't have to ask what that meant; he'd run into a few at the bars near the bases he'd been stationed at. They were girls looking for a husband as a ticket out of whatever hell they were living in.

Duane turned and looked Alex. "My best buddy in basic told me to stay away from her, but I never did listen to what other people said about someone I liked. Anyway, it was too late by the time I realized he was right. So, I often volunteered for deployments just to get away from her."

There was another period of silence before Duane said, "It had been a quiet night, but it turned into chaos. I was with a team of rangers who had been sent to get a high-value target. We were moving tactically single file up both sides of the dark road when a bearded Iraqi burst from a house with an AK-47 and a firefight began. None of our guys got hit that night, but return fire cut the bearded Iraqi to shreds. After the shooting stopped, a woman dressed in the traditional black hajib and a long black dress came out of the house, followed by a little boy, who looked to be around eight. She took one look at the bloody, mangled corpse and threw herself on top of him. She began to scream and wail with such pain and horror I can still hear it." Duane took a deep breath.

Alex said nothing but looked over at Duane periodically to let him know he was listening.

"The little boy was so confused and frightened that he climbed onto his mother's back and stared up at the group of scary men wearing night-vision goggles with such hatred. I thought if he wasn't born to be an insurgent, he would be now. I thought about Danny, who at the time was about the same age, and it really shook me. Then came visions of an Iraqi mother wailing over the body of her dead teenage son a month earlier and the shrieks of a soldier lying on his back, his legs shredded by an IED, and suddenly I wasn't sure what was real or in my mind. I turned away and walked down the dark street and knew then that I would forever be haunted by that woman's grief and all the others. That's when it started."

Alex squeezed Duane's shoulder. They were quiet for another few minutes before Duane said, "You know, this is the first time I've told someone about what happened and haven't had a racing heart, nausea, and sweat pouring out of me."

Alex waited a long beat before he said, "Your symptoms make sense given what you've been through. I want you to remember you're not alone. My door and ears are always open to you."

Duane relaxed against the seat back. "You've already done enough letting me use the truck. You're a real good man, Alex. No wonder your ex-fiancée went off the deep end when you deep-sixed her."

Alex's head swiveled to face Duane straight on and slapped his palm against the steering wheel. "Isn't there anyone in this county that hasn't heard about that?"

"Doubt it," Duane said with a chuckle. "Even my mother asked me if I'd heard about it."

Alex snorted, and they began to laugh as the truck crested the last hill to the winter pasture and the cattle came into view.

After discussing things with Cody, it was decided that Cody would take the herd to the summer pasture, and Alex would go to the hospital to support his mother and aunt. Cody would let Alex know when the herd was delivered, and Alex would send a truck to pick him up and trailer the horses back to the ranch. They agreed Carlos Banderas had the most skill and best temperament to act as trail boss when Cody left.

"I'll check how things are going with the drone, and if you need anything, just call me, and as long as it's not a horse, I can deliver it with the drone," Alex said before he drove away.

# Chapter 59

For the truly faithful, no miracle is necessary,
For those that doubt, no miracle is sufficient.
—*Nancy Reid Gibbs*

The waiting area at St. Vincent's hadn't changed much since the night seven years ago when Alex and his mother waited for word about Alex's father's condition. The racks of plastic pockets on the wall he passed in search of his mother and aunt had the same requisite pamphlets about heart diseases, HIV, drug and alcohol addiction treatment programs, and diabetes.

Scanning the overcrowded room, Alex spotted his mother, aunt, and Jesse at the far end, sitting huddled on chairs against the wall. Alex knelt in front of his aunt, took her hands in his and said, "Aunt Peg, I'm so sorry this happened. How is he?"

She looked up at him and wiped her eyes with a wadded-up tissue she kept folding and unfolding. "All the nurse at the admissions desk will say is that he's being treated, and the doctor will be out soon."

"I should have kept a closer eye on him," Alex said, casting his gaze to the floor.

Peg put her hand on Alex's shoulder and gave it a gentle squeeze. "It's a cattle drive. It's not a walk on the beach. Things are going to happen. I know that. And Jesse told us what happened and how you and Cody took care of Jake and brought him down and had him airlifted. You did everything you could."

Mary stood, and Alex rose to his feet. He put his arms around her and kissed her forehead. She patted his back and asked, "Will you go ask that nurse if there's an update on Jake? Maybe she'll tell *you* something."

As Alex walked to the nurses' station, he noticed a young woman cradling a crying baby, who was rubbing his or her ear with tiny, dimpled fingers. *Probably an ear infection*, he thought. There were dozens of others in various stages of distress, including lacerations, broken bones, and respiratory problems. An older man was vomiting into a trash can in the corner.

The nurse looked up from her keyboard when Alex cleared his throat. Her name tag said, Tea Williams, RN."

"Miss Williams, I'm Jake Patterson's cousin. Can you tell me what his condition is and what treatment he's getting?"

She smiled compassionately and said, "I'm sorry, but all I can tell you is that they're working on him, and the doctor will be out and speak to you."

"Can you just tell me if he's regained consciousness?"

Her smile faded. "I'm sorry, but that's all I can tell you," she said firmly and looked back at her keyboard.

Just then someone dressed in scrubs walked out of the door marked RESTRICTED AREA—AUTHORIZED PERSONNEL ONLY next to the nurses' station. Alex glanced at Miss Williams, who was focused on her keyboard, and slipped through the door as it closed. At the far end of the hallway was a set of double doors marked TRAUMA BAY. Alex approached the doors and peered through the square window in the middle of the door. An unconscious Jake lay on a gurney surrounded by a team of four people, who were wearing scrub gowns and masks. They were frantically working on him. Alex could hear a woman's voice yelling instructions. Another was suturing the gash on Jake's forehead. There was an IV inserted into his arm, and two IV bags hung on a stainless-steel pole.

A door to one of the rooms opened, and a tall, muscular young man dressed in scrubs yelled, "Hey, you. You can't be back here."

Alex turned and walked toward the waiting room. As he approached Aunt Peg, he noticed Jesse was gone and took his seat. Reaching for Peg's hand, he said, "I couldn't get any information from the nurse, but I slipped back there, and they're working on Jake. He seems to be stable. We should probably hear something from the doctor soon."

Peg closed her eyes and stretched her head back. "Alex, since you're back from the cattle drive, do you think you can help out at the Tavern until I can get back?"

"Of course. Whatever you need, you know that."

Mary smiled at him and took her sister's hand.

Jesse appeared with a beverage carrier filled with four cups of coffee. Sipping their coffee, they waited in silence, each lost in his or her own thoughts.

Finally, a woman dressed in scrubs appeared from behind the restricted door and called, "Jake Patterson's family."

Peg jumped up as if she'd been launched from the chair.

The group walked quickly toward the woman.

"I'm Dr. Morrow. I'm a trauma surgeon. Let's go into the conference room so I can speak to you in private," she said, directing them to a door on the opposite side of the nurses' station.

The small room had a table and four chairs. The doctor, Peg, and Mary sat down, with Alex and Jesse standing behind their mothers.

Dr. Morrow explained that although Jake had a head injury, the tests didn't show brain swelling, which was a very good sign. He'd have to be monitored though for at least two weeks to make sure a subdural hematoma didn't develop. After explaining what that was, she said, "You'll be given a sheet when he's discharged of what to look for. But while he's here, we'll monitor him for that Mrs. Patterson, your boy is young , he's strong and I'm confident he'll make a full recovery. Once he's transferred to the ICU, you can see him."

"How long do you think he'll be here?" Peg asked.

"We'll run some more tests tomorrow and have a neurosurgeon look at him, and we'll be able to tell you more about that tomorrow," Dr. Morrow said.

After the doctor left, they breathed a deep collective sigh of relief, but real relief wouldn't come until Jake woke up.

# Chapter 60

My faith didn't remove the pain, but it got me through the pain. Trusting God didn't diminish or vanquish the anguish, but it enabled me to endure it.

—*Robert Rogers*

At Peg's insistence, Alex was to drop Jesse off at her house, and Jesse was to pack a bag for her since she wasn't leaving the hospital until Jake awoke. Expecting nothing less from Peg, Mary sent Alex to pack her a bag because she wasn't leaving her sister's side.

"What do you think, Alex?" Jesse asked as they pulled out of the hospital parking lot.

"I think he'll be OK. I've known several guys who had serious concussions and came out of them OK," Alex said.

"If anything happens to Jake, I'm not sure my mom could handle it. She always says we are her reason for living," Jesse said, staring out the passenger's window. Then Jesse glanced over at Alex and said, "Do you believe in God?"

"Why do you ask?"

"Because I'm not sure I do. I know our mothers do, but I doubt there's a God up there who knows the number of hairs on *my* head. I mean, if there is a God, then tell me, why is there so much suffering in the world? Why do innocent babies and children die? Why are there religious wars? Where's the tangible proof that God even exists?"

"I hear you, Jesse, and I've struggled with the same thoughts. All I can tell you is what the chaplain in Afghanistan used to say when he was questioned about God's existence. He said, 'The tangible proof of His existence is the Bible and Jesus Christ. And consider this. I have come to know that despite a person's doubts, there are no atheists in fox holes.'" Alex waited a moment before he continued. "I think what he was saying was that it doesn't matter if you believe in Him or not, prayer can help you through bad times. And I can tell you it's helped me. And I prayed for Jake as I was driving him down to the pickup spot for the air rescue. And I will keep praying for him."

Jesse said nothing.

As they pulled into Peg's driveway, Alex asked, "Do you want me to pick you up after I get my mother's things and take you back to the hospital?

"No thanks. I'll need a car. Thanks for being there for us," Jesse said.

"Come on. Besides my mom, your family is all I have, and there's nothing I wouldn't do for you," Alex said.

Jesse's eyes were moist, and his mouth quivered slightly. "Alex, you wouldn't leave here, would you?"

"What do you mean?"

"I mean you told us you're in love, and she lives in Charleston."

"Don't worry about that, Jesse. I'm not planning on it anytime soon. I'll see you back at the hospital." He looked at his watch before he backed out of the driveway. It was six thirty, eight thirty in Charleston. He wanted to FaceTime Brooke but decided to call her on his cell until he got home.

Brooke answered on the first ring. "Hey, there. I wasn't expecting to hear from you so soon."

Alex told her about what had happened and about his conversations with Cody and Duane.

"You know, when you're in combat, you expect someone is going to get hurt or die. But somehow when I'm just living everyday life, it shocks me. Makes me realize how fragile life is and that we need to make the most of every day. Before Jake got hurt, I looked around here and thought how hard it would be to leave. And then something like this happens, and you realize what really matters is that you and I are together. It doesn't matter where."

Brooke was silent for a minute. "Odd. I've been thinking about it, too."

"And?"

"And it's as if something is pulling us together. Fate, destiny, a deity? All I know is, I'm not going to fight it. I want to see where this pull takes us."

To Alex's ears it sounded like a promise. For the first time since Jake's accident, he felt the tension that had coiled around his heart release its grasp.

Alex pulled into the courtyard and said, "Hey, I'm home. I've got to get my mother's things. Can I call you later?

"OK. But don't worry about getting back to me. You take care of yourself," Brooke said.

"Love you."

"Love you, too."

Alex felt strange entering his mother's bedroom. He couldn't remember the last time he had been in it. He went to her closet and pulled down the overnight bag from the top shelf. When he pulled it down, a box next to it fell to the floor, and its contents scattered on the carpet. Alex knelt to put what appeared to be letters back in the box and noticed they were in his handwriting. He knelt and opened one that appeared tearstained.

The thought of his mother crying brought tears to his eyes as he read,

Dear Mom,

Thank you for the care package you sent. The guys really enjoyed the homemade cookies. I'm sorry I haven't been able to write more. It's been busy. I've been out chasing the bad guys. Remember when I was little and Jake, Jesse, and I would form a posse and ride out to save a town from Jesse James and his gang?

I think about you and the ranch a lot. And how grateful I am that I grew up in a place where using a gun for hunting was a way of life. Some of the guys, whose only experience with guns is from basic training, seem traumatized when they have to fire it at a live target. I'm not. What I'm trying to say, Mom, is don't worry about me. When …

"Mr. Alex," Maria called from the bedroom. "Your mother called and told me what happened. She asked me to help you get her overnight bag together."

Alex got to his feet and put the letters back in the box, returning it to the shelf. "Maria, I'm in the closet. Be right out." He wiped his eyes with his palm, took a deep breath, and walked into the bedroom, where Maria was smoothing a nonexistent wrinkle on Mary's bedspread.

He handed Maria the overnight bag and asked her to meet him in the kitchen when she was finished.

Alex went to his room, showered, and changed his clothes. Before he took the stairs to the kitchen, he went to the window and looked out at the sky. It was ablaze with striated clouds infused with various shades of bright, gilded hues. Thoughts of his conversation with Duane, memories of those he'd seen killed, and confusion over why this had happened to Jake flooded his mind. "All I know," he said aloud, "is that trying to reconcile human suffering with the existence of a God who is supposed to love us is as insoluble as reconciling why we humans inflict so much pain on each other."

# Chapter 61

Grown don't mean nothing to a mother. A child is a child. They get bigger, older, but grown? What's that supposed to mean? In my heart it don't mean a thing.

—*Toni Morrison*

When Alex returned to the hospital, he found his mother, aunt, and Jesse sitting on a couch in the ICU waiting room. "Have you been able to see Jake yet?"

"No. Not yet," Peg said. "A nurse came out and explained that although their goal was to give us access to Jake as much as possible, since patients need the love and support of family, she said it was equally important that the staff be able to render care without having to work around family members. She said visiting hours are limited to when there aren't any procedures being done, and as soon as they're finished with him, we could go in."

Alex nodded in acknowledgment and sat on the chair adjacent to the couch. "Have you spoken to Cody?" Alex asked his mother.

"Yes. He called right after you left. I told him what we know and said I'd call him after we see Jake," Mary said.

A few minutes later, the ICU doors opened, and a nurse came to tell them they could see Jake. Peg trembled as the nurse walked them down a corridor and past rooms with glass windows occupied by unconscious and semiconscious patients attached to monitors. Some monitors made loud alarm sounds, and some connected to ventilators made loud pressure sounds.

Peg's eyes flooded with tears when she saw Jake through the window of his room. She rushed into the room and pushed past the nurse adjusting his IV. Peg held onto the bedrail to steady herself. Jake's eyes were closed, and he looked as white as the sheets he lay on. A bandage wrapped around his head covered the cut on his forehead.

The nurse said, "I assume you're Jake's mother." She handed Peg a tissue from the box on the bedside table.

"I am," Peg said.

"I'm Jo Daley, Jake's primary care nurse. He's still unconscious, but he can hear you. I'd encourage you to talk to him and get him to open his eyes. The longer he can stay awake, the sooner he can go to a step-down unit and then home."

"Oh, thank you. Thank you so much for everything you're doing for him. Oh, and I'm sorry if I bumped into you," Peg said.

"Don't worry about it. I'm used to mamma bears doing anything to get to their cubs," Jo Daley said. "I'll give you some privacy now. If you need me, just press this call button," she said, pointing to the white cord attached by a clip to the sheet.

Peg took Jake's hand, IV and all, and kissed the entire surface of his palm, then held his hand to her cheek. When she heard Jesse's sob, she looked up and waved him to her side.

Alex put his arm around his mother's shoulder and pulled her into his chest as she wept.

"I'm here, my baby boy," Peg said. "It's Mamma. Can you open your eyes for me? Come on, Jakey."

"Mom, you know he hates it when you call him that. If you want him to open his eyes, maybe you should just stick to Jake," Jesse said.

"I'm calling him that because I know he *hates* it. I'm not trying to keep him asleep. I'm trying to wake him up," Peg scolded.

"Look," Alex said, turning Mary toward the bed.

Jake's eyes fluttered.

"Come on, *Jake. Please*, open your eyes," Peg cried.

Jake turned his head toward his mother with a slight grimace and opened his eyes. His lips turned up slightly as he mouthed, "What happened?"

Jo Daley, responding to the call button Peg pressed, came back into the room. "Jake, welcome back to consciousville," she said, smiling broadly. Then, turning to Peg, she added, "I have to take his vitals and check his cognitive status. Why don't you go to the cafeteria and get something to eat?"

"That's OK. I'm not hungry. I'll be in the waiting room. Please get me when you're through," Peg said.

Peg slumped into a chair. Mary sat down on the couch, closed her eyes, and heaved a sigh.

"Well, thank God. Jake seems to be all right," Peg said.

"Yes, thank God," Mary agreed, opening her eyes.

Alex and Jesse exchanged looks.

"Alex, I know you have the ranch to deal with, and I want you to be honest about whether you have the time to help out at the Tavern. Nick is a quick study. Actually, I'm thinking of training him to take over as manager so I can take more time off. But at the moment, I don't have anyone. Can you help out?"

"Of course. Whatever you need," Alex said.

"Nick said he thought he could handle tonight, but we have a large anniversary party scheduled for tomorrow night, and I don't want to ruin their celebration by canceling it," Peg said.

"And I can hostess or do whatever you need," Mary offered.

Peg began to cry, and Mary pulled tissues from her handbag, dabbing her sister's eyes. She pulled out a few more and closed Peg's hand around them.

"I'm just so grateful to you all," Peg said. "But I'm worried about the possibility of a subdural hematoma the doctor talked about."

"I don't blame you. I'd do the same if it were Alex," Mary said. Turning to Alex, she continued, "I'm going to stay with Peg unless you need me at the Tavern. So, why don't you go and see what help Nick thinks he'll need?"

"I'm going to stay for a while. I'd like to see Jake again before I leave, and then I'll stop by, too," Jesse said.

"OK, then. I'll get going, but if anything changes with Jake or you need me for anything, call me," Alex said.

Mary stood and embraced Alex. Her voice cracked as she said, "I'm so grateful you're here."

*Oh, God,* he thought, *is this some sort of a sign to tell me not to even think about going to Charleston? Was Jake's accident preordained to show me just how much everyone depends on me? What the fuck am I supposed to do? Live my life to satisfy everyone's needs but my own?*

# Chapter 62

What you don't see with your eyes,
don't witness with your mouth.
—*Jewish proverb*

Alex dug his shoulder into the swinging door of The Cedar Tavern's kitchen. He'd barely taken a step in, his shoulder still holding the door open, when he heard, "Hey, Alex."

It was Nick calling from behind the bar. It was near closing, and there was only one group of women left, clustered in a booth on the opposite side of the room farthest from the bar. He noticed they looked over at him, but he didn't do more than glance at them out of the corner of his eye. He walked to the bar and sat down on a stool.

"How about a beer?" he said.

As Nick pulled the beer tap, he said in a low voice, "How's Jake?"

Alex told him what he knew and explained Peg's request that Alex help at the restaurant until she returned. Suddenly, he heard one of the women practically shriek, "You're kidding. That's him?"

"Seriously?" he heard another voice say.

"Yup. That's him," the first speaker replied.

Alex rolled his eyes and looked at Nick, whose eyes darted toward the women and then back to Alex. Nick shrugged. "I already announced 'last call.'" He walked over and said to the women, "We're closing now. How about settling up for the night?"

He came back a minute or two later, ran the credit card through the machine, and walked back to the booth with a receipt. "Good night, ladies," Nick said.

As Nick walked them to the front door, Alex overheard one of them whisper, "He's hot, and what a great butt. No wonder she's pissed he dumped her."

"Although I wasn't actively listening, I couldn't help but string together the pieces of their comments." Alex took a long sip of beer and said, "I don't care what they're saying about me. But I'm curious. Did you hear them say anything about Gwynn?"

Nick nodded, his gaze moving to the beer tap. "Want me to top that off?"

"No. I'm good. Well?" Alex said.

Nick looked down. "I haven't heard much until just now when they spotted you."

"Sheesh. You make it sound like I'm a fucking unicorn."

"To these ladies, you are," Nick said. "Give me a break. You have to know that Mountainville isn't exactly the rallying point for handsome, single, wealthy men. And most guys your age are married. And there is the elephant in the room."

Alex put his elbows on the counter and pulled at his lips. "Yeah, what's that?"

Nick's eyes moved quickly over Alex's face as he dipped his chin and said gravely, "That you employ most of the people in this town in some way or another."

A sickening feeling made the back of Alex's neck itch. Rubbing his neck, he took a deep breath through his nose and said, "And that makes me, what?"

"Get real. It makes you the target of their obsession. Anyway, we could use your help until Peg gets back. That is, if you're okay to do it," Nick said.

"I can work at the ranch until midafternoon, go and see Jake at the hospital, and then come here," Alex said.

"That'll work," Nick said. There was a pause that gave the air a heavy sensation. Then he said, "Um, when things here settle down, I've decided to go back to Virginia, pack up my apartment, and move out here permanently."

Alex's eyes grew wide as he choked down the mouthful of beer he'd just drunk. "Great," he said. "That's great."

"And," Nick continued, "I put a deposit on an apartment in the building they just finished over by the lake."

"Good for you, Nick."

"Yeah, well. I'm not going back to the way things were before I quit drinking. I like my life, thanks to you letting me stay in the carriage house and your mom and Cody making me feel like family. Like they wanted to be around me, even though I didn't want to be around myself. Drinking used to be the shortest way out of my own company, which I couldn't stand. The easiest thing for me was to do a deep dive into the bottom of a bottle."

Alex stood up and leaned over the counter, clasping Nick's hand. "You, my friend, would have given your life for me and the other guys. It's the least we could do for you. It's no less than you would've done for me. Like Donovan said, 'It's not bullets or protective gear that saved you in combat. It's the love we have for each other.'"

# Chapter 63

Everybody is aware of physical and emotional pain,
but that doesn't stop them from inflicting it on others.
—*Shon Meta*

When Susan Wright pulled into her driveway and saw that Gwynn's lights were still on, she was overcome with excitement. She couldn't wait to tell Gwynn she'd seen Alex. She knew she'd had a little too much to drink and was grateful that she'd arrived home without being stopped and cited with a DUI, so she felt a rush of luck and an urgent need to share her news.

Susan stumbled her way to Gwynn's front stairs. Holding on to the banister, she pulled herself up onto the porch and knocked on the door.

Gwynn opened the door and said, "Good Lord, Susan. A sommelier could probably guess the years of the bottles of wine you drank by the smell of you."

"Oh, yeah, I probably look a mess. I was out celebrating a friend's birthday at the Tavern. And guess who walked in?" Susan managed to slur as she steadied herself by holding onto the door frame.

Gwynn stepped back into the foyer and said, "Brad Pitt?"

Susan walked by Gwynn, collapsing into the first chair closest to the foyer. "Ha ha. But he's as good looking as him, your ex."

Gwynn had also had a few glasses of wine but was sober enough to wonder what Susan's agenda was. She was beginning to get suspicious of what was in it for her to see Gwynn get upset every time Susan gave her news about Alex. Susan knew how devastated and embarrassed Gwynn was over the breakup and that Gwynn was obsessed with anything related to him. "Are you sure? I thought he was on a cattle drive," Gwynn said.

Susan began to laugh. A sloppy, drunk laugh that made Gwynn angry. Gwynn's cheeks grew scarlet, and her eyes burned into Susan, who was so anesthetized by the wine that she was oblivious.

"Uh-uh. His cousin got hurt on the cattle drive and is in the hospital, and Alex is back." Susan looked up at Gwynn and felt the searing look in Gwynn's eyes have a sobering effect on her. Susan's eyebrows almost reached the ceiling as she pushed herself up from the chair and said, "Sorry, Gwynn, um, I just thought you'd want to know."

Gwynn stood back as Susan got to her feet and rushed past Gwynn and down the front steps.

Gwynn walked into the kitchen and looked at the empty wine glass on the counter. She picked it up and opened the refrigerator. After filling the glass, she went to her bedroom and climbed under the covers, resting her back against the headboard. Taking a sip of wine, she began to rock back and forth, staring at the wedding gown that still hung on the frame of her closet. Her mother had tried to get her to give it to Goodwill, but Gwynn wasn't ready to give up the fantasy that someday she'd wear it—when she married Alex.

Then she thought about the conversation with Alex at the coffee shop and what Terri had said to her in Charleston. Although Terri had called and left several messages, Gwynn hadn't returned his calls. "Maybe I will make an appointment," she said to the wedding gown. Nodding to herself, she continued aloud, "That will get my mother off my back, and then maybe I can get the counselor to invite Alex to a session. Yes, if I can manage that ..."

She took another sip of wine, and a slow smile began to grow on her lips. "All I have to do is convince Alex that I'm getting help and that I've changed. Maybe we can get back together." She put the wine glass on the bedside table and turned off the lamp next to her bed. "Yes, that's what I'm going to do, and I'll call him tomorrow and ask about his cousin. Shit. That idiot didn't tell me which one got hurt."

But instead of sleeping, she tried to think of what she could say to get the counselor to ask Alex to come to a session. She thought about it for a few minutes and sat up. She turned on the light and looked at the dress again. Slipping out of bed, she took the dress down and tried it on. "Damn, I've lost too much weight. I'll have to have this altered," she said to the mirror. "But I still look beautiful in it. And I'm going to wear it. I know I can get him back. By God, if it's the last thing I do, I am going to get him back."

She twirled around, went to the kitchen, and poured herself another glass of wine. Returning to the mirror, she raised the glass to herself and took a long drink. She unzipped the dress, and it fell to the floor. She stared at her body in the mirror, smiled, and said, "I know what he likes, and I know the power I have over him." She lifted the glass to herself again and smiled. "I have a plan now. Isn't that what Terri said I needed?"

She turned the light off again and thought, *You can make it happen. You have to.*

Waking up before the sun rose, Gwynn followed her morning routine. She went to the kitchen and made coffee, and while it was brewing, she brushed the cotton out of her mouth with her toothbrush and got dressed in running clothes. She thought about her plan and smiled at herself in the reflection of the window above the sink. *What psychologist could refuse a sobbing ex-fiancée who wanted a chance to talk to her ex so she could have closure and stop thinking of herself as a loser who deserved to be dumped? And I'm just the girl to play the role.*

For the first time since Alex had canceled the wedding and shattered her dreams, Gwynn felt like her life was becoming right again … and she'd be in control.

# Chapter 64

Yesterday is history, tomorrow is a
mystery, today is a gift of God,
which is why we call it the present.
—*Bill Keane*

Alex was up before the sun. He hadn't slept that well. He'd Face Timed with Brooke when he got home and talked for an hour. He missed her so much that he ached. All he could think about was getting through the next week and a half.

Throwing off the covers, he walked into the bathroom and stared at his reflection. It was as if he were looking at himself with new eyes. The face in the mirror smiled back at him, and for the first time he could remember, he felt authentic. He still felt conflicted and confused about how exactly things would work out for him and Brooke, but he also felt a conviction they would.

His phone rang, and he glanced at the caller ID.

"Hey, Cody. How's it going?" Alex asked.

"It's going fine. Just checking in. Did you hear anything about Jake overnight? I spoke to your mom last night, and she said he was waking up and that they were gonna do more tests today."

"No. But I'm going to the hospital in a little while, and I'll call you if anything has changed. How far from the summer pasture are you?"

"We're about a day out from the Ponderosa tree line."

"Boy, you're making good time."

"They're a good crew. By the way, what'd you say to Duane? He was tellin' stories last night about other drives he's been on. I didn't know he had a sense of humor."

"Nothing. I just listened," Alex said with a smile on his lips. "Listen, I'll fly the drone up ahead of you later and let you know if I see anything of concern."

"Anything in particular you worried about?" Cody asked.

"That cougar has me worried. I'm going to concentrate on the wooded area and undergrowth to see if there are any more cougars or black bears. I was thinking that, although the bears have been out of hibernation a couple of months, you never know if they're still hungry from it."

"That's not a bad idea."

"I'd better get a move on. Mom wants me to stop and get the nurses donuts."

Alex could tell Cody was smiling as he said, "Well, tell her I said hello."

An hour later, Alex carried two dozen donuts through the corridor to the ICU. His mother and Peg were in the waiting room. His mother stood as he approached and took the donuts from him.

"Thanks, Alex," Mary said.

"Why are you out here?" Alex asked.

"They're taking Jake for a brain scan because he had some fluctuations in his vital signs. They want to make sure he doesn't have a brain bleed," Peg said solemnly.

Alex swallowed the lump in his throat. "Oh," he said. "When do you think he'll be back?"

"We're not sure. If you have to do something, go ahead," Mary said. "We'll call you after he's back and the doctor comes by with the results."

"Okay, I have to fly the drone up the trail and do a few things at the ranch."

"That's fine. We'll call you if anything changes," Mary said.

★★★★

When Alex got back to the ranch, he noticed Nick's truck was gone. Alex knew Nick didn't start work until four and guessed he'd gone in early to cover for the things Peg normally did. *Funny how things work out,* he thought. *If he hadn't planned on marrying Gwynn, he wouldn't have asked his buddies to come to the ranch. And if he hadn't, he wouldn't have gone to Charleston and met Brooke and wouldn't have had a chance to help Nick.*

As if on cue, his phone rang. Glancing at the caller ID display, he said, "Give me a fucking break."

"Hey, Gwynn, how are you?"

"I'm fine, Alex. I'm calling to find out how your cousin is. I heard he was injured on the cattle drive."

"Yeah, he's in the hospital, and they're monitoring him for a brain bleed," Alex said.

"Oh, I'm so sorry. How're your aunt and mom holding up?"

Alex tilted his head and almost asked why the sudden interest in his family since she'd showed no interest in any of them when they were engaged. But the words stayed on the tip of his tongue, filling the back of his mouth until he swallowed them down his throat.

"They're fine."

"Please tell them I asked about them, and I'm praying for them," Gwynn added.

That comment caused Alex to check the caller ID display. *Yup, it's Gwynn, but it sure doesn't sound like her,* he thought.

"Look, Gwynn, I don't mean to be rude, but I'm in the middle of something."

"Oh, I understand. I also wanted to tell you I decided to take your advice and see a therapist. And I was wondering if the therapist thought it would help me if you'd agree to come in for a session."

Alex shook his head and thought, *Fuck, I don't like not knowing what to do or say.* And then he thought about what he'd gone over with Brooke about using the LEAP. *OK*, he thought. *Try delaying an answer.*

"I'm happy you're getting help, Gwynn. I'm not sure about coming to one of your sessions though. I mean, isn't therapy supposed to be only between you and your therapist?"

"Um, yes, but if the therapist thinks it would help me understand some things in order to feel better, would you come?"

"If he calls me, I'll certainly talk to him, and we'll see," Alex said, sandwiching himself between the truth and a lie.

"OK … well, I won't keep you. Thanks, Alex," Gwynn said.

★★★★

She'd pulled off the first step of her plan. Now all she had to do was get the therapist to get Alex to come to a session and see for himself how she'd changed. She'd manipulated him into an engagement once, she could do it again. All she needed was access to him.

# Chapter 65

When one door of happiness closes, another opens,
but often we look so long at the closed door that we
do not see the one that has been opened for us.

*—Helen Keller*

After an hour of flying the drone over the tree line and the underbrush of the trail, Alex spotted bear tracks in the soft spots of earth under the tree canopy. He hovered the drone over the tracks and saw there were smaller tracks alongside the larger ones. It looked like a mamma and her cubs. Checking the map stretched out on the bed of the truck, he marked the site. Then he adjusted the camera lens to home in on the tracks leading to one of the tallest white pine trees.

Alex smiled as he recalled being around twelve when riding with his father to check fencing; they had followed the tracks of some steers that had wandered through a broken fence to graze on the other side of it. At that point, he'd read all about bears in books and had seen their heads and hides mounted on walls, but he'd never seen one up close—until then. He knew when mamma bears led their cubs away from a den, she used a tall white pine with strong, rough bark as a "babysitter" tree, where her cubs could take refuge from danger while she foraged for food. She'd rake a bed at its base for herself and her cubs, who could climb to safety if a predator came. That day when Alex's horse stepped on a branch and startled the three cubs, he watched in amazement as the cubs used their powerful limbs to rapidly hunch upward in successive hugs and claw their way to the crown of the tree. His father explained this was where the term "bear hug" came from.

Alex pulled out his cell and phoned Cody. "I found a mamma and her cubs located at quadrant one hundred fifty-eight."

"We're about five miles from there," Cody said. "I'll tell the boys to keep the herd on the other side of the pasture. If we stay away from her babies, we should be fine. Did you see anything else?"

"No, but I haven't taken the drone all the way up to the summer pasture yet. I wanted to call you and give you a heads-up about this."

"I talked to Carlos about acting as trail boss once we make the summer pasture."

"What'd he say?"

"He wanted to thank you. He was real happy. He's a good choice."

"Well, move 'em on, head 'em up, and get those doggies up to the pasture and back here as soon as you can. I think Mom could use your support right now," Alex said. "I'll call if I see anything else."

After another hour of carefully scanning the area up to the pasture, there was nothing to report. Alex brought the drone in and drove back to the ranch. After he put it away, he called Brooke.

"Hey, beautiful, good morning," Alex said.

"Hey, cowboy, it's afternoon here."

"Oh, yeah, sometimes it's hard to remember the time difference because when I think of you, it's like you're here. Remember, I carry you in my heart."

There was silence on the other end, and Alex heard a sniffle. "Are you crying?"

He heard an inhale and exhale, then Brooke's voice. "I'm not crying. I'm tearing. I didn't think cowboys said things like that. I mean, you say things that go to the heart of me."

"That's because you *are* the heart of me. And I don't know why you wouldn't think a cowboy would say things like that. We may sit up straight on a horse and have steely resolve, but we're extremely sensitive when it comes to our women and family, especially if anyone hurts them, in which case we kill the person and eat their heart."

Brooke laughed and said, "So, I'm learning."

"You know what I saw today?"

"What?"

Alex told her about the bear cubs, the origin of "bear hug," and how energized he felt when he was out in nature. He told her how he longed for her and that he wanted to show her all his favorite places, just as she had shown him hers when he was in Charleston.

"I can't wait to come out there. And Hollis is all over it. She actually bought a cowgirl outfit from Amazon. You think I need one?"

"Uh, no, as long as you bring a pair of jeans and heeled boots." He paused, "Oh, you may want to bring something to wear to the square dance."

"The square dance?"

"Yeah, my aunt is putting on a big shindig for the Fourth. That is, assuming Jake is out of the hospital and all."

Then he told her about Gwynn's call and her asking him to go to a session.

"Sounds like you handled the call with Gwynn the best way you could. You didn't say no. You deferred," Brooke said.

"I don't know. I have a tight chest every time I talk to her."

"That's understandable. You have a lot of history with her that gets stirred up every time you do. But you're doing the right thing by trying to help her," Brooke said. There was a pause, and then she said, "All any of us can do is our best."

"You're the best thing that ever happened to me. I'm thinking our meeting each other was kismet."

"Kismet, huh? All I know is that what happened with us you can't plan for. It was like it was preordained."

"So, that means there's got to be a way we can work out this distance thing. Because when you're not with me, it's like something uneasy is burning through my belly."

"And for me it's like my insides are limp," Brooke said.

"I can tell you what's limp on me without you," Alex said.

He could hear her laughter and waited for her to say something. Then she did. "You are *so* bad."

"You make me that way."

"And you make me laugh like no one else ever has. I love you. Now go do whatever cowboy thing you have to, and we'll FaceTime tonight."

"Don't forget I have to help out at the Tavern tonight. So, it will be close to midnight your time."

"My time is *anytime* you have time to call," Brooke said softly.

# Chapter 66

Eventually, there is one principle, and one principle only on which the world is hinged: things will work out as they should, provided we do as we should.

—*Manrett Sodhi Someshwar*

The next few hours went by in a blur. After Alex went to the hospital to find there was no sign of a brain bleed and that Jake had improved to the point of being transferred to the step-down unit later in the day, he went back to the ranch. He planned for the culled cattle to be sold and then arrived at the Tavern in time for the dinner crowd.

Alex parked in the back and came in through the kitchen. The chef they called "Chef" was at his station, and Jesse was at the sous-chef station busily cutting and chopping vegetables.

"Hey, there. You heard the good news about Jake?" Jesse asked.

"Yeah, I stopped by the hospital earlier. That's great news."

"You want to hear some bad news?"

"I don't know. Do I need to hear it?"

Nodding, Jesse smirked. "Think you'd better."

"OK then, spit it out. Or do I have to guess if it's Colonel Mustard in the library?"

"Ha ha, very funny. I never could figure out how you always won at Clue. But that gives me an idea. I'll give you a clue. It's a smokin' hot chick dressed to kill at the bar, and she's asking for you with determination on her face."

"Gwynn's here?"

"She is. She's with the other girl who comes in here a lot. I think her name is Susan something."

"Sheesh. Um, why don't I do that, and you can wait tables," Alex said without a momentary lapse.

Jesse undid his apron, threw it at Alex, and said, "You got it. But what do you want me to tell her?"

*Tell her to fuck herself because I will never fuck her again,* Alex thought. But instead, he said, "Tell her I'm held up at the ranch and not coming in today." Wrapping the apron around his waist, he pulled the strings tight. *Shit*, he thought. "Forget it, Jesse. I'll handle it."

Alex walked down the back hallway to a door located to the left of the bar used by barbacks. He took a deep breath and opened it to see Nick making a Manhattan. Nick caught Alex's eye, blew out a breath through pursed lips, and nodded toward Gwynn, who was sitting with her back to Alex and talking to the woman next to her. Alex walked behind the bar and stood in front of Gwynn.

"I heard you were asking for me," Alex said, looking at Gwynn and glancing at the plain-looking woman next to her, who he guessed must be Susan.

"Yes, I was. I wanted to ask how Jake is doing," Gwynn said. She leaned in, her cleavage on full display. Cupping her mouth, she whispered, "And I wanted to thank you for saying you'll consider coming to one of my sessions."

Alex stepped back, stood up straight, and nodded. "Jake is out of the coma and doing well. Thanks for asking. I'm sorry, Gwynn, but if that's it, I've *really* got to get back to work. Have a nice night, ladies." And before Gwynn could say anything further, he walked through the barback door to the kitchen.

"How'd it go?" Jesse asked, his face serious.

"It went," Alex said, heading for the sous-chef station.

Alex was grateful that the restaurant was so busy since it made the hours fly by. But periodically, despite how he'd focused on his work, the feeling that Gwynn was stalking him kept creeping into his mind, causing an uneasy feeling in his gut. He was cleaning up his workstation when Chester Evans, the chef, came over and patted him on the back.

"Thanks for helping out, Alex. I hear you have friends coming in soon," Chester said.

"Yeah, in a hundred and ninety-two hours, but who's counting?"

Chester lifted a brow. "Well, I'm going to make a special western menu for them with all the bells and whistles." He paused and smiled. "I'll make my special Rocky Mountain oysters."

Alex chuckled, remembering the meal at Pearlz. "That'd be great."

"I'll make my special rainbow trout. We can go over the menu when Peg gets back." A pained look passed over Chester's face. "Do you have any idea when that will be?"

"Um, probably not for a week or so. Even if Jake is discharged in the next few days, she'll probably insist that he stay with her at her house."

Chester shook his head. "I have to speak to her later today about a few candidates Nick and I interviewed to be a sous-chef and servers. We're getting so busy that we need more help. You of all people shouldn't be in here chopping vegetables."

"And why not?"

"Because of who you are."

"And who do you think I am?"

"Well, I mean, your family is one of the richest in the state."

"And that disqualifies me from helping my family when they need it?"

Chester blanched and sucked in a noisy breath. "No. No. That's not what I mean."

Alex noticed his eyes looked confused, and he saw small beads of perspiration spring on Chester's brow. "I'm sorry. It's been a hard couple of days. I didn't mean to take it out on you. Look, all I should've said is that my family *is my* wealth. And what gives me more pleasure than anything I can buy with money is doing something for them when they need me."

Chester's voice cracked as he said, "I'm sorry. I didn't mean any disrespect."

"Neither did I," Alex said gently nudging him on the shoulder with his fist. "I have a call to make, so I'm going to go. I'll see you tomorrow."

★★★★

"Hey, it's only eleven here. Finish early?" Brooke asked.

"I worked in the kitchen and it closed at 9 tonight. Guess who showed up at the bar tonight?"

There was silence and a sigh before Brooke spoke. "Gwynn," she said dryly.

Alex told her about the brief conversation.

"I have to tell you I'm a little concerned about Gwynn showing up there after you spoke to her," she said.

"Yeah, so am I."

"This may be because I've watched too many *Forensic Files*, but she doesn't have a gun, does she?"

"Brooke, this is Montana. You can carry a loaded gun anywhere except in municipal, state, and federal buildings without a permit. Almost every woman has one in the glove compartment. In fact, Gwynn is a Realtor, and she told me she carries one when she's alone while showing a property just in case some wacko tries something. So, yeah, she does."

Alex heard Brooke's voice crack. "I don't know. I think, given how unstable she seems, maybe someone should see if her mother could take it from her."

"Good luck with that. Her mother is Gwynn's biggest enabler. Besides, I think that would set Gwynn off. If she's getting therapy, shouldn't the therapist feel out whether she could be a threat to someone?"

"You ever hear the phrase 'garbage in, garbage out'? It's the same with a patient in therapy. If they don't tell you the truth, there's no way you could make that determination. I'm going to have to think about this."

"Well, you can think about this while I think about how excited I am to see you. I'm counting down the hours. When does your plane land so I can add the minutes?"

They talked until Alex pulled into the courtyard and said, "I'm home. Do you want to FaceTime when I get inside?"

"Oh, I don't know. It may make me sad that I can't kiss your handsome face," Brooke said. "You get some rest. Sounds like you have a busy tomorrow."

"OK. Talk to you in the morning. Love you."

# Chapter 67

Your life doesn't get better by chance;
it gets better by change.
—*Jim Rohn*

One hundred and ninety-one hours and fifty-five minutes later, Alex rose after a fitful night. He walked into the kitchen to find his mother and Cody there.

"As the song says, 'What a difference a day makes,'" Mary said as she poured Alex and Cody coffee. "Now that Jake is home and the cattle drive is over, I feel so relieved. Things can get back to normal."

"Normal? On this ranch?" Cody asked.

"Well, you make a good point," Mary said with a chuckle.

"Have you heard anything more from Gwynn, Alex?" Cody asked.

"No. Why do you ask?"

"I'd bet my saddle on her having heard that your friends are coming for the Fourth of July celebration. I'm a little worried that if she sees you with Brooke, she may not take it well," Cody said.

"Hopefully she's dealing with some of her issues in therapy." *At least that's what she said she was going to do. But come to think of it,* Alex thought, *a therapist never did call me to come in for a session. Screw it. I'm not going to worry about it. Brooke will be here soon.*

"Has she been back to the Tavern?" Cody asked.

"No," Alex said. "Not that I know of. And since it seems Gwynn gets all the news about what's going on with me from her friend, there's no need for her to go."

"Well, I do worry about what she may do," Mary said.

"Gwynn's angry, bitter, and sad, but she's not Betty Broderick. Besides, weren't you and Dad the ones who taught me I can only control the problems I can fix? And if I can't fix it, letting the problem control me isn't going to help."

"Yes, we were," Mary said, smiling. "Oh, by the way, Peg said she's hired a couple of new people, and you won't have to help out anymore. So, you'll have all the time you want with your friends."

"Have you decided what you're going to do with them?" Cody asked. "Do they ride?"

"I asked Brooke, and she does. I thought we'd do things around here first. Then if the others ride, we'll head up to the hideout, show them the ranch from the air, and take them to the July third rodeo. After that, I'm sort of torn. I thought about taking them to Billings and to the Pictograph Cave State Park and the Little Bighorn Battlefield National Monument. But then I love the Glacier National Park and the Going-to-the-Sun Road. I don't know. I want Brooke to fall in love with Montana."

Mary smiled. "Alex, she fell in love with you, and you *are* Montana. She will."

"Yeah, but you haven't seen Charleston. It's so full of history and so happening and romantic. I want to show her Montana may be different, but it has as much to offer," Alex said.

Cody cleared his throat and smiled at Mary in a way Alex had never seen but always suspected was behind his steely exterior. "I think what your mom is saying is that it's not our geography that makes Montana so special. It's Montanans."

"That's the fucking truth," Alex said.

"Alex, do you kiss Brooke with that mouth?" Mary asked.

Cody and Alex were laughing as Maria entered the kitchen.

"Good morning," Maria said, eyeing the three of them. "It's nice to see everyone so happy."

Mary titled her head and nodded. "Yes, it is."

# *Chapter 68*

We all take different paths in life,
but no matter where we go,
we take a little of each other everywhere.
*—Tim McGraw*

All Alex could think about on the morning of Brooke's arrival was that the gnawing yearning he's felt since he left her would subside. He smiled as he sent her a text.

*Alex*

*ONLY SIX MORE HOURS.*

*Brooke*

*THAT'S 360 MINUTES, BUT WHO'S COUNTING?*

*Alex*

*IT SEEMS LIKE FOREVER SINCE WE'VE SEEN EACH OTHER. IN CASE YOU DON'T RECOGNIZE ME, I'LL BE THE ONE IN THE STETSON. OH, THAT'S RIGHT, SO WILL EVERY OTHER GUY THERE. I'LL BE THE ONE WITH THE LOVESICK LOOK ON HIS FACE*

*STANDING AS CLOSE TO THE SECURITY EXIT AS POSSIBLE.*

*Brooke*

*I'LL BE THE ONE MAKING A BEELINE FOR YOUR ARMS, LOOKING FOR A 'BEAR HUG'! GOT TO GO. DONOVAN IS HERE TO TAKE ME TO THE AIRPORT. HE'S BUMMED HE CAN'T COME WITH US. LOVE YOU.*

*Alex*

*LOVE YOU TOO.*

He was standing behind the security checkpoint in almost the exact place Cody and his mother had stood when he returned from Charleston. He was holding two bouquets of flowers. The one for Brooke: a dozen red roses. The one for Hollis: Gerber daisies. He wasn't sure whether it was the scent of the roses or the daisies that made him feel like a schoolboy on prom night. It may have just been the giddiness he felt that the wait was finally over. She'd be walking toward him in just a few minutes.

And suddenly, she was there. She wore a light-blue blouse tucked into blue jeans and secured with a tooled leather belt with a large silver buckle. She was drenched in the midafternoon light filtering through the large aquarium windows that lined the waiting area. She looked so beautiful and so happy that Alex started to choke up. He noticed several people, women and men, were staring at Brooke. Although he felt a twinge of protectiveness, he thought, *Who can blame them? We live in a visual world, and she is a vision.*

She ran up to him and wrapped her arms around his neck, pulling his face to hers and nuzzling his nose. Then she pressed her lips against his.

"Hey, you two," Hollis said, tapping Brooke's shoulder. "Let me give this guy a squeeze. We've missed you, Alex."

Brooke stepped back, and Alex handed the roses to her and the daisies to Hollis. Hollis hugged Alex again and said, "It's so good to see you. I wasn't sure whether Brooke was going to be able to stand being away from you another minute. Blake has diagnosed her with lovesickness, and it's *terminal.* Get it. We're in an airport … *terminal.*" Hollis began to laugh at her joke.

"Sorry, Alex," Blake said, extending his hand. "She's corny, but she's a *trip*, and I love her."

"Ha ha, a *trip*? Mine was funnier," Hollis laughed.

"OMG. You should have heard all the lame airport jokes Hollis was coming up with in Charleston. Seriously pathetic," Brooke said, chuckling.

"What? It killed the time, didn't it? I bet Alex knows this one. What is the most ordered food in an airport?" Hollis asked.

"A *plane* bagel," Alex said. "I think I heard that one in the third grade. Let's get your bags. My mother has lunch ready, and if we're late, I'll say it's not my fault or yours. It was the airport's '*asphalt.*'"

"Oh, e-n-ough," Brooke groaned as Alex, Hollis, and Blake laughed.

When Alex pulled out of the parking lot, Brooke's reaction to Montana's natural beauty was all Alex had hoped for. He heard her gasp and looked over to see her eyes had grown wide, and her mouth was slightly open.

"Oh, Alex, this is spectacular. For as far as I can see in every direction, the sky is so blue and bright, it almost hurts my eyes. And those mountains towering in the distance are so … majestic. But that word doesn't do it." Brooke stretched her neck to look at them. "I don't know. It's like they're silently watching us, like the gods on Mount Olympus."

Hollis said, "I agree. There's something eerie about how they seem to be watching us."

"Those mountains *have* seen everything century after century," Alex said solemnly. "Every homesteader's struggle to survive, every act of kindness, every act of cruelty, especially to the Native American Indians."

"Many Indian tribes believed mountains were sacred and part of their ancestor worship. What Indian tribes lived here?" Blake asked.

"This area was a common hunting ground for many tribes: Blackfeet, Salish, Crow, to name a few," Alex said. "If you all are up for it, I thought it would be fun to ride up the mountain near my ranch where my grandfather built a cabin. You can see a lot from there."

Collectively they replied, "Yes."

The rest of the way to the ranch, Brooke, Hollis, and Blake continued to comment on the beauty of the landscape, the open spaces, and the bison and herds of sheep they passed as well as the bald eagle that flew above them. As Alex approached his driveway, Hollis asked, "Is that a resort up ahead?"

"Um, no, that's my ranch," Alex said.

"Holy shit," Hollis said. "That doesn't look like any ranch I ever saw in the movies or in magazines."

"Well it was built in the late 1840s after my great-great-great-grandpappy discovered gold, and it was the fashion then to build a house that looked European, since a lot of the architects who came out west were trained in Europe," Alex said.

The group grew quiet as their eyes darted from side to side, taking in the trees, the lawn, the vast pastures. As the house came into view, Brooke said, "Alex, this is breathtaking. It's so beautiful. Donovan showed me pictures, but they didn't do it justice."

"When my mother brings her friends here for the first time and they 'ooh and ah' over it, she dismisses their compliments, saying, 'It's no different than your house. It keeps the rain out,'" Alex said, laughing.

He pulled into the courtyard, and Mary and Maria were standing at the back door. Mary came down the steps and waited while the group got out of the truck. After Alex introduced them to his mother, she said, “Welcome. We’re so happy to have you. Now, let’s get you settled. We have lunch waiting for you. Maria will show you to your rooms.”

Then Mary extended outstretched arms to Brooke. “I am so happy you’re here, Brooke. You’ve made my son so happy. I cannot tell you what that means to me.”

“And I am so happy to meet you, Mrs. Whitgate,” Brooke said, returning the hug.

“Please, call me ‘Mary.’ How beautiful you are,” Mary said, stepping back and touching Brooke’s cheek.

Maria was standing at the top of the stairs with Blake and Hollis.

“Brooke, why don’t you go with them and get settled? Maria will show you your room,” Mary said.

“She’s exquisite,” Mary said to Alex, who stood next to her and beamed. “I only hope Gwynn never sees her.”

“Why?” Alex asked.

“Because I don’t think Gwynn could handle someone more beautiful than she is being with you. Women are funny like that.”

# Chapter 69

Heaven is under our feet as well as over our heads.

*—Henry David Thoreau*

Alex opened the door to his room, and Brooke turned to face him. "Alex, this room, this house—it's gorgeous."

Alex took her hand and led her to the settee at the end of the king-size bed. "I know it's way too soon to ask you whether you could imagine yourself living here and on what schedule, but while you're here, I'd just ask that you take everything in and think about it. We can talk about different possibilities about how to split our time between here and Charleston before you leave. But we need a plan, and I want you to be honest with me about how you feel."

While Alex waited for Brooke to answer, he felt as if the air in the room crackled with tension.

"I will. Think about it. The whole idea about me coming out here was so we could discuss different options once I saw your home and Montana. And of course, I'll be honest with you. I always am. Long-distance relationships are hard. But I think people who live unhappily under the same roof experience more distance between them than we will."

Alex raised his eyebrows and nodded. "You have such incredible insight. You amaze me."

Brooke looked up from their intertwined hands and said, "As you do me, cowboy." She leaned in and kissed him on the lips.

There was a knock on the door, and Hollis called, "Are you two ready to go down to lunch? I'm starving."

Brooke kissed Alex on the lips again and said, "No one should ever get between Hollis and her vittles."

"Vittles, huh? That's what we say out here," Alex said.

"I'm trying to learn your language, cowboy," Brooke said, pulling Alex to his feet.

"The only language you need to learn is my love language," Alex said, smirking.

"Are you guys coming?" Hollis called.

"We'll be right there," Brooke said. "Go ahead down."

Brooke tilted her head. "Did you take the Five Love Languages quiz?"

"I did," Alex said.

"Well, we'll have to talk about *that* later," Brooke said.

Alex and Brooke walked into the dining room to find Hollis and Blake at the buffet Maria had set out.

Hollis looked up at them and smiled. "OMG. This food looks amazing. Look, there's machaca in a burrito, red rice, refried beans, discada, and cochinita pibil."

"Maria will be thrilled that you like it," Mary said as she sat down at the head of the table with her plate of food. "Alex, please take care of getting our guests what they want to drink. Maria put the choices at the end of the buffet."

Hollis and Blake walked to the table with their plates, and Hollis asked, "Is there any special place you want us to sit?"

Patting the placemat to her left, Mary said, "Please sit here, and Blake can sit next to you. Then Brooke can sit to my right with Alex next to her."

While Alex got the drinks, Mary began a conversation with Hollis and Blake in between bites of food. "So, Hollis, I understand you're a nurse, and Blake, you're a doctor. Do you work together?"

Hollis explained that they both worked at the same hospital but in different specialties. Then she went on to tell Mary how they had met and fallen in love and how happy they were. Alex invited them to come to the ranch. Blake looked lovingly at Hollis and just smiled. When Mary tried to ask him a question, Hollis answered for him. Mary, being Mary, looked at Blake and said, "I love to hear about young people falling in love, and I'd love to hear how it happened for you, Blake."

Blake put down his fork and smiled. "Mrs. Whitgate, it may seem to a lot of people that Hollis and I rushed into this, that it's too quick, but until I met her, I was a lonely guy. I'd been living in a world of insanely competitive people, who were willing to eat your liver if it meant they would get a better internship and residency. When you're accepted to medical school, everyone high-fives you and thinks it's great. And don't misunderstand me. I love being a doctor and helping people, but it comes at a huge cost personally and financially." Blake took a sip of the beer Alex had placed in front of his plate.

He looked around the table to see all eyes riveted on him. "I'm sorry. I don't mean to bore you."

"You are *not* boring us," Mary said softly. "Please, go on."

Blake sat back in his seat. "Up until I finished my residency and moved to Charleston, I survived on takeout pizza, Chinese food, and easy nurses looking to marry a doctor." Blake stopped abruptly and looked sheepishly around the table. "Oops, maybe I shouldn't have said that." After everyone laughed, he continued after nodding to the beer glass in his hand. "And beer. That is, until I met Hollis. Then suddenly, it was as if all the fun and joy I'd suppressed to get ahead popped, like a cork from a bottle of champagne. Every day her effervescence tickles me and makes me smile."

Mary sat up in her chair. "I'm ashamed to admit I've always taken it for granted that when I needed a doctor, they'd be there, never really giving much thought to what it took out of them *to be* there. You've given me a new perspective. Thank you, Blake." Mary turned to Alex and asked, "What are you going to do for the rest of the afternoon?"

Alex said, "I was thinking of going for a plane ride over the ranch." In response to the questioning looks they gave him, Alex explained that the ranch had an airplane, and he'd been flying with his father since high school. He took his pilot's license out from his wallet and showed it to them. "Trust me. I'm a good pilot, and I don't take risks," Alex said, glancing at Brooke. "Well?"

After they collectively agreed, Mary said, "First, Maria made her famous Pastel de tres leches."

"Three milks cake. I haven't had that in a long time," Blake said, licking his lips. In response to Hollis's quizzical look, he added, "I also lived on Mexican takeout."

After lunch, Alex drove them to the fenced airfield a few miles from the house. Travis Chapman, the ranch's full-time mechanic, was just moving the airplane from the hangar.

"Howdy," Travis said as the group got out of Alex's truck.

"Howdy, Travis," Alex said. After introducing everyone, Alex said, "Is she all gassed up?"

"She sure is. And I just did the maintenance on her, so she should purr for you," Travis said.

"OK, then," Alex said, "all aboard."

After everyone was buckled in and Alex went through his preflight check, he piloted the plane to the runway for takeoff. A minute later, they were in the air. Ahead of them was the sweeping panorama of mountains, rolling valleys, trees, pastures, and every complementary color of green possible. They flew over a mountain lake so still and clear that it mirrored the blue sky. The cabin of the plane was silent except for the oohs and ahs.

"What do you think?" Alex asked as he banked right to take them up and over the summer pasture.

"I don't know about the girls, but every time I have a chance to witness nature's beauty like this, I'm in awe. Who owns all of this land?" Blake asked.

Since Alex had skirted Brooke's questions about the size of the ranch to avoid questions about the size of his wealth, he hemmed for a minute before saying, "We do."

"How many acres is it?" Blake asked.

"Three hundred and fifty thousand," Alex said.

"Holy shit. That's five hundred and forty-six miles," Blake said.

"Yeah, well, it's not a straight line. It's across and up. Speaking of up, up ahead in that valley, there's a herd of wild horses. Look over there at the river. The water is so clear there that you can see the trout."

"This is amazing," Brooke said. "I always thought that nothing can be as meditative as the sound of the ocean waves surging to shore and receding, but I have to say the majestic silence of these mountains and the natural beauty beneath us makes me feel as meditative here as the ocean at home does."

Alex looked over. "I'm glad to hear that."

"Look," Hollis said, "there's a herd of cattle."

"That's the summer pasture. That's where I was headed when Jake had his accident," Alex said. "Let me fly over it and take a video."

"Where's your camera?" Blake asked.

"Mounted on the bottom of the plane," Alex said. He explained that the plane and drones were used as vital pieces of modern farm equipment and all the functions they had with respect to ranching.

"I had no idea ranching had become so high tech," Blake said.

Turning slightly to glance at Blake, Alex said, "Just like medicine. There's a lot of digital diagnoses now, isn't there?"

"More and more," Blake said.

"Um, I'm sorry to announce this," Hollis said hesitantly, "but I have to use the restroom."

"Be back on the ground in a flash," Alex said, turning the plane and accelerating speed.

# Chapter 70

Heaven has no rage like love to hatred turned.

—*William Congreve*

After they returned to the ranch, Mary told them that Peg had called and arranged for a private dinner in the terrace room. Jake was feeling better and complained that he had cabin fever and wanted to get out of the house and meet Alex's friends. After freshening up and dressing for dinner, the group met on the lanai for drinks before going to the Tavern. They were taking in the perfectly gorgeous Montana evening air typical for July. The thermometer on the wall read sixty-eight. The sun, still high in the cloudless sky, wouldn't set for hours.

"I thoroughly enjoyed the day," Blake said. "I can't wait to ride up to the hideout and see nature from the back of a horse. Your ranch is really something. I mean, I expected something like a dude ranch experience, not the lap of luxury."

"It really is fantastic here. Thank you so much for including us," Hollis said.

Brooke smiled at Alex, who sat next to him on the couch. "It really is an amazing place, Alex."

Alex took Brooke's hand into his. "I couldn't be happier that you're all here." Brooke leaned on his shoulder.

"Howdy, you all," Cody said, escorting Mary up the stairs to the lanai.

As Alex and Brooke stood to give Mary and Cody their seats, Mary said, "Thank you, but we'd better get going. Peg wants to take Jake home as soon as dinner is over so he can rest."

When they arrived at the Tavern, the parking lot was packed. Mary said, "Peg said to come in through the terrace. She left the door open."

They walked around to the side of the building and entered the side room through the terrace. Jake and Jesse were standing at the bar set up in the corner.

"Hey, there," Alex said, walking toward them while holding Brooke's hand. Blake and Hollis followed him. "How are you feeling, Jake?"

"Like I'll lose my mind if my mother doesn't get off my back. She's driving me crazy. She acts like I'm going to break," he said.

"Oh, shut up. She's just worried about you. You've got another week before they sound all clear on your head. In a way if this hadn't happened, I'd never have known you actually had a brain," Jesse said, flinching at the shot in the arm Jake gave him.

"Who is this beautiful lady, and what is she doing with an ugly guy like you, Alex?" Jake said.

"Brooke, this is my cousin, Jake. He's going to be a great trail boss someday."

Jake's eyes grew wide, and his face lit up with a smile.

"That is, if he can learn to stay in the saddle," Alex finished.

Jake punched Alex in the arm. "I'll have you know, beautiful lady, that it wasn't my fault. This man should be reported to OSHA because his saddles don't have seat belts."

Jesse took drink orders and acted like the bartender as Peg chatted with Brooke.

"Although I haven't seen much of the restaurant, it looks a lot like the replica of The Cedar Tavern at Disneyland," Brooke said.

"Well, after my divorce from my first husband, I took the kids to Disney and saw the one in Epcot. And I loved it so much that I've tried to imitate it. Of course," she said, looking around, "it could never be confused with the original on Cedar Street in New York. The one where Jackson Pollock was banned for tearing the bathroom door off its hinges and throwing it at Franz Kline," she added, laughing. Then she said, "OK, now, let's take our seats."

The table was set with an arrangement of flowers and cascading ivy on either end of the vase, votives, a red-checkered tablecloth and napkins, and place cards. The champagne glasses had been filled. Cody sat at the head of the far end of the table. Next to him on his right were Mary, Jake, Jesse, then Peg at the opposite end of the table. To his left were Brooke, Alex, Hollis, and Blake.

Peg tapped her glass and stood. "I'd like to propose a toast to everyone's health. Recently as you know, I came to realize that health is something we tend to take for granted. And we shouldn't. It's something to be grateful for every single day. I also want to toast my sister, Mary, who has stood by me in good times and hard times."

"Come on, Mom," Jesse whispered, "the food's getting cold."

Peg gave him her half-closed right-eye stare the boys called "the stink eye." She cleared her throat. "Finally, I want to raise a glass to our guests, Brooke, Hollis, and Blake. I hope you enjoy your time here as much as we enjoy having you."

After all of them raised their glasses and touched rims, Alex turned to Brooke, raised his glass to her, and whispered, "To the beautiful lady who has upended my life and stolen my heart." Then he leaned over and kissed her on the lips. It was a long, lingering kiss that caused Peg to say, "Alex, let the girl breathe."

For the next several hours, all of them ate, drank, laughed, and were lost in nonstop conversation. They talked about the cattle drive and Jake's run-in with a cougar. Cody told his cowboy stories. When Jesse asked him to tell the one about the black bear, Cody explained that when he was around fifteen, he was looking for his dog, who'd run into the woods. Cody dismounted his horse because he was afraid there may be gopher holes in the underbrush his horse could step in. He said it wasn't until he was face-to-face with the bear that he realized his dog was probably just following the bear's scent.

"What did you do to get away? Did you play dead?" Blake asked.

"I learned at Daddy's knee that you never play dead if you come face-to-face with a black bear. That's only if you come upon a brown or grizzly bear. Bears just want to be left alone. First thing you do is stand your ground and not run. Then I talked to him to let him know I was human and not a prey animal. I told him I was sorry for trespassing on his turf and that I'd best be leaving. I moved away slowly, taking side steps so I could keep an eye on him. Side steps are the away to avoid threatening the bear. When I did, he turned and walked away."

"What happened to your dog?" Hollis asked.

"I whistled for him when I was back in the saddle, and Old Bongo came running. Then I high-tailed it out of there and went home and changed my underwear," Cody said as everyone broke into laughter.

Suddenly, Alex noticed Diedre was standing in the open French doors. He jumped to his feet. "Diedre?" he said.

The room fell silent as everyone turned to look. Diedre stood still, her face set and grim.

"Diedre is there something I can help you with?" Alex asked.

Diedre quickly raised both hands. Her right one held a gun, her left a cell phone. On the cell's screen was a picture of Alex and Brooke kissing.

"How could you do this to my daughter?" Diedre cried. "How could you?"

"Deidre," Alex said calmly, "let's go outside and talk about this."

"The time for talking has passed," Diedre said in an eerily calm tone. "Someone sent this to Gwynn. She is out of her mind with rage." The text on the screen read:

> *YOU ARE SUCH A BITCH AND A LOSER. HE'S MOVED ON. HA HA. GET A LIFE. BUT IT WON'T BE WITH HIM!*

Diedre shook her head as her searing eyes remained focused on Alex. "Do you have any idea what you have done to my daughter? You murdered the woman my Gwynn was supposed to become." Her eyes began to water, and she wiped them with her sleeve. "So now I have to kill you, or she will."

Alex noticed Cody's gaze dart between him and Diedre as Cody slowly rose from his seat.

"You sit still, Cody. I don't want to hurt *you*. I'm here to do what my daughter plans on doing." Diedre faltered a second, blinking back tears. "Gwynn's convinced herself the only way to stop obsessing over getting you back is to make it impossible for anyone to have you."

Alex heard his mother gasp as she began to stand, but Cody grabbed Mary's hand and pulled her back down as he took his seat.

"Diedre," Brooke said quietly, "you have every right to be upset with Alex for causing your daughter so much pain, but hurting someone else won't make her pain go away."

Raising the gun, Diedre sneered. "*You! You shut up!*" Diedre hissed as she aimed the gun at Brooke, "If Gwynn can't have him, no one else is going to."

"Diedre, listen to me," Alex said as he wrapped his foot around the leg of Brooke's chair. Alex pulled the chair's leg out, sending Brooke to the floor.

Out of the corner of his eye, he saw the muzzle of Diedre's gun blow a cloud of yellow-white discharge from its chamber as he threw his body over Brooke's.

His cheeks, flushed with heat seconds earlier, grew cold. He felt as if the air were leaving his body. Screams drifted around him as he tried to lift his heavy eyelids. A thick, warm liquid pooled in the back of his throat, and a rusty, metallic taste filled his mouth. Then he felt a peaceful, detached calm settle inside him. He took a breath, and his body shuddered as his heart stopped.

# Chapter 71

Be still prepared for death: and death or
life shall thereby be the sweeter.
—*Shakespeare*

Alex awoke to the sound of repetitive beeping and hushed voices. His throat burned, and pain seared his chest. He struggled to raise his hand to his eyes to see something other than the black curtain in front of them.

"Alex," Brooke whispered softly as she gently lowered his arm to his side.

Her voice and her soft touch caused him to try to sit up, but as he did, he began to cough violently.

"I'm here, Alex," Brooke said. "Don't move. They taped gauze pads over your eyes so they wouldn't dry out. Lie still so I can take them off."

But before Brooke could remove the gauze, Alex heard his mother's voice, thick with emotion, whisper, "Thank God, thank God." He felt her move closer until he felt her breath in his ear and wetness against the side of his face he thought must be her tears. "Oh, Alex, I was so scared."

When Brooke removed the gauze pads, it took a few moments before his eyes adjusted to the light. He blinked a few times before his vision cleared, and he squinted up at Brooke and his mother.

Then a woman wearing scrubs came into his peripheral vision. Her eyes didn't move from the monitor. "My name is Doris Reichly. I'm your primary care nurse. You are one lucky son of a gun. Oh, sorry about the pun. One more inch, and the bullet would have gone through your heart."

"Well, Cupid recently shot his arrow through it, so there wouldn't have been much left to injure," Alex said hoarsely.

Doris nodded, her right eyebrow arched so sharply from where he lay that it looked like it touched the ceiling. "Well, that's a wound I hope never heals. I have to get some supplies to change your dressing. I'll be right back."

Alex looked around the room. His mother had stepped back and was hovering around the door, whispering something to Peg. Hollis and Blake stood behind them.

Brooke was still holding his hand. "How long have I been here?" Alex asked.

"Four days. They put you in a medically induced coma to protect your brain from blood loss. The bullet nicked an artery, and your heart stopped from the blood loss," Brooke said. "They took your breathing tube out yesterday and began to bring you out of it. We've been waiting for you to wake up."

Alex looked at her. "What happened?"

"What do you remember?" Brooke asked.

"Not much. Diedre with a gun. That's about all."

"Diedre tried to shoot me, but you protected me. Thank God, Hollis and Blake were there. They put pressure on your wound to stop the bleeding and gave you CPR and used the AED you had your aunt buy for the restaurant to shock your heart after it stopped from the blood loss," Brooke said, taking his hand to her lips.

"What happened to Diedre?" Alex asked.

"They arrested her. I think they're going to charge her with attempted murder now. They've been by every day, checking on whether you were going to survive." Brooke hesitated before she added, "One of the detectives said that when Gwynn told her mother what she intended to do, Diedre felt the only way her daughter was going to get better was to eliminate you. She wanted to protect Gwynn."

Alex turned his head away from Brooke and sucked in a deep breath. "I did this to them," he said, a tear rolling down his cheek.

Brooke grabbed a tissue from the bedside table and wiped the tear from his cheek. "You didn't do this. The seeds of their illness were sown long before you ever knew them. *I'm* the one who feels guilty. I opened my big mouth. I thought if I could empathize with her, I might disarm her." A tear from Brooke's cheek fell onto Alex's face. She stood over him to wipe it away. Looking into his eyes, her voice pensive, she said, "I've decided something, cowboy."

When she didn't say anything further, he asked in a gravelly voice, "What's that?"

Bending close to his ear, she whispered, "That a moment with you in Montana … is worth a lifetime without you in Charleston."

Alex turned his head to look into Brooke's eyes.

Tears trickled down both their cheeks. When Nurse Reichly returned, she asked, "Is he in pain?"

"No. In love," Alex said.

"Same difference," Nurse Reichley said, a wry smile on her lips as she shook her head.